A SHOT AWAY

Pierre Ouellette

A SHOT AWAY

A CRIME NOVEL

ISBN-13: 978-1-7331007-5-5

Library of Congress
Control Number: 2021946234

Cover design: Keith Carlson, Pierre Ouellette

Formatting: Keith Carlson

First edition

JORVIK PRESS

5331 S Macadam Ave., Ste 258/424,
Portland OR 97239

JorvikPress.com

About the Author

Pierre Ouellette lives in the Portland, Oregon Metro Area and is the author of seven previously published novels that span a diversity of subjects and settings. He served for two decades as the creative partner in an advertising and public relations agency focused on science and technology. Prior to that he was a professional guitarist and played in numerous pop bands and jazz ensembles, including Paul Revere and the Raiders, Jim Pepper and David Friesen.

Also by Pierre Ouellette

Haight St.

Bakersfield

The Deus Machine

The Third Pandemic

The Forever Man

Writing as Pierre Davis

A Breed Apart

Origin Unknown

Dedicated to my four sons,
Jean-Pierre, Jesse, Justin and Julien.
Each a fine lad in his own right.

1.

CHICAGO
FALL 1966

A relentless beating. Not of the body but of the mind. No, not of the mind but of the spirit.

Matt Carson's vision shrunk to a single tile of linoleum, scuffed, stained and dust-laden. His interrogators disappeared from view, but their voices carried on. Strident, indignant, salted with rage.

"So once again, you went to war of your own volition. Correct?"

"Not exactly," Carson said. "I was drafted."

"So why didn't you resist? Why didn't you refuse induction? What was wrong with you?"

"I don't know. I never thought about it."

"Never thought about it?" a second voice chimed in, a female voice a single beat away from hysteria. "How could you not think about it? How could you not notice the imperial slaughter of thousands of innocents?"

"I didn't know about it." When he'd received his draft notice, Carson had to look on a map to find Vietnam.

"And just what does that say about you?"

"It says I didn't know," Carson repeated.

"Wrong!" a third voice shouted. "It says you were ignorant. It says you ignored all the suffering. It says you went ahead like a good Nazi and did whatever you were told."

"Did you ever kill anyone?" a fourth voice piped up.

The room sank into an earnest silence. None of them had ever killed anyone. Most had never even struck someone in anger. They were nearly all college students, children of upper and middle America. Not Carson. He came from more modest origins, from people still immersed in the biblical edict of the sweat of thy brow. Physical violence always dwelled close by. He was the ancient reluctant conscript. Weaponry naturally slid into hands used to clutching tools, just as issuing orders came naturally to those sitting behind desks.

Ultimately, the war broke him and snapped him. He came apart at Landing Zone Albany, when he loaded a mutilated soldier onto a chopper. The kid kept insisting that his girlfriend wouldn't care if he was missing a couple of limbs. Carson knew better. If that was true, the guy wouldn't be repeatedly going on about her steadfast devotion. Through the chop of the rotors and the sporadic gunfire, he could hear the subtext: *Please tell me she won't leave me.* And he could not.

As the war slid ever deeper into anarchy, so did Carson. Unlike other returning combatants, who stoically healed as best they could, he became an open sore, raw and festering with bad intent. So began his silent war on all those who wore uniforms of any stripe, all those who insisted on order in the ranks, and all those who imposed their will from a privileged stratum high above.

Carson lifted his gaze up from the floor. The mechanical click of a relay broke the expectant silence. It triggered the quiet roar of a gas furnace in the far corner of the room where his inquisitors formed a semicircle around him, maybe a dozen or so. They all sat hunched forward on metal folding chairs that occasionally creaked as their weight shifted.

"Yeah, I killed someone. And then I killed someone else. And so on. Get the idea?"

He panned their faces, right to left. Most avoided eye contact. He was different, and they knew it. The Weatherman leadership had adopted this style of criticism/self-criticism created by the venerable Mao Tse-tung, whom they greatly admired. The target was stripped bare and rebuilt in the image of the faithful follower, a true disciple of the revolution. But Carson had a hardened casing that deflected any such attempt to penetrate it. In truth, they envied him. When subjected to this same ordeal, many of them had collapsed into tears. Others fled like wounded beasts, never to return. But Carson did neither, and this perplexed them. More ominously, they sensed a capacity for bedlam that far exceeded their own, one that he could willfully exercise with virtually no civilized restraint.

Yet they shared a critical bond with him, a deep loathing of the established order, of those who held common sway over their lives. The moral imperative that once united the nation was rapidly disintegrating, and they saw themselves at the vanguard of its dissolution. They understood implicitly that Carson might be a tool of necessity in the coming revolution.

"I shot them," Carson continued. "And I blew them up. I had advanced training in munitions and explosives. I was good at it. I was good at my job. We all want to be good at our job now, don't we?"

"But you had their blood on your hands," a young woman ventured.

"Wrong. I had their blood all over me. I drowned in their blood and that's why I'm here. I'm a ghost come back to find justice for those who died. All of them, our side and theirs. I'm to be the instrument of their revenge."

He scanned their faces once more, and his eyes came to rest on the girl he'd had sex with the previous night. She'd been part of an awkwardly engineered "orgy" designed to sever monogamous relationships in the Weatherman organization and focus members exclusively on the cause. Their coupling was perfunctory at best, and he couldn't even remember her name, but now her eyes signaled genuine interest.

A male student attempted to relight the offensive. "Tell us some of the ways you've failed the movement."

"I've failed to kick ass when called for. I've failed to mow down all those who oppose me. I've failed to watch their heads roll down the street."

"And do you feel regret for your failings?"

"Yes, I do. And I can tell you right now, they won't be repeated."

The student nodded and squirmed uncomfortably. He was one of the local leaders, and Carson was supposed to be one of the devoted followers but was morphing into something altogether different.

"So, what else?" Carson demanded of the group.

The student leader looked at his watch. "It's late," he declared. "Let's get stoned."

"Well yeah," someone in the back agreed. "Orange Sunshine, comin' right up."

The group dispersed and headed up the stairs to the main floor of the old house, a cheap rental on the fringe of downtown. The girl from the previous night lingered. "You've really given yourself over to the cause," she told him. "Totally. I can tell. I wish I had your purity of thought. Sometimes I have my doubts."

Carson placed his hands on her bottom and drew her close. "Maybe we could work on that."

She gave him a timid smile. "Maybe we could."

"I can really dig what you said downstairs," a redheaded guy told Carson when they reached the main floor. "It's hard for us to grok all that. We weren't there, so we can't know, not really."

"No, you can't," Carson agreed. The student's hair bloomed in a red-orange foam that rendered him slightly comical, along with his pale complexion and blue eyes welded wide open.

"You said you worked with explosives," the guy noted. "Was that part of your regular gig?"

"Nope, I picked it up on the fly. Not much to it, unless you fucked up. Then you were dead or in pieces or both."

"Wow," the redhead said. "Well, I'm glad you're on our side now."

"Me too."

. . .

The redhead left the old house and walked down the sidewalk through the chill evening air. A slight mist muted the glow of the streetlights. After two blocks he entered a convenience store and changed five dollars into quarters. He avoided the payphone out front. The clerk might wonder why he needed all that change to make a call. The clerk might remember what he looked like if later questioned.

Three blocks further, he entered a glassed-in phone booth, closed the folding door behind him and placed a stack of quarters on the little shelf beside the phone. Making an overseas call could be a tricky business, especially from a payphone; but by now he was thoroughly acclimated to the international telecommunications system and its various idiosyncrasies. Within ten minutes, he was patched through.

"Yes?" said the voice on the other end.

"Sing a song," the redhead directed.

"Of sixpence."

"Very good. I think I've found a promising candidate. Ex-military. Angry. Radicalized. Experienced with explosives."

"You think he's approachable?"

"Absolutely. He's Weather Underground. He's one of us."

"Good. Your people are definitely buying what we're selling, so go ahead and make him an offer."

"Will do."

"Let me know immediately if he accepts. We'll have to take certain steps to arrange the particulars."

"Understand."

"You're doing the right thing; I hope you know that. You're acting for the common good."

"I do know that."

"Alright then, goodnight."

"Yes, goodnight."

The redhead hung up and started back down the sidewalk at a leisurely pace. If he could pull this thing off, his contribution would be openly celebrated and rewarded when the revolution came. And the revolution was definitely on the way. The people were going to take to the streets in a seismic upheaval. The established order would topple. The megalithic corporate conspiracy with its iron grip on the monolithic government would come to an abrupt and terrible end. Scores would be settled. Debts repaid.

The movement's leadership, from Ayers and Dohrn on down, had no idea what he was up to. Nor did they need to. When the new order arose from the smoking rubble of the old, his actions would be self-explanatory.

The night chill came on strong now, and he shoved his hands into his coat pockets. His vaporous breath fled into the nocturnal air. By any measure, he was a hero.

2.

SAN FRANCISCO
SPRING 1967

James Stone watched in wonder as the hippie chicks launched into their rapturous choreography. Their limbs traced random arcs through the warm air in the open field at the east end of Golden Gate Park. What would Lawrence Welk or Arthur Murray think? All sense of order, pattern and predictability were gone. The same could be said of the entire Haight-Ashbury culture, which had sprouted as suddenly as a psilocybin mushroom after a summer downpour.

Stone shifted his focus from the dancers to the musicians on the makeshift stage above. They called themselves the Grateful Dead, and they were in serious violation of music industry norms. They were playing for free. And in doing so, they were liberated from all the usual constraints brought on by monetary compensation. They played songs that went on for ten or twenty minutes, as opposed to the two and a half minute hits you heard on AM radio. All with no chord changes whatsoever, long modal adventures full of brilliant guitar improvisation and raw vocals. Sinatra and Dino not spoken here.

As a record producer, Stone couldn't help but view them as freshly extracted ore, waiting to be refined and shaped into something more commercially viable. It took him back ten years to Bakersfield, when he came upon a fabulous cache of young country players performing in the honky-tonks along Chester Avenue. People like Buck Owens and Merle Haggard.

He was a cop back then, but a cop with a finely tuned musical ear. Earlier in his career he'd worked Hollywood Vice but wound up on the wrong side of LAPD politics and was exiled to Bakersfield, where he was hired into Homicide. An ugly little job in an ugly little city. However, the curse morphed into a blessing when he discovered the music. He eventually quit the force, started a small record company and quickly hit pay dirt with what became nationally known as the Bakersfield Sound. Capitol Records bought him out, and he went back to LA as a full-fledged producer charged with finding the next big thing.

Could he pull off another Bakersfield? Good question. One he hoped to answer here in San Francisco. Like all record executives, he came stamped with an expiration date, but he had no idea what it was.

He turned to Christine, who stood next to him nodding her head in time to the music. "So, what do you think?"

"I think they might be a little ahead of their time," she said. "And I suspect that, somehow, pharmaceuticals are involved."

Stone smiled. She was probably right on both counts. These guys would be pretty difficult to mold into the mainstream. As for the pharmaceuticals, she should know. She was a doctor, a female doctor, still a rare species. Best of all, she was his longtime lover, partner, companion, and God knew what else. They'd met back in Bakersfield, where she worked as the county's forensic pathologist while he was a homicide detective. She'd stuck with him through a very ugly and protracted episode involving murder and sexual perversion in high places. They never married, by mutual consent, and he sometimes grew weary of trying to explain their relationship to those of a more conventional persuasion. As proof of concept, he would point out that they'd seen many a divorce come and go and here they were, doing just fine.

When the concert ended, they drifted with the crowd out of the park and onto Haight Street, which was starting to resemble a carnival at the edge of the known universe. Men in top hats two feet tall. Biker thugs burbling by on chromed monsters. Women in skirts that barely cleared their mons pubis. Transvestites walking small dogs dressed in clown suits. Stone was certain the tour buses weren't far behind.

By the time they had covered a half dozen blocks, Stone understood that this place and the music oozing out of it were like some very unstable chemical isotope. Highly exotic and doomed to a relatively short life span. If he wanted in, he'd have to act fast.

Later they took a taxi back to their hotel in downtown and wound up at the House of Prime Rib, with tuxedoed waiters sporting perfectly barbered gray hair. No upstarts or amateurs allowed. After a very gratifying dinner of prime rib and Yorkshire pudding, Stone leaned back and lit a Marlboro. Christine used to caution him about smoking but had eventually given up. She patiently explained that it probably increased your risk of lung cancer. She didn't quite have the science to back it up but said the data was all headed in that direction. Stone told her that when it arrived, he'd seriously consider quitting. He didn't resent her concern, which he knew was born out of love.

"Would you mind living here for a while?" he asked her out of nowhere.

Her eyebrows elevated ever so slightly. Lovely. Ten years on, he still found her extraordinarily attractive.

"And why do you ask?" she queried.

"This place is the new center of the musical universe. Forget about LA. Every major label is sending their excavating equipment up here to dig up the next Beatles or Stones. The only way to play the game and win is going to be to swim in it. Long distance just won't work."

"I'm sure you're right," she said. "It's definitely worth a thought."

Stone nodded. This was Christine's shorthand for 'I'm going to carefully consider it before I respond because it's a really big deal'.

"Fair enough," he said. He already knew it was a done deal. She loved the city and her medical life in LA was limited to volunteer work at a few clinics for the very needy. If she returned, it would be there waiting.

Good. Because he needed to be here right now. Tomorrow would be too late.

In fact, it might already be too late.

3.

HAVANA, CUBA

Carson stared at the large framed print of Che Guevara with its blood-red background and face rendered in stark black and white. It owed its origin to Alberto Korda's famous photograph of the man. Dark, curly hair in wild profusion. Beret stretched in a defiant arc across the forehead. Eyes ablaze under a slightly furrowed brow. Mouth teetering toward a scowl. A perfect encapsulation of the fulminating rage of the oppressed masses. If someone chiseled a new Mt. Rushmore somewhere in the Andes, Che Guevara would be the first face up. He currently floated in a brilliant cloud of unabashed idolatry, a fierce crusader for social justice fused with a smoldering sexuality. Romance and revolution perfectly entwined. What could be better?

Outside, Carson could hear the insistent buzz of traffic along the aging arterial in front of the capitol building in the center of Havana. He'd been waiting for twenty minutes in this modest meeting room just off the main corridor. Not a problem. At this moment, he was the envy of virtually every member of the U.S. radical movement.

He turned to the sound of the door opening. Fidel Castro strode in briskly, trailed by two other men who seemed of little substance in the presence this iconic figure with his broad face and dark, bushy beard.

"Forgive my English, Mr. Carson. I seldom resort to it these days." He gave Carson a firm handshake.

"Not a problem," Carson replied.

Castro pointed to the print of Guevara on the wall. "A great man, may he rest in peace. An inspiration to us all. A man of action." He turned back to Carson. "I'm told the same is true of you. Am I right?"

"Depends on who you ask," Carson said. The two men in the background visibly tightened at Carson's aggressive response to the supreme leader of this nascent Communist state.

Castro laughed and patted Carson on the shoulder. "Very clever." He gestured to a pair of leather armchairs. "Have a seat."

Once they settled in, Castro leaned forward, elbows on his knees. "Your lovely Miss Dohrn paid us a visit a few weeks back. She spoke of open revolution on American soil, of armed battle with the police. And you know what we told her?"

"No, I don't." Carson knew only that Bernadette Dohrn sat somewhere atop the Weather Underground leadership. He had yet to meet her or any of the others in power.

"We told her to forget it," Castro continued. "Why? Because the public in your country isn't ready for open confrontation. Other options must be explored."

"Such as?" Carson asked.

Castro smiled once again and pointed to the two men in the back by the door. "Reynaldo and Miguel will guide you on your journey." He stood up. "You've chosen the path of true class struggle. I congratulate you and wish you well. Goodbye."

That said, he did a quick pivot and left the room, while the two others remained. One of them came forward, a wiry middle-aged Cuban who had met him at the airport and been his constant escort for the past two days. He introduced himself only as Reynaldo. No surname. In the days to come, Carson would meet numerous others with only a single moniker.

"You've been afforded a great privilege," Reynaldo told Carson in Hispanic-flavored English. "You've met the heart and soul of world-wide revolution. Hold this moment close."

His trip to Havana had been arranged and executed in total secrecy. A law firm in Chicago sympathetic to the cause had financed and booked it, no questions asked. His contact, the redheaded student from Chicago, had explained the need for total anonymity. If something went wrong in the future and he was apprehended, it was imperative that no evidence of this trip remain. Any covert connection between Carson and a hostile communist nation would be an enormous propaganda victory for U.S. imperialism.

Reynaldo looked to the second man, who appeared to be of Afro-Cuban extraction. "This is Miguel. He's been assigned to assist in refining your skills."

Miguel gave a sober nod. He was dressed in military fatigues and combat boots in contrast to Reynaldo's untucked cotton sport shirt and black slacks. Carson himself came off more as a tropical tourist, with a T-shirt, khaki shorts and sandals.

Reynaldo looked at his watch. "It's getting late. I'm going to take you back to your hotel. Miguel will pick you up tomorrow at 9 a.m. in the lobby. Have a good rest."

. . .

Carson walked slowly along the beach in front of the Hotel Nacional de Cuba, where they had put him up. Out to sea, a flock of seagulls traversed the bluish green waters with their wings cutting gracefully through the salty air. Compared to Chicago, the sun shone upon him with an almost miraculous warmth. It reminded him of Vũng Tàu on the Vietnamese coast. But the memory threatened to send him tumbling back into those terrible days in the jungle, and he cut it short. He only went there when he felt an ebb in his resolve to slash and burn.

He turned back toward the hotel, a capitalist relic from the Batista days, when American gangsters packed the clubs, and the liquor and women flowed freely. In the current ethos, it represented a wasteful extravagance, but that was lost on Carson. Politics registered only dimly in his world view, despite his association with the Weather Underground. He drifted through an ambiguous region between the poles of codified justice and free-form vengeance. His vision extended no further than the next violent act of retribution. Whatever followed thereafter played no part. He tired of dreamy declamations about some kind of egalitarian society where all was good and righteous, where the residual darkness had drained from people's souls and fled to some unreachable part of the universe.

He himself seldom dreamed. And when he did, he wished he hadn't.

Miguel drove them along the coast road west of Havana in a Gaz-67, the Soviet equivalent of an American jeep from World War Two. For the first half hour, he made no conversation and let the blast of wind around the open vehicle speak for itself.

When they slowed to drive through the town of Mariel, he abruptly turned to Carson. "So you fought in the war, right?"

"Yeah, I fought in the war," Carson answered.

"Then we're both men of the military," Miguel declared. "And what did you learn?"

"I learned how easy it is to lead pigs to the slaughter," Carson replied without hesitation.

"So it is for wars of imperial aggression. Always. Here in Cuba that was not the case. I fought in a war of liberation."

"And that makes it different?"

"Yes. We only did what was necessary. No more."

They had reached the other end of the town, and the wind blast took over once more.

. . .

The man named Reynaldo sipped his coffee and surveyed the broad plaza across the street from his outdoor table. It centered on a massive monument to one General Maximo Gomez, who led the nation's army in the war of liberation against Spain.

"Now that you've spent some time with him, do you still think he's a good investment?" the man next to him asked. His name was Chavenko, and he was attached to the Soviet embassy.

Reynaldo smiled at the question. The pair shared an amiable professional bond. He worked for the IDG, Cuba's central intelligence agency, while Chavenko represented the Soviet KGB.

"He's like all investments," Reynaldo replied. "It's simply a matter of risk versus gain. You know the risks going in and hope for the best coming out."

Chavenko grinned through slightly crooked teeth. His pale Slavic skin had never yielded to the tropical sun. "You had better be careful using capitalist metaphors. You never know who's listening."

"No, you don't. Which is why we're sitting outside next to a busy street. Ah well; it's no worse than Batista's secret police."

"Probably not. Did Fidel make the proper impression on the young man?"

Reynaldo took another sip of coffee. "Fidel always makes the proper impression. That's how he got to be Fidel."

"So, tell me this," the Russian said. "How did Che get to be Che? I mean, he made a real mess out of that business in the Congo, but no one seemed to notice." He snorted. "I suppose it helped a lot to look like a fucking movie star."

"It did. But not with Fidel. He got sick of all that Maoist stuff about revolutions that go on forever. He's got a country to run, and that meant taking a more pragmatic view of the world. It meant making deals with you people while Che blundered around out in foreign jungles."

"Fidel has it right," Chavenko said. "Revolution is a process, not an event. Look at the United States. They made a big mistake going into Vietnam and riled up their political left. But will it lead to a revolution? Not likely. Revolutions happen when the masses have nothing left to lose; and in America the masses are driving big cars, shopping in supermarkets and mowing their very own front lawns. People like the Weather Underground are romantic revolutionaries. They don't see the political reality of their situation."

"So why spend so much effort on our angry young friend? What's the payoff?" Reynaldo asked.

"It's a long-term proposition," Chavenko replied. "It's all about social and political destabilization. If you do it for long enough, the country starts to fall apart from the inside. You create conflict, you encourage chaos. And that's where people like our Mr. Carson fit in. If he learns his trade well enough, he'll be able to make bombs that do some really serious damage. Suppose he and his friends pull off a bombing that kills a hundred or so people. The federal government will go wild. They'll give Hoover and his FBI carte blanche. So much for the constitution, so much for civil rights. It'll launch a wave of repression that pushes the whole country that much further toward the edge."

"Basically, what you're saying is that it's a lot easier to slowly poison your enemy than to risk a shootout," Reynaldo summarized.

"That's exactly what I'm saying."

. . .

Miguel pulled off the main highway near the town of Sandino and drove north for a mile toward the coast. A few minutes later, they turned onto a rutted road that took them to a locked gate with a sign that shouted ADVERTENCIA! Carson couldn't read the text in Spanish below the warning, but he got the general idea. Miguel unlocked the gate, and they continued over a rise to the beach, where the breakers did a lazy roll into the gritty sand. After a brief trip to the east, they parked in front of a windowless building constructed of corrugated metal.

"So where do we start?" Carson asked the Cuban as he unlocked the front door.

"Come in and grab a chair," Miguel responded. "We'll sit out here. We'll talk about first things first."

The building's interior looked like an inventor's basement, with a workbench, tools and shelves full of electrical devices, along with a safe that undoubtedly held explosives. Carson set up the folding lawn chairs on a concrete apron out front while Miguel reached into an ice chest and fished out two bottles of Coke, the one product that apparently transcended all borders and political persuasions.

Once seated, Miguel took a swig from his bottle and told Carson, "Let's start at the beginning: what really is an explosion?"

The simplicity of the query caught Carson off guard. "I'm not sure what you mean."

Miguel gave him a stern smile. "And that's why I asked the question. Basically, it is energy traveling from one place to another at very high speed. You create the energy though some kind chemical reaction that turns a solid or liquid into a gas. But it's the speed part that's critical. If you burn a log in a fire, you produce heat and light but don't get an explosion because it happens gradually. Even with gunpowder all you get is a big flash and some smoke. But now think about a pipe bomb full of powder. At the moment it's ignited, all the energy is stuck inside. An instant later, the pipe can no longer contain it. It's released all at once in a single wave. You have an explosion."

Carson nodded. He already knew all this. Still, he was a guest here and had best reciprocate by paying close attention. He'd already built one bomb of serious dimension, but it failed to explode due to technical miscalculations. He hoped to learn enough during his stay to avoid repeating the error.

"Now let's talk about chemicals, one of my favorite subjects. I was a chemist before the revolution and wound up applying my knowledge to help end the oppression visited upon the common people. The energy of the explosion is locked in the atoms, waiting to be released. If a compound is unstable, all it takes is simple motion to upset the order of things. Nitroglycerine is a good example. It's too volatile to be safely handled. But if you combine it with a few other substances, you can make dynamite, the bomb maker's best friend, powerful yet easy to handle."

Miguel took another sip of his Coke. Carson couldn't help but see the irony in an Afro-Cuban communist swigging capitalist America's favorite soft drink.

Miguel put down the bottle and went on. "Now if the dynamite is at peace with itself, how do you get it to explode?" He got up from his chair. "Wait here." He went back into the building and reappeared with a small metal cylinder with two wires protruding.

"You use a blasting cap. When you hook the wires up to a battery, electric current flows into the cap and creates enough heat to set off an initiation compound, which then sets off the primary and base explosives. You get a big enough bang to trigger the dynamite."

"What if I want to use something more powerful than dynamite?" Carson asked. He was thinking back to the deal he'd made with a Hells Angel for the Semtex he'd used in his original bomb.

"Yes, there are substances more powerful, like C4 and RDX. But most of them are tightly controlled and hard to come by. And if you try, you risk getting caught. Not so with dynamite. You can walk into a construction supply place, show some ID and you're set." He managed a wry grin, revealing perfect white teeth set against his dark skin, where brown approached pure black. "So you see, there are certain advantages to your free market system."

As the day went on, the sun threw long shadows down the length of the beach as Miguel continued his overview of the art and science of bomb making. He covered basic schemes for igniting the blasting cap. He went on to discuss timing devices that would close the circuit and deliver electric current to the cap.

Finally, he crossed over from hard science to pure horror, and described the role of shrapnel, which would tear, rip, puncture, and shred human flesh to devastating effect. He explained that the blast wave was seldom enough to do serious harm. It might fracture a few limbs and break some eardrums, but little more. You needed something like nails, ball bearings or roofing staples accelerated to murderous velocity to truly make your point.

He concluded with a rhetorical question: Why bomb at all? Simple. Because it exposes the vulnerability of the ruling class. It renders law enforcement impotent and seriously erodes the public's sense of personal security. "With most people, if they know they're okay, then they'll obey," he quipped. During the revolution, he'd engineered a whole series of bombings that the Batista regime was powerless to stop, and the people took note. They weren't okay and weren't going to obey.

He declined to mention that many of the blasts killed innocent civilians.

. . .

A week later, Carson's instruction was complete, and Reynaldo walked him to the gate at José Martí International Airport for his flight to Mexico City. At the last moment, the Cuban agent handed him a card with a hand-written phone number.

"If you ever find yourself in serious difficulty, call this number. But only if you have no other option. Understand?"

"Understand."

"Tell him you met at Alegría de Pío. Got it?"

"Got it."

4.

BERKELEY
MAY 15, 1969

"I'm starting to think I'm screwed," Stone said to Christine.

"And why's that?"

"All the decent talent has been sucked up. Unless I get really lucky and find the next John Lennon holed up in a basement somewhere. If he's been out in broad daylight, someone's already seen him and signed him."

"That bad?"

"As Robert Johnson once said: 'Woke up this morning and all the crawdads were gone. Someone been fishin' in my pond'."

Christine smiled. "I think he was referring to something a lot naughtier than record deals."

Stone's mood brightened a little. "I think you're probably right." She'd yanked him back from the edge. She was good at that. He downshifted their VW bug from fourth into third to slow their descent on the winding street out of the Berkeley Hills. Occasionally they got a glimpse between houses of the UC Berkeley campus below. They'd been visiting an old friend of Christine's who taught microbiology there. The man and his wife, a history professor, had seemed distracted and the conversation kept drifting back to local politics.

A couple of years back, the student-driven Free Speech Movement had pitted the administration against student activists, who wound up occupying a key campus building for several days before police drove them out. Since then, a semblance of order had been restored, but the campus remained on edge. The governor, Ronald Reagan, didn't help matters by labeling the students as pro-communist perverts.

Eventually they left the hills and rolled out onto Piedmont Avenue which would take them south toward 580, then over the Bay Bridge.

A block later, Stone spotted the helicopter. It appeared to be a military model, and it came in low just a few blocks ahead. They could feel the insistent thump of the rotor blades as it veered west toward the downtown area and stopped to hover.

"Not good," Stone commented.

"What's the problem?" Christine asked.

"That's not a civilian chopper. It's either Army or police. Something's wrong."

The traffic up ahead came to a complete halt. Police cars, both county sheriff and state patrol, had blocked off all the surrounding streets. "Well, whatever it is," Stone said, "we're now part of it."

He spied one remaining parking space to their immediate front, pulled in and shut off the engine.

"You think it's some kind of student thing?" Christine asked.

"I think that's a pretty good bet," Stone replied. "Let's go check it out."

"You think that's a good idea?" she asked.

"We'll be on foot, so we can keep our distance. We might even get to witness some local history in the making."

"But we stay out of it, right?"

"Absolutely. Spectators only."

"Good. I'm relying on your previous experience in the law enforcement profession to keep us out of hot water."

"As well you should. Let's do it."

They heard the sirens the moment they got out of the car and started down the sidewalk toward a roundabout. An ominous whining crisscrossed the late afternoon. Up ahead, stalled traffic choked the roundabout's circular path. People had begun to emerge from their vehicles.

And old man with an ample belly stepped out of a decrepit camper and looked around. "It's the goddamn hippies. Gotta be. They're at it all over again."

Stone and Christine picked their way through the cars to the far side, where a woman in a Mumu stared down the street to the west while she puffed on a filtered cigarette.

"What's going on?" Christine asked the woman.

"People's Park," she said. "The students took it and now the cops want it back."

"Where is it?" Stone asked.

The woman pointed straight down the street. "Coupla blocks down there. They put up these big fences to keep 'em out. Now they're really pissed."

In the distance, clusters of red and blue lights put out a frantic flicker. A column of dark smoke rose from a burning sedan. Water shot out of an open fire hydrant in a powerful white arc. Overhead, the chopper left its hover and drifted in a lazy circle only a short distance above the buildings. A white fog flowed out of its fuselage and dispersed into a fine mist that refracted the sun into a glittering rainbow.

"Tear gas," Stone said.

"Yeah," the woman said. "Seen that before."

Stone turned to Christine. "We better take the long way around."

"No fooling."

They continued south for a few more blocks until they reached Derby Street and stopped at the corner. An occasional concussive pop erupted from off in the distance. Stone pointed west. "The main drag's down this way. We'll take it slow."

"I would certainly hope so," Christine said with a generous dose of cynicism. Her enthusiasm for this exploit was rapidly dissipating.

"We're far enough from the major battle we should be okay," Stone said as they walked toward Telegraph Avenue.

Wrong.

When they started down the last block, a chaotic crowd of students appeared on the main drag in a kind of defiant retreat. As they went, some scooped up tear gas canisters and threw them back up the street, beyond Stone's view. Others walked backwards, shaking their fists and flipping the bird.

Then the shooting started.

"Down!" Stone commanded, and they ducked behind a VW bus. The source of the gunfire wasn't yet visible. But its impact was. Students twisted and fell and clutched their arms, legs and torsos. Their retreat turned into a route, with the wounded struggling to their feet, helped forward by their fleeing comrades.

As the students faded away, the source of the gunfire came into view. A small army of helmeted cops strolled forward, many toting shotguns. Some casually reloaded while others fired. The report of their weapons echoed off the nearby buildings. They seemed to be in no hurry now that they had the upper hand. Eventually they passed from sight, like some terrible dream of robots from hell.

Stone and Christine slowly stood up in silence as they tried to absorb what they had just witnessed. They whirled around at a clattering sound on the sidewalk behind them. Three young men wheeled a fourth on a portable gurney. A red blanket of blood glistened on his left side and his face was drawn into a mask of unmitigated suffering.

Christine did not hesitate. She strode over to the group and announced "I'm a doctor. Let me see him."

When she gingerly lifted his shirt, Stone could see the perforations in the wet cloth. Buckshot. As an ex-cop, it wasn't the first time he'd been exposed to it. "What happened to him?" he asked the group.

One of the men spoke up in urgent tones. "A cop shot him. I was there. We were up on the roof. We weren't doing anything. The cop didn't care. He was down on the street right below us with a shotgun and he just started blasting."

If it was true, it was absolutely murderous, since 00 buckshot has the power to maim and kill, as opposed to birdshot, which produces more superficial wounds. A lot of the wounds just inflicted out on Telegraph Avenue were probably birdshot – but not all. That army of cops out on the avenue was peppered with stone killers. But which ones? No one would ever know. Civil chaos always casts a dense cloak of ambiguity that stymies any quest for accountability.

Christine put the victim's shirt back down. "I'm sorry, there's not much I can do for him right here. He's sustained a lot of intestinal damage. You need to find an ambulance."

"Yeah, sure," one of the other men said in total frustration. "The last one left before we could load him on."

Stone sensed motion on the street and looked up. An ambulance. A remarkable tumble of the die. He flagged it down and went around to the side as the driver rolled down his window.

"We've got a guy here who's in really bad shape. You got room?" Stone asked.

The driver looked over to the blood-soaked gurney on the sidewalk. "We'll make room," he said.

. . .

Matt Carson stared at the blood on the adjoining roof. The sun and asphalt tile had already baked it brown. Somehow, they had managed to get the guy down and onto a gurney, but he was in bad shape. Gut shot. By one of the pigs. He probably wouldn't make it. Carson could tell. He'd seen hundreds of wounds and become an expert judge of their mortality.

Telegraph Avenue was clear now. The pigs had blasted their way south. Carson sat alone on the roof of the old theater. The time had come. The carnage today in the street was the final validation. He was ready to do some blasting of his own.

. . .

As Stone crossed the Bay Bridge on the way home, he watched a towering fog bank roll in and envelope the city. It muted the sun dull orange and turned the water slate gray.

He'd like to think that today's upheaval on the streets of Berkeley was an isolated incident, a social anomaly of some kind. But he knew better. Chaos, confusion, senseless violence. It was a harbinger of dark times ahead. He could feel it in his bones. He considered himself a person of good intentions, but what were such people to do right now?

He had no idea. And that was the worst of it.

5.

HOLLYWOOD

"Yeah, I would've thumped on 'em for sure," Murphy said. "They're a bunch of spoiled communist punks. But that's a lot different than killing them. You gotta give 'em a chance to grow up and see how fucked they are."

"Yes, you do," Stone agreed. He'd just told Detective Sgt. John Murphy what went down during the People's Park march in Berkeley last week. It was going on fifteen years since the pair had worked together in Hollywood Vice. In the interim, Murphy had moved over to Homicide, where he was cruising along toward his pension. It looked like an easy ride – right up until recently.

Stone looked out the window onto Vine Street from their padded booth in Hody's Coffee Shop. An old woman with silver beehive hair beat on a parking meter with her cane. A lesbian couple glided by in matching outfits and sunglasses. Stone smiled. Welcome to Hollywood. He chose this spot because it was within walking distance of Capitol Records, where he had a meeting later on. Given a choice, Murphy would have opted for a dive bar down on Santa Monica, where he could down a little afternoon nip.

"So now you're smack in the middle of this Manson thing," Stone said. "How'd you come up with an indictment?"

"Oldest trick in the world," Murphy said. "One of his hippy chicks, name of Atkins, started blabbing to her cellmate down at the jail. She spilled enough stuff that we nailed the whole bunch of them, Manson included. I'm telling you they're downright fucking evil. I mean, how do you stick a fork in the belly of a pregnant woman?"

"I don't know," Stone said. He'd read the gruesome details several times over in different media. It only added to his despondence about where the world was headed.

"Know what else?" Murphy said. "A couple of your buddies up at Capitol are out on the edge of this thing."

"Oh yeah?"

"Oh yeah. You know Terry Melcher?"

"A little." Stone had met him a couple of times when they crossed paths in the studio. Melcher was Doris Day's son. He produced several of the Beach Boys albums, which made him a big deal around the company. Was he any good? Hard to tell. Brian Wilson was the real driving force behind the Beach Boys' sound.

"And what about Dennis Wilson?"

"Same." Stone had met the Beach Boys' drummer on several occasions and found him to be an arrogant jerk but decided it best to keep his opinion private.

"Well here's the real deal," Murphy said. "Wilson's out driving around in his Ferrari looking for some easy pussy and he picks up a couple of Manson's chicks. Next thing you know, Manson and his harem move in at Wilson's place, trading tricks for rent. Sounds kind of like our old gig in Vice, right?"

"Yeah, it does."

"Well it gets better. Seems Charlie fancies himself a rock star, and Wilson bites. He brings in Melcher and sets up an audition. Manson flunks the test. He's more than a little pissed. Then the murders go down and now Melcher's completely freaked. He's gone into hiding along with a couple of bodyguards."

"You blame him?"

"Can't say as I do. Anyway, just thought you'd like to know."

"Got it. Thanks."

Murphy took the last bite of his key lime pie and washed it down with some coffee. "Know what I think? You can dink around all you want with this record business. It won't make any difference. You're still a cop. You should get back down here and get it on."

Stone had to smile. "Maybe." In truth, he couldn't rule it out. Not entirely. He'd put in too many years behind the badge to ever get away clean.

Outside, he gave Murphy a pat on the back and sent him on his way. The giant clown head on top of Hody's looked down on him with its tiny top hat and ominous smile. Did it know something he didn't? He started down the sidewalk toward the Capitol Records Building, a Hollywood landmark from the day it went up.

. . .

Stanley Gortikov definitely looked the part. Broad face with a leisurely tan. White receding hair. Impeccably tailored suit. An entertainment industry veteran. An archetypical native of Southern California.

"Jimmy! Come in," he greeted Stone. Behind him, the curved windows of his office on the top floor of Capitol Records swept across an impressive arc of the urban core. An office truly befitting the president of a major label.

Gortikov guided him to a small meeting table. "Have a seat. Anything to drink?"

"No thanks," Stone said. This was already going badly. His golden ear picked up the artifice of formality in the executive's voice.

"So how are things up in the city by the sea?"

"Let's just say they've been better," Stone responded.

"Yes, I read about that business last week over in Berkeley. Very disturbing."

Stone knew that wasn't the issue at all. The real issue was: Where's the talent?

"Well, you've certainly had your day up there," Gortikov continued. "Even the Beatles have gone psychedelic on us. It makes me wonder if there's still some gems for the plucking." He looked up at Stone expectantly. "What do you think?"

"Could be," Stone responded. "Time will tell."

"Time. Yes, time," Gortikov said in a reflective mode. "You know, some parts of the music market are damn near timeless, like the classics. But not the pop music side. It's one revolution after another. You're late, you're dead. That's just the way it is. Agreed?"

"Agreed." He could almost hear pulleys squeak as the guillotine blade reached full height.

"I don't like to say this Jimmy, but we've gone from being a little late to too late in the Bay Area. And you know what you do with a mine when it stops producing?"

"You shut it down," Stone suggested. He could hear the blade whistling down the rails.

"You've got a lot of talent, Jimmy. Everybody says so. It just needs to find the proper home. You did a great job up in Bakersfield. You should look around for a label that's big in country."

Boom! His head rolled across the tastefully carpeted floor.

"Yeah, maybe so," he uttered. It was the best he could manage.

Gortikov stood up, signaling an end to the meeting. "I think you'll be quite happy with the severance package we've put together. Your service to this company has not gone unappreciated." He held out his hand. "Good luck."

Stone gave it reluctant shake. "Thanks."

. . .

James Stone walked back down Vine Street to where he'd parked his rental car near Hody's Coffee Shop. He looked up at the giant clown with its curved teeth and black lips set in a leering grin.

"You knew all along, didn't you?"

6.

SAN FRANCISCO

The cat had made a mistake. Stone was sure of it. The animal padded cautiously up the stairs toward the porch, where Stone sat smoking a cigarette. Its eyes fixated on the ashtray that Stone had brought out with him. The cat obviously thought it was yet another dish holding a kitty treat of some kind. Fresh milk, a little tuna maybe.

They had abbreviated the cat down to Kitty, because it wasn't an official member of the household. It operated as a freelance hustler, seeking booty all up and down the block. Stone or Christine's arrival at the curb out front triggered Kitty to come forth, leap up the stairs and wait expectantly for a handout. Inevitably, they would go inside and bring something out for it to lap up or munch on. They found its arrogance and sense of entitlement hopelessly endearing.

Kitty reached the top of the stairs and stopped short of the ashtray, realizing it had been duped. It lingered long enough to register its disgust before bounding down the stairs and strolling off in search of more promising opportunities.

"Well, at least you have a job," Stone told the retreating animal, which was more than he could say. For some inscrutable reason, his biggest takeaway from his meeting with Gortikov at Capitol had nothing to do with being summarily executed. Instead, he wondered how the man found the time to maintain his marvelous tan.

He stubbed his cigarette and caught a pleasant whiff of ocean air. Their rental house was about six blocks off the beach and a couple of blocks south of Golden Gate Park. A comfortable, quiet neighborhood, a good place to seek refuge from the endless urban hustle.

Christine would be home soon from her new job in the ER at the UCSF Medical Center, which was close by. She'd decided she needed something that pumped a little adrenaline into her work, and the ER was doing just that. Each evening, they had a drink while they fixed dinner and she recounted the day's episodes, which ranged from humorous to horrifying. But last night was different. His dismissal at Capitol took precedence over their customary patter and they pondered where he might go from here. He told her that, at forty, he wasn't ready to cash in his chips just yet. Fortunately, money wasn't a problem. Besides her medical income, Christine had received a hefty divorce settlement from her ex, a Los Angeles real estate developer, which was prudently invested. And Stone had managed to set aside a generous portion of his compensation in the music industry.

The real question was where did he go from here? Christine counseled patience. Since they weren't living paycheck to paycheck, he could take his time as he mapped out his future. Christine, as usual, was right. Besides, he'd just started reading a new novel called *The Godfather* by this guy named Mario Puzo and now he could buzz all the way through it with no distractions.

. . .

"Well boo hiss on Capitol," Rhonda Savage said when Stone told her what went down. "You're one of the best things that ever happened to them."

Stone managed a modest laugh. "I think the Beatles and the Beach Boys might take issue with that."

Stone and Rhonda went way back. All the way to Bakersfield over twelve years ago when she was just thirteen and wound up ensnared by a group of wealthy perverts with a penchant for very young girls. He'd extracted her and helped launch her on a new life in Los Angeles. Sadly, it didn't take. She'd done all right up until her young husband-to-be was killed in Vietnam, and then she unraveled. He'd encountered her a couple of years ago on the street in Haight Ashbury, where she'd become entangled in an even uglier situation. Once again he interceded, and this time it looked like a keeper. She was working as the executive assistant to the legendary rock promoter Bill Graham, who was quite happy with her performance.

He had coffee with her every other week or so at this little place on Geary Street, a short distance from Graham's premier music venue, the Fillmore. Over time, they'd settled into something approaching a father-daughter relationship. Stone had no children of his own, so Rhonda was about as close as he was ever going to get.

"And speaking of music and money," Stone said, "how is Mr. Graham these days?"

Rhonda grimaced. "He's pissed."

Stone laughed. "The way I hear it, he's pissed pretty much all the time."

"No, I mean seriously pissed."

"Oh yeah?"

"Oh yeah. You know about the upcoming Rolling Stones tour, right?"

"How could I miss it? The media's going nuts."

"There's a guy named Scully. He's one of the Dead people and he pitched Jagger on ending it with a big free concert in Golden Gate Park. Bill thinks it's a terrible idea, and so does the city. They applied for a permit and got turned down cold, so now the Stones people are looking around for another venue."

"I see. Now didn't Bill get in a brawl with one of the Stone's managers when he put on their show in Oakland?"

Rhonda had to smile. "We don't talk about that around the office."

"I bet you don't."

"There's this weird guy named John Jaymes who seems to be in the middle of all this," Rhonda said. "He's connected with the Stones, but I don't know exactly how. Anyway, he had the chutzpah to call me yesterday, even though Bill's in an uproar about anything connected to this free concert idea. Jaymes. You ever heard of him?"

"Can't say I have. What was his pitch?"

"He's looking for security people."

"But they don't even have a venue yet, right?"

"Right. It's all very strange. I'd really like to know what's going on – and so would Bill."

Stone smiled. "Ah, I see. A chance to shine for the boss."

"Something like that," Rhonda revealed with a knowing grin.

"Maybe I can help."

"Oh yeah?"

"I'm an ex-cop, as you know. If he's looking for security people, I'm a prime candidate. Give him my number, and in the meantime I'll see what I can find out."

"You sure?" Rhonda asked hesitantly.

"I'm sure. No harm in asking, right?"

"Right."

She was beaming. Wonderful. Stone had to admit he definitely liked being her hero. Always had. He couldn't help it.

. . .

Stone's encounter with Mr. John Jaymes started strange and only got stranger. It began when Jaymes phoned him the next day and gave a very hazy outline of his plans for the concert. In turn, Stone briefly presented his credentials, and Jaymes liked what he heard. A meeting was set up for later in the day downtown at the Hilton.

When Stone arrived, he got his first hint of things to come. Jaymes wasn't staying in one of the hotel's standard rooms. He occupied an executive suite on the top floor, with all the requisite perks. A living room separate from the bedroom, done in the most tasteful of furnishings. A dining area with a polished wooden table. A kitchen with a refrigerator, cupboards and sink.

One look at Jaymes told Stone that the man had already grazed through the entire room service menu. The guy had long ago crossed the dietary line into the realm of obesity. His loud, blousy shirt sported a paisley print that reflected the style of the moment but failed to conceal the ominous bulge beneath.

"Mr. Stone, good to meet you." He looked to be about thirty and had a handshake both cool and clammy. His wiry brown hair descended to a set of mutton chops, a lame attempt to be hip and with-it.

"Have a seat." Jaymes gestured to some chairs at a table on the far side of the room. The table itself was littered with the remnants of recently consumed menu items: a hamburger, a grilled cheese sandwich, pepperoni pizza, melting ice cream. "Could I get you anything?" he asked.

"I'm fine," Stone answered. He suddenly felt less than hungry.

"Here's the deal," Jaymes started. "Like I said on the phone, I'm involved with pulling off this free concert for the Stones here in the Bay Area. One of my areas of responsibility is security. I already have some people on retainer from other events that I've done in the past but, given the scale of this thing, I'm going to need more help."

"Sounds pretty interesting," Stone said. "So, how'd you get hooked up with the Stones?"

"I became involved with their management people some time back and we've formed a partnership. I've taken over security and transportation, and it's turned out to be a great relationship."

"Where's this thing going to be held?" Stone asked.

"Our first choice was Golden Gate Park, but there turned out to be some technical difficulties. We currently have several other venues under consideration."

"Let's talk about the money. How much for how long?"

"Two hundred dollars for a single day's work. Cash. It should be easy money. These kinds of events are pretty mellow. Look at Woodstock."

"And who does the paying?"

"I do, as soon as the gig's over."

"Why don't you tell me a little about these other people I'd be working with? I always like to know who has my back."

"Sure. They're all ex-cops of some sort, most of them through my connections on the East Coast. Good guys. You'll like 'em."

"Okay then." Stone rose to leave. "Tell you what: As soon as this thing gets settled and you got a venue nailed down, let me know, okay?"

"Will do." Jaymes rose laboriously to his feet, struggling to hoist three hundred pounds against the omnipresent force of gravity. "Talk to you soon."

. . .

Stone smiled to himself as he rode the elevator back down to reality. The guy was a complete enigma, floating in a world where truth and fiction freely intermingled and had little hybrid babies. Nothing he said was verifiable in any reasonable way. Based on his years with Hollywood Vice, he saw a classic con artist at the peak of his powers.

If this was the best the Stones people could do with their concert, they were heading for a real disaster.

7.

FLINT, MICHIGAN
DECEMBER 27, 1969

The Council of War had convened, and the Giant Ballroom on Saginaw Avenue went from being a boarded-up relic to occupying the center of the American radical universe. Its dance floor was cold and drafty, but a furnace of unmitigated rage provided more than enough heat for its 300 occupants.

The Chicago cops had killed Fred Hampton, their black brother-in-arms, and now his image, done in red and black, glared down at them from posters plastered to the walls. They had already forgotten that he'd called them "adventuristic, masochistic, and Custeristic." His violent apotheosis carried the day.

One by one, the Weatherman leaders went to the podium and stoked the faithful. They made it clear that the SDS, the Students for a Democratic Society, was moribund, ineffectual and irrelevant. Its Weatherman branch would now sever completely and become the Weather Underground. They would transform into fugitive guerrillas, roaming the underbelly of the urban landscape in combat with the established order, known collectively as "the pigs." Politicians, businesspeople, educators and parents had now joined the cops as icons of imperialist decadence.

Matt Carson sat toward the back with his girlfriend from the Chicago sessions, Alice. She bent forward and nodded her head in earnest agreement with the stream of rants coming from the stage. Finally, she could contain herself no longer and leapt to her feet.

"All white babies are pigs!" she shouted. The crowd cheered in agreement. Fred Hampton had it right. A subliminal masochistic streak ran rampant through the entire movement. Carson knew it but didn't care. They were finally moving toward some serious violence, as he'd hoped they would. He sensed that all the rhetoric and hyperbole were running out of gas, leaving little choice but to resort to action. It was the only way to truly shed their "white-skin privilege" as they called it. Ultimately, he regarded these people not as comrades but as allies fighting against a common enemy. He had no problem with his white skin but an enormous problem with the incalculable arrogance and cruelty of those who prosecuted the war.

He looked over to Alice, who'd gone back to nodding her head in automatic assent to whatever was spewing from the podium. She fit the mold almost perfectly. A trust-fund baby living on daddy's tab while she crusaded for social justice, whatever that was. Her family lived in Chicago, where her father earned hefty sums as an attorney in a partnership specializing in corporate law. On the flip side of the family ledger, her mother spent hefty sums on chic clothes, club dues and their frequent trips to Europe. Shopping in Rome, sailing in Sardinia, skiing in the Alps.

A natural extension of this lifestyle was to send their only daughter to Bryn Mawr, where she quickly started to unravel. The bohemian life beckoned, although Alice's limited intellectual capacity kept her out on its periphery. To compensate, she quit school and volunteered for a charity in Costa Rica, where she learned the hardscrabble reality of life outside the American bubble. She came to believe that all the poverty and suffering she saw resulted from U.S. imperialism and its callous economic grip on these hapless people. And with this belief came a growing rage at the injustice of it all. When visiting home, she became an embarrassment at dinner parties, a source of parental anguish, and prime bait for outlier politicians of virtually any stripe.

Still, her parents loved her and had to believe that this whole radical thing was just a phase. They determined that they would see her through it. She received financial support on a regular basis, which she regarded not as an act of love but as a just entitlement in her quest to purge Amerika of all that ailed it.

And by pairing with Alice, Carson became an indirect beneficiary of the best that white privilege could buy. He no longer had to work odd jobs or curl up on park benches. Their relationship was not one of love but of mutual convenience. She got a partner who would tolerate her slavish devotion to political causes, and he got one who propped him up financially. He also got someone who would accommodate his growing use of street drugs, like various flavors of amphetamine. Psychedelics were fine for college kids, but he was not a college kid. He'd grown up in a wrecking yard owned by his stepfather in El Paso, where he helped the old man crush the mechanical life out of aging automobiles. Twisted steel, spent motor oil and shattered glass defined his days. In that particular world at that particular time, alcohol and speed were the drugs of choice. He'd dabbled with smoking heroin in Vietnam but preferred to shoot for peaks rather than dreamy valleys. While the booze supplied the buzz, the speed put the pedal to the metal.

The rhetoric from the stage droned on and washed out over the eager audience. It's revolution time, we're going to be the new Viet Cong right here in River City. Carson considered most of it to be a histrionic shuck embedded in theatrical jive. They could talk the talk, but could they walk the walk? Some had confronted the cops on the streets of Chicago a couple of months back. Some had even been superficially wounded and jailed. But then the family attorneys showed up. Charges were dismissed. Life had returned to normal. Their platform of support remained firm.

Had any of them loaded someone missing multiple limbs onto a chopper with bullets whizzing and mortar rounds spraying shrapnel? No.

At least, not yet. When the final reckoning came, some would stay the course while most would drift away. The real army would assemble, and Carson, who had fought a real war, would join forces with them. They were trending in the right direction. It was just a matter of time.

On stage a strikingly attractive woman in her mid-twenties approached the podium. Bernadette Dohrn. Supreme empress of the radical left. The ultimate combination of sex and intellect. All the men wanted to have her. All the women wanted to be her. Lust and gravitas condensed into a single package wearing a miniskirt and knee-high Italian boots.

Her impassioned speech immediately grabbed Carson's attention. She berated the liberal community for not avenging Fred Hampton's murder, for failing to take to the streets and burn Chicago to the ground. They were all a bunch of scared honkies. It was time to quit cowering and take up arms and be a fighting force alongside the blacks.

Carson liked what he was hearing. At last, someone in the leadership swept aside the last vestiges of peaceful political action and advocated outright war, with all its attendant horrors. Dohrn confirmed this declaration with a stunning reference to none other than Charles Manson as a model for revolutionary zeal. His cult-driven murder of Sharon Tate and friends served as the new standard for radical justice from the street.

"Dig it," she said. "First, they killed those pigs and then they ate dinner in the same room with them, then they even shoved a fork into a victim's stomach. Wild."

Wild, yes. The vision of a fork plunged into Tate's pregnant belly resonated perfectly with the fevered mood of the crowd. In no time at all they were raising their hands in a four-fingered salute, signifying the tines of a dinner fork. Alice, of course, was no exception.

· · ·

That night, they retired to the nave of a nearby Catholic church, where rows of stained-glass saints looked down in sorrow upon the vigorous coupling in the pews below. Women straddled the seated men and bounced with a ferocity previously unseen. They were going to war.

Alice played the part perfectly, with eyes closed and parted lips that expelled one gasp after another. Carson grasped her hips as she thrust herself onto him. All around them, others did much the same. A giant asynchronous engine of wanton sexuality. Carson wondered what the local priest would think of it. Would he be aghast? Would he join in? Would he peep from concealment? Probably the latter.

Later, they clustered in small groups and speculated about what the leadership was planning. They resembled excited little children, wondering about what their parents had in store for the big summer trip.

Carson was pleased to hear much conjecture about a bombing campaign. At last, they were on the right track.

At this point, he could not know that within the coming months all but a small minority of them would be purged. Those clinging to the lush life of the bourgeoisie, those dedicated to family, and those who questioned the leadership; all would be surgically excised. Only those utterly devoted to the revolution would survive. These chosen few would then split into even smaller groups, each plotting their very own insurrection.

An insurrection mostly centered on bombs.

8.

ALTAMONT
DECEMBER 6, 1969

"It's a done deal, finally," Rhonda told Stone over the phone. "They're going to put it on at Altamont."

"Where's that?" Stone asked.

"It's a race track out east past Livermore. It'll be all over the media by tomorrow."

"And what about that Jaymes guy? I never heard back. What about security?"

"They're hiring the Hells Angels."

"They're what?" Stone asked incredulously.

"They're hiring the Hells Angels," Rhonda repeated.

"Let me get this straight. They're hiring an outlaw motorcycle gang to do security at a major concert."

"You got it. And it gets better. They're paying them five hundred dollars' worth of beer for their services."

"Unbelievable." All Stone's suspicions about Jaymes were confirmed. He was in charge of basically nothing.

"Give me a guess: How many people?" Stone asked.

"For a freebie headlined by the Rolling Stones? At least a couple of hundred thousand," she responded.

"Jesus," he muttered.

"Yeah, they're going to need Jesus times ten to pull it off," she said. "Bossman Bill had it right all along."

"So it would seem," Stone said. "You find out anything more, you let me know, okay?"

"You got it. See you," Rhonda said.

Stone hung up and turned on the TV before shuffling into the kitchen. CBS News anchor Walter Cronkite was saying something about a Soviet nuclear test. It didn't sound good. It never did.

Stone ignored it. This Altamont thing consumed him. He'd been in the business long enough to know how complex it was to stage an event of this magnitude. The fact that someone like Jaymes had wormed his way into the middle of it was a very bad sign. And the Hells Angels as security was an even worse sign.

Oh well, at least they were going to have shrimp linguini tonight. He always sautéed the shrimp while Christine cooked the pasta and made the sauce. He decided to get it all in gear by pouring a glass of midrange Bordeaux and tossing the shrimp in the pan.

The front door opened, and Christine came in, still wearing her signature white lab coat from work. Stone heard a plaintive meow from behind her. Kitty. Christine smiled sympathetically. "I'll get it," she said and crossed to the refrigerator, where she fetched milk, poured a little in a saucer and set it out for the freeloading cat.

"I just talked to Rhonda," Stone told her as she shut the door and took her coat off.

"And how is Rhonda?"

"Rhonda's fine, but she had some really weird news about that free Stones concert that's coming up."

"Oh yeah?"

"They switched it to a race track out east of Livermore, and they've hired the Hells Angels for security. All for five hundred bucks' worth of beer."

"Really," she said as he poured herself a glass of wine and sat on a stool by the kitchen counter.

Stone caught a measure of neutrality in her response, like maybe it wasn't such a big deal. "So what do you think?" he asked.

"I think you better have another sip of wine, maybe a big sip."

"And why's that?"

"You remember Dr. Richard Fine?"

"You mean that left-wing guy who's Janis Joplin's doctor?"

Christine took a generous sip of wine before answering. "The same. He's putting together a pro bono medical team in case they need help."

"You're talking about the concert, aren't you?"

"Yup. The concert."

"And you signed up?" Of course she did. Christine was a compulsive volunteer.

"Yup."

"Shit." Stone paused. "And does Dr. Fine have any idea how fucked-up this thing might be?"

Christine shrugged. "Probably not."

Stone sighed and stared down at the raw shrimp in the pan. "You know I can't let you go alone."

"I do know that." She came off the stool and kissed him warmly on the lips. "And that's why I love you so very much."

Stone managed a wistful smile. "I sure hope so."

"And if we do go, there's a consolation prize."

"Like what?"

"A free helicopter ride."

"Now that's better," said Stone as he poured a little oil in the pan to fry the shrimp.

. . .

One could live a lifetime and never behold anything close to what was unfolding below. Especially without access to a Bell 212 helicopter, a favorite of CEOs, global arms traders and rock royalty.

Stone had managed to commandeer the copilot's seat, which afforded a spectacular view. One look ahead told him why they needed to fly in. Tens of thousands of cars jammed the freeway east toward the speedway. The freeway north was no better. Most had given up and pulled off like little grains of rice flung to the side of the road. Their occupants streamed out and set forth on foot toward a massive rite dedicated to the new and unholy trinity of sex, drugs and rock 'n' roll. Since the recent summer of love, hedonism and spiritualism had fought an epic battle for the souls of the young, and hedonism had clearly won. The beast slouched on toward Altamont.

At this altitude, the crowd shrank to anonymous dots and formed squirming rivers that flowed through the brown, barren hills to a giant bowl beside the speedway track. Here they pooled into a great pointillist ocean of colored grain. A hundred thousand or so, with many more still streaming in through the brisk morning air.

As the chopper descended, the stage area came up, flanked by twin towers constructed of scaffoldings that held lighting gear. The crowd pressed right up to the edge of the stage and oozed around to the sides, where a barrier of service vehicles kept it partially in check. It reminded Stone of a military camp under siege by an insurgent mob.

They flew on and landed in a nearby open area where the rotors threw up big clouds of dust. It still hung in the air as they departed and made their way toward a hillside to the left of the stage. Here a large tent had been hastily pitched. As they climbed the slope, Stone took measure of the assembled mass of humanity out front. Its scale was nearly beyond reckoning.

"I hope this ends well," he remarked to Christine.

"Me too," she said, with a trace of doubt.

Ahead, someone opened the tent flap to greet them. A long series of agonized howls rolled out. "They're going to eat me! Oh God! Oh God!"

Once inside, they encountered six rows of portable cots and some makeshift counters made of stacked boxes. Several cots were already occupied, including one holding the screamer, a long-haired young man wearing cowboy boots and faded blue jeans. "Please get them off me," he begged as he covered his face with his bony hands. "Please, please, please."

Stone turned to Christine, who was putting down her medical bag and pulling out a stethoscope. "So, what do you think?" he asked.

Before she could answer, a sudden blast of music erupted outside the tent. Stone identified it instantly. "Santana." A wall of percussion overlaid by a vibrant guitar tone gave them away immediately.

"Tell you what," Christine said. "This is doctor stuff here. Why don't you go hang out with your music pals and check back later?"

"Good idea," Stone said. He'd been around the scene long enough that he was bound to know people in the stage area.

. . .

As he threaded his way through the trucks and busses behind the stage, Stone saw the first sign of trouble. No badges, no ID. At any event this size, the organizers always printed up laminated backstage passes, which hung around the necks of the anointed. Not here. People wandered around in perfect anonymity. The thing had come together too quickly, and no one was at the helm, not really.

When he reached the back side of the stage, he encountered something much more worrisome. It was only about three feet off the ground. Most venues put up stage platforms rising six feet or more to keep even the most rabid of fans at bay. This one put you just a hop away from becoming part of the show.

Stone jumped up in a single leap and found a spot near some equipment cases at the rear, where he had a decent view. Santana had launched into a searing guitar solo in the middle of "Evil Ways," their signature song. Out front, the crowd already pressed tightly against the shallow stage, like an incoming tide. At this point, only one thing held them back from becoming one with the band.

The Hells Angels.

You couldn't miss their jackets with the winged skull plastered on the back. Or their long greasy hair and nasty demeanor. They paced like vicious animals along each side of the stage. Some clutched pool cues, the weapon of choice. Right now, their presence was enough to give pause to anyone thinking of leaping onstage. But Stone knew that wouldn't last. It was still early, and the full impact of all the drugs and booze had yet to manifest.

Stone noted the faces and body language of the bikers and sensed something that others might have missed. They were scared. As they scanned the front, they kept glancing up at the incredible mass of people that stretched into the distance and up the surrounding hills. For all their macho posturing, they understood that a single large wave pulsing through the massive crowd might be the end of them. Literally. No amount of tough-guy action would save them from being crushed as the wave broke over the shallow stage. They'd done plenty of ad hoc security at gigs in Golden Gate Park, where they did things like guard the power cords leading to the stage. But this was different, totally different. And they knew it.

. . .

"Hey bro, wanna hit?"

"Sure." Carson accepted the jug of white wine from a guy walking next to him up the final hill to the concert. He took a generous swig and handed it back. "Thanks."

A dark walrus mustache drooped down the guy's chubby chin and bowed outward as he grinned. "Party time."

Carson nodded and felt a warm inner gush as the wine settled in. He had a bottle of his own in his backpack, along with some sleazy prefab sandwiches they'd bought at a convenience store back in Castro Valley. One of the latest Weatherman precepts dictated that women would no longer be enslaved in the kitchen.

"We're just one hill away now," Alice said from beside him. "I can feel it."

"Good," Carson said. They'd made the trip out here with another couple in the local Weatherman cell, one of maybe a half dozen scattered around the country. This one stood out as first among equals because Bill Ayers and Bernadette Dohrn sat atop it. Which didn't matter much to Carson, because most of the political discourse was lost on him. He was a tactician, not a strategist. While others fervently read the works of Debray and Marighella, he studied manuals on the application of various explosives.

"I can't wait for the Stones to come on," Alice said dreamily. "Mick Jagger's going to speak the truth. He's going to bring real revolution to all these people. Then they're going to go home and spread it everywhere. Just listen to 'Street Fighting Man.' It's all there."

She'd played the tune repeatedly for Carson and made him take careful note of the lyrics. It spoke of a palace revolution that trumps a compromise solution. It announced that the time was right for fighting in the street, all the while shouting and screaming, "Kill the king." The tune's final line lamented there's just no place for a street fighting man, but Alice skipped over this.

Carson reached into his pocket, pulled out a small tin, and consumed a couple of Benzedrine tablets. The alcohol had injected the fuel and the bennies would furnish the ignition. He didn't know it, but the wine he'd consumed also contained a generous dose of LSD. It wouldn't take long before he found out.

Overhead, the sun picked up speed as it shone through a high veil of wispy cirrus. Yes, there would be a revolution today, but of a very different sort.

. . .

From his vantage point on the stage, Stone watched the naked fat man as his billowing folds of white flesh lurched through the packed crowd near the stage. He reminded Stone of an albino walrus blundering along a beach packed with seals.

At the same time, the Hells Angeles spotted the man, and the day's troubles began in earnest.

Like a pack of animals on the hunt, they leapt off the stage, stalked him, knocked him down and beat on him without mercy. Bystanders recoiled in horror but did nothing to intervene. They were here for the music, not to fight. Stone resisted an impulse to wade into the melee. The odds were hopeless.

Finally, someone with the concert staff jumped in and got the Angels to back off. Amazingly, it worked. Except that the fat man turned and punched an Angel before waddling off into the crowd. By way of retribution, the Angels turned on the staffer and the pool cues came out.

All the while, Santana thundered on.

Stone looked out over the crowd and didn't like what he saw. Countless jugs of wine, something you seldom encountered at the free concerts in Golden Gate Park in years past. You could almost feel the collective mood of the spectators giving way to the most primal of impulses. It was only a matter of time before they launched tentative assaults on the stage itself.

. . .

I don't know where I'm goin' next. I don't know who I'm gonna be.

So sang the Jefferson Airplane. And their words became notes, and the notes became missiles reigning down on Carson where he sat on the hillside with Alice.

Words, notes, missiles.

Mortar rounds! They were under attack.

"Fuck!" Carson screamed as he bolted up. "Haul ass! Head for the tree line!"

Only there wasn't any tree line, except in his profoundly altered neurons. The booze had dissolved his inhibitions, the speed amped his paranoia, and the acid put him back in the jungles of Vietnam.

"Hey," a guy behind him yelled. "Down in front!"

"Up yours!" Carson yelled. "We're under fire."

"Oh yeah?" The guy retorted as he rose to challenge Carson while clutching a half-empty wine bottle.

Carson kicked him in the stomach, and he crashed down onto the people seated behind him. His wine bottle flew loose and sprayed out over the crowd.

Alice stood by dumbfounded as Carson grabbed her arm. "Go! Now!"

He led them through the random maze of seated bodies, leaving a trail of chaos as he went.

"What are we doing?" Alice asked.

"We've got to get to cover," Carson mumbled. "We're dead if we don't."

"You've gone crazy!" she yelled at him. By now, they had reached the hillside to the right of the stage.

"No way," he said. His eyes darted around in the dance of the truly deranged.

Alice saw a way out. Up ahead, two big tents sat next to each other. One had the universal symbol of the Red Cross emblazoned on its side. "We've got to get you to the medics," she pleaded.

Carson came to a sudden stop. "The medics," he said. "Yeah, the medics." It made some kind of twisted sense.

"Straight ahead," Alice directed, and Carson complied.

Carson's agitation was gaining momentum by the time they reached the tent. "We're fucked," he declared. "No air cover. We're screwed."

A medic in a white lab coat stood at the tent's entrance. "We're full up," he said and pointed to a second tent just to the rear. "Next door."

. . .

Christine applied the fourteenth and final stitch to the forehead of the young woman with frizzy red hair. Between whimpers, she'd said her name was Ola and she came from Oklahoma City. She wouldn't give any details about how she'd acquired the laceration. Christine swabbed on some disinfectant and taped a bandage into place. "Okay we're all done. It should be okay. If it starts to look like it's infected, you should see your doctor about it."

"I don't have a doctor," Ola declared.

"Well then you should go to the emergency room. Infections are nothing to fool around with. Good luck."

They were sitting in a pair of director's chairs in a makeshift treatment area. "Thank you," Ola said as she rose to leave. "Thank you so much."

"Not a problem," Christine said. She stood and surveyed the matrix of cots. Most were occupied. Cuts, bruises, punctures, drug overdoses, general hysteria. Compared to other rock concerts, this was quickly turning into a disaster of unprecedented magnitude.

A nurse came up. "Doctor, you ready for the next one?"

"Yeah, I guess so," Christine said wearily. She'd been at it for hours without a break. "Bring 'em on."

The nurse escorted a young man and woman over to her. One look at the man's darting eyes and the woman's anxious demeanor gave her a good idea of what was wrong.

. . .

"Yeah, I saw it myself," the roadie was saying to one of his peers. "That Angel guy punched out Marty. Right in the middle of a song! Un-fuckin' believable."

Stone caught their conversation as he came down off the rear of the stage. They had to be talking about Marty Balin, one of the Jefferson Airplane. Stone thought about asking but demurred. He'd heard and seen enough already. Things were only going to get worse.

"I hear the Dead are gonna cop out," the other roadie said as Stone drifted out of earshot. "They heard what happened with the Airplane and…"

Stone considered the irony of this last remark as he walked out of earshot. The way Rhonda told it, the Dead were tight with the Angels. They considered them to be fellow outlaws, one gravitating to music, the other to motorcycles, and both to underage girls. It was the Dead's management that helped sign them on as security here.

On stage, the Airplane had regrouped and were well into their last song and chanting the refrain, "We're Volunteers of America." Which was precisely what Christine and her fellow medical workers were. He climbed the hill toward their tent. The winter sun had dipped to the south and cast its thin glow across the surrounding topography. The big lighting towers threw fractured shadows across the restless crowd.

The Flying Burrito Brothers launched into their set, and Stone stopped to listen. They were a hippy-country band and it made him think of his Bakersfield days. In a humorous twist, they played "Lucille" by Little Richard, a hard-core black R&B number that would have been lost on Buck Owens or Merle Haggard.

When he reached the tent's entrance, Stone noted that they had posted a security person, which suggested that things were not improving. After he passed muster and entered, he spied Christine at one of the cots near the front. A young couple sat on it, and she was kneeling so she could talk with them at eye level. The girl, who had long hair and wire-rimmed glasses, held the hand of a gaunt man who was staring off into some unimaginable distance. Without warning, he shot to his feet and screamed "Look out!" The girl patiently pulled him back down, and Christine touched her gently on the arm and delivered some kind of advice that Stone couldn't hear. The noise in the tent blended with the blare of the nearby music. Screams, drum rolls, yells, guitar licks, groans, pedal steel riffs.

Stone made a tactful approach, and Christine got up and came over to him. "You're just in time," she said.

"For what?"

She nodded in the direction of the couple. "The guy's having some kind of psychotic reaction. He thinks he's being hunted." She sighed. "She says they didn't take any psychedelics, but there's a good chance he got some second hand. A lot of people are spiking their wine with acid and then sharing. Not much I can do for him. We don't have anything like Thorazine around here."

"So, what can I do?"

"They've set up a kind of psych ward in some tents up above us. Four psychiatric residents from UCSF and a bunch of drug counselors. They're a lot better equipped to deal with him than we are. Would you mind taking him up there? I don't want him to get lost on the way and I'm not sure she can control him."

"Not a problem," Stone said. "You look done-in. You ought to take a break."

"Maybe later." She squeezed his hand. "Thank you."

On the trip up the hill, Stone made only one attempt to communicate with the guy, whom the girl called Matt.

"How you doing?" he asked the guy.

Matt stopped abruptly. "Fuck you," he said. "Stay back."

Stone raised his hands in concession. "You got it." The guy had unkempt hair hacked off halfway to his shoulders and a thin beard over pale skin. His blue eyes screamed trouble and his taut lips did the same.

Stone started back up the hill and the couple followed. He had this uneasy feeling that he'd encountered this guy somewhere before. It bothered him that he couldn't nail it down. Cops, past or present, were supposed to be good at that kind of thing.

They reached the first of the four tents, and a middle-aged woman came out to greet them. She had an almost preternatural calm about her. A definite asset in this line of work. "Hi, I'm Denise," she said. "What can we do for you?"

"I'm bringing this gentleman up from the medical tent," Stone explained. "They said you might be able to help out."

Denise looked directly at Matt. "I'm sure we can." Her placid demeanor seemed to have a calming effect on the guy. In an instant, he went from extremely mad to lost in grief. "He was all hacked up," he sobbed. "I put him on in pieces."

"That's very sad," Denise sympathized. "Why don't you come in and we can talk about it?"

Without a word, Matt started toward the entrance. Alice followed, but Denise caught her hand. "Why don't you give us a little time alone? It seems to work better that way."

"Are you sure?" Alice asked.

"I'm sure."

Alice turned to Stone. "We've got friends down there. I need to tell them what's going on."

"Go ahead," Stone said. "He's going to be fine right here."

"Thanks," she responded. "I can't miss Mick Jagger. It's really important."

"I'm sure it is."

They headed back down and stopped in front of the medical tent. "You going to be okay?" he asked her.

"I'm fine." She took a step down the hill, stopped, and looked back at him. "There's going to be a revolution."

The conviction and finality in her voice caught Stone off guard. Before he could respond, she'd already turned and started toward the crowd.

. . .

Stone assumed his vantage point at the rear corner of the stage platform, which gave him a decent view of Crosby, Stills, Nash and Young. Out front, the Angels continued their forays into the nearest ranks of the crowd. Their pool cues were out in force now and had become standard procedure.

The group was halfway through "Down by The River" when he felt a tap on his shoulder. It was Jaymes, the ersatz security manager who'd tried to hire him. Unbelievable. Stone would have thought the guy would be halfway to Rio by now, considering what was going down.

"Stone, right?" he yelled over the music.

"Yeah, Stone." He had to marvel at Jaymes' chutzpah.

"Great show, huh?" Jaymes said without even a hint of irony.

"You've got to be kidding," Stone said.

Jaymes pointed to his ear. "Can't hear you." He gestured to the rear. "Let's step to the back."

At three hundred pounds, Jaymes had to gingerly work his way off the back of the stage and onto the ground. Stone jumped down after him. How could this man remain upbeat given the churning horror out front?

"So where are all your hired guns?" he asked Jaymes. Stone had seen a few token security cops, but the Angels were clearly the dominant force.

"They're around," Jaymes answered ambiguously. "We're making adjustments as we go."

"Like hiring a biker gang?"

James shrugged it off. "I wasn't involved in that decision. And at this point, it doesn't really matter. We're all going to have to improvise to pull this thing off."

"Yeah, I guess so," Stone said. His cynicism sailed right over the top of Jaymes' mutton chopped head. "And just what are you going to do when it gets dark?" Every cop knew that if things are bad during the day, they were only going get worse when night fell. The shadow side of humanity roams free after darkness descends.

"I think by then we'll have picked all the bad apples," Jaymes said.

Stone pointed over Jaymes' shoulder. "Looks like you've already found a barrel for 'em."

Jaymes turned to face a spot between two buses where a group of Angels hovered over some of their most recent victims. All were bruised, swollen and crusted with dried blood from head wounds. The naked fat man sat among them, still bleeding rivulets of fresh blood from the corners of his swollen mouth. Stone guessed his front teeth were probably a thing of the past.

"That's for repeat offenders," Jaymes explained. "Just a precautionary measure."

"Right," Stone said dryly. "I heard that the Dead aren't very happy about your biker pals. I heard they're not going to play. That right?"

"The way I hear it, it's a matter of negotiation right now," Jaymes said. "There's been no final decision. They're searching for some kind of consensus. It's in everybody's best interest for them to go on. So, myself, I'd bet on a positive outcome."

"You would, huh?"

"Yes, I would," Jaymes said with great sincerity.

Stone didn't bother to respond. The man was an absolute master of obfuscation. He turned away and looked up the hill to the medical tents and the makeshift pyscho ward up above it.

The evening was coming on. He could only hope they were ready.

. . .

The slender hippy woman sobbed and screamed and bobbed in the folding chair facing Denise. "No, no, no!"

Denise sighed. She'd tried repeatedly to break through to her, with no luck at all.

At least she wasn't violent. The residents were almost out of Thorazine and saving it for the very worst cases.

The light grew dim inside the tent as evening came on. The music had stopped for the moment. She gave the woman a pat on the hand and looked over to where she'd parked one of her other cases, the Vietnam vet suffering paranoid hallucinations.

He was gone.

. . .

Night fell, and with it came the Rolling Stones.

The packed crowd became a sea, and its waves washed upon the stage. A rare demonstration of human dynamics in motion. Stone had never seen the likes of it.

Nor had the Hells Angels, who became more agitated than ever.

By the time "Sympathy for The Devil" rolled around, the crowd had developed a will of its own, and the Angels knew it. Multiple confrontations between fans and bikers simmered close to boiling point.

Pleased to meet you. Hope you guess my name.

A nude woman, all pink and pale, wrestled her way forward and mounted the shallow platform. The bikers kicked her back down. In a perfect nod to the growing anarchy, a stray dog appeared out of nowhere and casually made its way across the stage.

But what's puzzling you is the nature of my game.

The fighting boiled over. The music stopped. Mick Jagger called for calm. Keith Richards rewound to the opening lick and fired the tune back up.

Stone watched it all from his vantage point near the back of the stage. It looked like maybe Jagger had succeeded. The audience's temperature fell from boiling to merely boisterous. It stayed that way for the next two tunes.

Then came "Under My Thumb."

I say it's all right.

But it wasn't. Not now, not ever.

It started with a bright green flash out of the corner of Stone's eye. A black man in a lime-colored suit rushed the stage near the monitor speakers. An Angel grabbed him and punched him back down. The crowd parted where he flew back. A pack of Angels descended in pursuit.

What happened next reminded Stone of something a veteran cop told him when he first joined the force: Real violence happens real fast.

Stone's vision was obstructed to the point where he couldn't see the pistol, or the stabbing. The bikers formed a hideous scrum around the downed man and kicked him viciously. One of them held up the man's pistol as a symbol of justification: Angels club and stab, but they don't shoot.

The Angels faded away. A few fans scooped up the body and deposited it on the side of the stage. The music stopped. Jagger and Richards looked on in absolute horror.

Stone thought about summoning Christine, but Jagger himself called over the PA for a doctor, which brought a young resident to the stage. Apparently, the victim was still alive, because the doctor picked him up and carried him to the rear, where he was loaded into a station wagon that headed up toward the medical tent.

Stone left the stage and trotted along behind the station wagon. Down below, the music started once more.

Under my thumb...

· · ·

Carson dropped to his knees some ten meters short of the stage. The speed, acid and booze ran rampant in his fevered brain. A brilliant light bathed the stage, which towered into the infinite blackness above.

Under my thumb...

The music surged and threatened to turn his ears inside out. Up ahead, a giant reptile tried to scale the speakers lining the stage, a bright green gecko lizard. A second creature hovered directly above it, an insect encased in a shell with a winged skull emblazoned on the back. One of its barbed limbs shot out and delivered a savage blow to the lizard, which toppled backward into the crowd. People parted to avoid the falling reptile and sent ripples out in the process.

Carson rose back to his feet as an entire swarm of the insects clambered off the stage in pursuit of the fallen lizard. Their attack became a kaleidoscope of black and green as they immersed themselves in the furious struggle.

When it was done, the scene froze and did a sudden flip inside him. The green object became a man, a black man, now sprawled lifeless in the harsh artificial light. The insects became bikers, Hells Angels.

They turned in unison and stared at him with glowing red eyes. He was next.

He didn't wait for them to charge. He turned and fled into a night gone terribly wrong.

. . .

When Stone reached the medical tent, he found Christine conferring with Dr. Fine, who had organized their presence here. Behind them, the Angel's victim, now stripped of his bright green suit, lie on the nearest cot.

"How bad?" Stone asked.

"Multiple stab wounds, massive head injuries," Christine said. "I don't think he's going to make it. His only chance is emergency surgery in a hospital. Right now."

"Any way they can airlift him?"

"Someone's trying to set that up with the tour people. There were two choppers, but the Grateful Dead grabbed one and skipped out."

"What about the other?"

Stone could see her anger mounting. "They say it's reserved for the Stones. And nobody knows how to get it unreserved. It's a complete mess." She sighed deeply. "Fuck!"

Her expletive caught Stone by surprise. She usually had an amazing capacity to take almost anything in stride. But now, this place, this time, this event had sapped all her reserves and rubbed her raw.

. . .

Hey! Think the time is right for palace revolution...

The lyrics brought Alice to her feet and a great thrill surged through her. Mick was singing his apocalyptic gospel to this enormous crowd. From where she sat on the hillside, he appeared as a distant speck, but his words assumed a dimension scarcely imaginable. Pop and political culture had fused to create a shock wave that would roll across the entire nation. She was sure of it.

It seemed absolutely fitting that this was the last song of the night. Surely, they had planned it that way all along. She gathered up her things and thought about Matt.

He'd flipped out during the Jefferson Airplane set and must still be at that tent up on the hill.

She asked the other couple to hang on for a couple of minutes while she went to round him up.

When she reached the tent, its population was nearly drained, and a few propane lanterns illuminated the interior where an exhausted Denise sat in a folding chair.

"Hi," Alice said. "Remember me?"

"Oh yeah," Denise said wearily. "You were with the veteran. He took off about an hour ago."

"Did he say where he was going?" Alice asked.

"You've got to be kidding." Denise was now running on reserves.

Oh well, he knew where they parked, Alice thought as she started back down the hill. He'd find his way back.

And if he didn't, that was okay too. Somebody would give him a ride. Thanks to Mick, they were all now bonded and pledged to the same purpose.

No more compromise solutions.

. . .

The abrupt chill of the night wrapped itself around Stone as he slowly walked down the hill. Up above, Christine was helping pack up the medical gear so they could strike the tent. There would be no chopper for the return trip. Dr. Fine had arranged for a bus to take them back to the city.

Below, the roadies were tearing down the stage and sound gear. They did it in an elegant kind of way that required little supervision. Everyone knew their part and they labored in relative silence.

From the center of the field, a large bonfire cast its flickering light over their labors. The Hells Angels gathered around it in drunken celebration of a distant past when savagery and survival gleefully embraced each other. As Stone watched, some hapless hippy tried to join in and was thrown down and stomped. His screams filled the now deserted space. All that remained were the bikers, a few stragglers and tons of discarded trash.

When Stone reached the bottom, he heard another scream, very close by. He headed in its direction toward an area illuminated by one of the speedway's overhead lights. Two Angels with pool cues swung viciously on a downed man next to a pickup truck and a downed motorcycle.

For Stone, it was his personal tipping point. He'd remained neutral all day and could do so no longer. This time, there was no one else to intervene.

"Hey!" he yelled as he moved toward them. The Angels stopped swinging and looked up at him. "Back off!" he commanded.

They took it as a joke. Stone was a man of medium height in early middle age and clad in casual attire. They broke into mindless grins as he approached. A bad miscalculation. While Stone wasn't large, he was stunningly fast, a gift that had served him well in his cop years.

Their grins faded the closer he came. His confidence threw them off balance. "So what the fuck's your problem?" the taller of the two asked. "You buddies with this piece of shit?" The man on ground lay on his stomach with his face concealed in the crook of his arm.

Stone moved within striking distance of the taller one and nodded toward the pickup. "That your ride?"

"Yeah, that's my ride," he said and pointed to the fallen motorcycle. "And that's my bike. He fucked with my bike, man. Nobody fucks with my bike."

"Fine," Stone said. "Now get the hell out of here."

The Angel's left eyebrow gave him away. It elevated slightly as he started to strike. Once the cue had cleared his shoulder, Stone's right hand shot out and grabbed it. At the same time, his right foot delivered a decisive kick to the man's crotch. As the man went down, Stone clubbed him on the skull with the cue. He immediately sank to his knees with his palms resting in the dirt.

The shorter Angel got the point. He dropped his cue in surrender and stared in disbelief at Stone and his fellow biker. But then, his expression took an odd turn. He smiled and his eyes lit up. "Hey, I know you," he said to Stone. "You're the record guy."

"Oh yeah?" Stone challenged him.

"Yeah. You're Stone. You auditioned my brother's band. I was there."

"You were, huh?" Stone had no such recollection, but it was certainly possible. He'd gone out and listened to maybe fifty bands before Capitol let him go.

"Yeah. Super Streak. Remember them?"

"Nope," Stone answered. He looked down at the victim, who was starting to move. "We're all done here," he said to the biker. "Get moving. Now."

Stone watched as the Angels loaded the bike onto the pickup and drove off. He turned to the victim, who was sitting up and holding his bloody face in his hands. "What happened here?" he asked.

"I don't know," the man answered and went silent.

Stone's years on the street told him the guy was in shock and there was no use pushing the point. He helped the man to his feet, and they started off toward what was left of the medical tent.

On the way, Stone pondered the mystery of the shorter Angel's behavior. In a single paradoxical instant, the man had gone from vicious thug to genial rock fan. And thought nothing of it.

. . .

Carson trotted, then stumbled through the night. A big hill loomed ahead, clogged with dark streams of people heading toward the highway. He smelled the hot, rotten breath of the Angels, who were gaining on him. When they caught him, they would club him senseless and eviscerate him, leaving a steaming pile of entrails beside his spent body.

The music was done, the concert was over. Only the collective mutter of the departing fans remained. Somewhere in the mix, the Angels howled and laughed as they pressed forward, unstoppable and resolute.

Carson saw that he was on a dirt road now, one that followed the hillside up and over the crest. If he could reach the highway on the far side, he just might escape. But right now, he was wading through gelatin. They would overtake him long before he cleared the top of the hill.

A car. He needed a car. Anybody's car.

And there it was, parked just off the shoulder. A late model Plymouth. A product of divine intervention. He grabbed the door handle on the driver's side. It swung open and the dome light ignited like a miniature sun. He slid in and felt for the ignition key, and there it was, already inserted. He brought the engine to life and turned on the headlights. Their twin beams revealed dozens of walkers, the departing pilgrims.

He caught a gap in the crowd and pulled onto the center of the road. As he drove forward, people on the road reluctantly yielded to his approach. Some glared over their shoulders at him. Fuck them. He was running for his life.

He checked the rearview mirror. Some shiny specks dotted the darkness. They moved about in tight yet random patterns. Motorcycle headlights. He was sure of it. The bikers were no longer on foot. They were going to close the distance, cut him off and chop him down.

He sped up. The car bounced and lurched on the unpaved road. The foot traffic grew more panicked and literally dived for the shoulders to avoid him. Directly ahead, the road crossed the crest of the hill. Freedom. He jammed down the gas pedal and clutched the wheel as he flew over the top.

He got one brief view of the campfire before he hit it. Six souls sat there frozen in horror as he plowed into them. He heard a sickening thump as they collided with the bumper and grill. The car skidded to a halt in the barren ground.

Ghosts, he thought. Beings from another world, here to save him from the Angels. He got out and went around to thank them for their incredible sacrifice.

Two dead. Two grievously injured. Two intact.

Triage set in and the first responders focused on the injured. Carson explained to one of the cops that the Angels had been after him, that they'd best be on the lookout for them. The officer told him to stay put and turned his attention back to the victims.

Carson wandered off and headed down the hill toward the highway. Bright flashes invaded his peripheral vision. His equilibrium kept swaying then steadying. His insides ballooned and pressed against his cranium.

He plowed ahead, on the way to nowhere in particular.

. . .

Stone and Christine got off the chartered bus in the parking lot of the USCF Medical Center. There had been little conversation among its passengers on the ride back. Stone and Christine were no exception. The enormity of the day's events defied any simple commentary. Meredith Hunter, the man in green, had been pronounced dead before the Stones even finished their set. Then came word that two other people died in a case of vehicular homicide on the way out.

"You okay?" Stone asked Christine as they headed for their car.

"Not really," she said after a moment of hesitation.

"Me neither," Stone said.

And they let it go at that.

The Sleeper was America personified. He barbequed. He bowled. He hand-washed his car. He attended community meetings. He installed air conditioners for a living. People liked him. He had a winning way about him. Because, after all, America was all about winning.

Only his memories might betray him, so he kept them close and tightly sealed. He lived in his persona rather than himself. But in the quieter moments, the private moments, he let them loose and wandered around inside them.

Miami. He grew up there, the only offspring of a naturalized Cuban and an American mother. His father worked as a clerk in the employ of the gangster Meyer Lansky, who controlled a vast gambling empire in Havana. America's elite flooded its hotels, casinos and brothels, wallowing in the decadence and high life forbidden them within their own borders. It produced millions for Lansky, and his father labored to keep it free from scrutiny and properly accounted for. All the while, he lived in constant fear of reprisal if he betrayed even the most irrelevant confidence. He compensated for his cowardly attitude on the home front, where he lashed out at The Sleeper and his mother, a dreamy idealist who longed for a better world. Over time, The Sleeper came to realize what a fearful and petty little man his father was and resolved to move in the opposite direction.

When he started college at the University of Miami, he heard certain professors speak of socialism as the savior of modern societies. They pointed to the revolutionary struggle in Cuba, just ninety miles to the south as a prime example. The Sleeper began to read about the brave souls out in the jungle revolting against the cruelties of the dictator, Fulgencio Batista, who operated in league with his father's overlord, Meyer Lansky. It presented the perfect opportunity to redeem his family's honor. He vowed to join them as soon as he could. His bilingual upbringing meant that he spoke both English and Spanish fluently and flawlessly. Surely this would somehow be an asset in the people's struggle against their oppressors.

And sure enough, it was. In the end, it brought him here to San Francisco, the most permissive and decadent of American cities, where rampant capitalism brewed the moral rot that would lead to the culture's ultimate downfall. Only a handful of the populace grasped the magnitude of the coming collapse, mostly students across the bay in Berkeley and traumatized Vietnam vets. But he dared not share his mission with them. Their ranks were riddled with informers, and he ran the risk of being exposed.

In fact, he might already be compromised. Lately, he'd noticed strange cars parked on the block where he lived, always occupied by a solitary male driver. He'd also detected faint clicks and pops on his telephone line. He doubted that they had any grounds to arrest him because of the unique nature of his role here. Other agents engaged in pilfering or copying classified documents, and the repetitive nature of their work left them vulnerable to investigation.

His talents were reserved for cases of a different sort.

9.

BERKELEY
FEBRUARY 12, 1970

Thirty minutes to go.

Carson still had his combat eyes. He spotted the two men the instant they rounded the corner and started down the sidewalk toward him. Even in the dim light, he picked out enough detail to identify them as the pair tasked with planting the bombs. They both wore sweaters and had their hands shoved into their jeans to ward off the modest chill as midnight approached. Just a couple of college kids walking home after a beer or two. Or so it seemed. Carson knew them only by their pseudonyms, the ones they took when the organization set up in the apartment on Pine Street over in the city. Jerry and Chris.

When they came near, he briefly flashed the parking lights in the rental car he was driving. He'd acquired it in Oakland with fake ID fabricated by another of the Pine residents, a woman with considerable graphics skills.

The pair glanced around, climbed in the back seat, and slumped in exhaustion as the tension abated.

"How did it go?" Carson asked.

"Good," Jerry answered as he raked his long hair out of his face. "We're all set."

Carson had his doubts. At best, these people were earnest amateurs. If they'd been part of his squad in Vietnam, they would have been dead in no time at all.

"No surveillance?"

"Nope," Chris replied. "They've got the place pretty well walled up except for the entrance by the Old City Hall. No gates, no cameras. We just walked on in."

He went on to describe how they trotted along the rear parking lot behind the old building, and on to a second lot where the cops parked their off-duty cars. Here they were exposed under the overhead security lights and had to move quickly. One bomb went next to the nearest car and the second was tossed between two cars further down the row.

"How far down?" Carson asked.

"I don't know," Jerry said. "I didn't stop to count. We had to haul ass."

"Yes, you did," Carson agreed. The biggest risk in the whole operation was that the two of them would get caught in the act, with the bombs as evidence. All it would take was a single cop stepping out the rear of the police headquarters for a smoke break.

"How long?" Chris asked and Carson checked his watch.

Twenty minutes.

. . .

Detective Sgt. David Verner of the Berkeley Police Department slid the report out of the platen on his typewriter. It described an incident where an intoxicated individual threw a brick through the rear window of his neighbor's car. That would have been the end of it, except that the aggrieved neighbor fetched a shotgun and blew a sizable chunk out of the brick thrower's calf. The majority of the drama had been witnessed by numerous neighbors drawn outside by the commotion, and Verner patiently took all their statements.

"Hey," he said to Sgt. Vincent Martino at the next desk over. "How long until they get us electric typewriters?"

Martino looked up to 11:50 on the wall clock. "Not on this shift, that's for sure."

"No, I'm serious," Verner said. "How long?"

"About the same time you get a personal secretary. So don't hold your breath."

Verner had to laugh. Martino's cynical humor always lightened him up, especially when it got late. As usual, he was beat and ready to put the day behind him.

"You good for a beer?" he asked Martino.

"Only if your old lady says it's okay," came the quip.

"Why don't you phone her and ask her?" Verner countered.

"Because my life insurance isn't paid up."

"Now you're starting to make some sense."

The two men stood up from behind their desks and went to grab their jackets.

Four minutes to go.

. . .

Carson watched as Chris and Jerry took off to remove themselves from the upcoming crime scene. He checked his watch.

Two minutes.

He gave this whole thing about a fifty-fifty chance of working. The bomb making had been really sloppy. The devices were crude and assembled on the fly with little thought given to their design. He'd made some suggestions but was always overruled by this pushy guy named Mahler that they'd brought in from the East Coast. He was an Ivy League intellectual by temperament and always had to have the last word, even though his technical skills were almost non-existent.

Each bomb consisted of two sticks of dynamite inserted into a capped steel pipe. The pipe would both amplify the explosion and create a spray of metal fragments. A blasting cap was inserted in one end, with its wires attached to a battery and an alarm clock that acted as a switch. There was no shunt or safety circuitry, meaning that the bomb might kill its maker just as easily as its target. Accordingly, Carson made sure that the plan didn't involve himself being anywhere near the bombs when they were transported from Pine Street to Berkeley. His principal role was to linger and survey the damage after the detonations.

As the operation came together, it became apparent to Carson that the leadership had made a critical shift in policy about bombing. This time, there would be no warning, no phone call in advance. This time, it would be murder pure and simple. The intent was to kill the pigs, just as the pigs had killed at People's Park. A war of homicidal retribution was officially underway.

Carson cranked down the window and just let the cool air flow in. If a bomb went off, he didn't want to just hear it. He wanted to feel it.

. . .

Thirty seconds.

Detectives Verner and Martino filed down the hallway behind a couple of dozen other cops, most uniformed patrolmen. Their shift had ended, and a good-natured buzz filled the space.

The two men emerged into the night and started down the concrete steps to the parking lot level. Verner wouldn't leave the electric typewriter thing alone. He deserved one, they all deserved one in their struggle against untold reams of paperwork.

They had just cleared the bottom step when the first bomb exploded.

. . .

Carson felt a slap on the side of his face when the blast wave slammed in through the open window. It packed enough power to rock the car slightly as it rolled past and on down the block. Several nearby windows shattered.

He closed his eyes and visualized a scene of chaos and carnage in the parking lot. They had crossed the line. There was no going back.

. . .

Neither Verner nor Martino heard the explosion. Its dense wall of compressed air perforated their eardrums before the sound could fully express itself. All that remained was a screaming buzz in the center of their heads. Both flew back and slammed into the pavement with a painful blow to the back of their skulls.

Verner managed to sit up and sat stunned as he tried to collect himself. All over the lot, other officers were also struggling to right themselves. Several people had come running out of the building in response to the blast. Verner could see their mouths form shouts but could hear none of it. The screaming buzz in his ears cast a brilliant sonic fog over the whole scene.

He looked over to Martino, who remained flat on his back and stared up at the sky through glazed eyes. Shock. But from what? Verner got on his hands and knees and crawled over to check him out. Sure enough, he had a massive injury to the lower portion of his right arm. Shrapnel from the detonation had shredded his jacket sleeve and revealed a mass of bloody pulp which had begun to pool on the pavement.

Verner tried to ask him if he was okay but couldn't hear himself speak. Martino tried weakly to mouth a response, but it remained inaudible. His arm gushed blood in regular pulses, indicating a severed artery. He needed a tourniquet. Verner came to a kneeling position and ripped off his belt to form one.

He had just looped it through the buckle when the second bomb went off.

. . .

Carson had just about given up on the remaining bomb when it finally detonated. He visualized the hour hand on the alarm clock as it rotated into a position where it made contact with a pin drilled into the clock face and completed the ignition circuit. The work had been crudely done and left all kinds of room for failure.

A second burst of compacted thunder rolled down the street. By now, neighbors had drifted out onto the sidewalk in response to the first blast. He heard screams of shock and saw arms instinctively rise to cover faces. Good. All the distraction would keep them from noticing a stranger in the neighborhood.

He got out of his car and started a roundabout route to the blast site. Timing was important. He needed to get a good look at the damage before the area hardened into an official crime scene, with yellow tape strung hither and yon.

. . .

Verner noted a large abrasion on his forearm as he struggled back upright. All over the lot, cops were kneeling or wandering aimlessly in drunken staggers. He still held the looped belt and looked over to Martino, who remained down and gushed blood. He felt a tap on his shoulder, and someone took the belt and applied it to Martino's upper arm. He wanted to say thanks, but all he could hear was the persistent shriek of tinnitus.

It would never go away completely.

. . .

Ambulance sirens wailed as they rushed past Carson on their way to the blast site. Spectators had begun to congregate on the far side of the block holding the police complex. As of yet, the cops had failed to cordon the area off, and Carson noted a large gap where the explosion had breached a concrete wall surrounding the parking lot. Already, several people had crossed the street to peer in, and Carson joined them.

He quickly took in the craters in the pavement and shrapnel-pocked vehicles. Terrible. The placement of the devices couldn't have been worse. In one case, the explosion had occurred between a car and the concrete wall. In the other, it went off between two parked cars. In both, the spray of shrapnel from bursting pipe metal was largely constrained.

Amateurs, fucking amateurs. Next time, they would do it his way and get it right.

And next time was only a week away.

10.

LA HONDA

Stone drove south from the city down I280, which parallels the hill country between the valley and the Pacific Coast. At Hwy 84 he turned off toward La Honda, a little town nestled up in the wooded hills about 20 miles distant.

There he would give the music business his last best shot.

As he made the turn, he considered dropping off to see an acquaintance who lived along the way, a scientist steeped in the arcane depths of semiconductor physics.

He'd recently given Stone a shorthand tutorial on the subject and told him he should look into the business side if he was planning a career change. It seemed that you could now cram thousands of transistors into a very small space and have them do any number of things that might generate very large sums of money. He said new companies were popping up all over down here in the valley to get in on the action.

When Stone asked what kinds of things, he learned that you would soon be able to shrink a computer the size of refrigerator into something about the size of a postage stamp. Maybe. Stone had his doubts. This guy also smoked large quantities of weed. You could never be sure if you were talking to the scientist or the stoner.

The two-lane road twisted through dense stands of trees, both pines and deciduous. The sun peeked through the marine overcast, and an occasional squirrel or chipmunk bounded across the road. Stone was beginning to understand why Ken Kesey, literary hero to many, had moved up here. Already, the city seemed no more than a busy memory. That said, you also had the option of reversing course and landing in Haight-Ashbury within an hour.

But Kesey wasn't the reason of this trip. It was Jerry Garcia, the lead guitarist and prime engine of The Grateful Dead. He frequently hung out up here at what was alternately known as the "ranch" or the "farm." It served as a sort of psychedelic launching pad, offering service from the sylvan hills of Santa Cruz to the surface of Jupiter, all for the price of just a few micrograms.

Stone's reluctant descent into the abyss of Altamont had permanently soured him on the mainstream music industry. In all his years as a cop, he'd never witnessed anything quite so disturbing. It was as if the gates of hell flew open and a vile black flood rolled out over the entire nation. At a less profound level, it was the result of bad business practices, endemic corruption and ethical collapse, all tied into a Gordian knot of prodigious proportion. In any case, Stone wanted out.

What remained was his love of music, especially new music bubbling up from the streets. As it ascended, it had a purity about it that dissolved as soon as big money and fame showed up. He decided that if he stayed in the music world, it would be to chart these moments of ascension and exit before the downside presented itself.

Garcia's music represented just such an opportunity. While the Dead were contracted with Warner, the restless Garcia embarked on numerous side projects into genres as diverse as jazz and bluegrass. Most of this work quickly faded into obscurity, but Stone thought it didn't have to. With the proper production and promotion, it would earn its rightful place in the pantheon of modern music. Stone had connected with Garcia about a year ago at a concert at the Filmore. It turned out that Jerry was a big fan of the Bakersfield Sound, which Stone had helped pioneer. As a result, Stone had been able to arrange this meeting through Rhonda, although "meeting" was the wrong descriptor. In this outlier world, you drifted in, you hung out, you smoked a little weed and just saw where it all went. The business stuff was just kind of an afterthought.

Maybe. He had learned that you had to play both sides of the fence to pull these things off.

Stone almost missed the place coming around a curve. The driveway consisted of a wooden bridge that spanned a creek along the roadway. Unkempt piles of orange and yellow leaves bordered the entrance. On the far side, a large one-story house sat in rustic splendor, with raw unpainted siding and stone chimneys at each end.

Stone crossed the bridge, parked in front and got out with a copy of Kesey's big novel, *One Flew over the Cuckoo's Nest*. Christine was a consummate reader and insisted that he get the book signed by the master himself.

It turned out the master was absent at the moment, out buying beer somewhere. Hardly the kind of thing you'd expect from a literary deity. Stone had knocked, but no one answered, so he opened the front door and walked through the smell of spent firewood and out onto a planked deck in the back. And there was Jerry, beer in hand, sitting at a primitive table with his signature burst of black hair and beard.

By ten minutes into their encounter, Stone had deduced the sad truth. His years as a detective for Hollywood Vice spelled it out. Forget about Orange Sunshine, Nepalese hash and Maui Wowie. Think China White. The man was a flat-out junkie. He had a pinkish flush, and his pupils were tiny black dots. When Stone talked, the artist hovered on the verge of nodding off and kept absently scratching his arm. After a short time, their conversational thread unraveled into utter randomness.

Stone gave it a few more minutes, then excused himself. Too bad. The guy was a brilliant player but a serious business risk. In the end, the dope would take him down. It always did.

He went back out, climbed in his car and plopped the unsigned book down on the passenger seat. No Garcia. No autograph. Not a good day. He sighed and drove back out over the wooden bridge to the main road.

And around the bend came the Hells Angels.

They lined up in a column two bikes wide to cross the bridge, maybe a dozen of them on their snorting mechanical beasts of chrome, metal and rubber. All wore sunglasses, unkempt hair and an obscene assortment of beards and mustaches.

They waited for Stone to pull out so they could occupy the bridge. He obliged and started down the opposite lane, which took him past each successive pair of riders. Over time, he'd heard references to a big party up here, where Kesey and the Angels had melded with a grab bag of famous writers and artists. Now here was the biker contingent, fresh from Altamont, right in front of him.

The third pair he passed were the two Angels he'd confronted at Altamont.

The taller one looked straight over at him. Had he been recognized? With the sunglasses, he couldn't be sure. He sped up and shifted the little Volkswagen into fourth, all the while glancing into the rearview mirror. He lost sight of them around a curve and sped back toward La Honda, which was about a mile off.

. . .

By the time he reached the edge of town, he remembered that there was hardly any town at all. Just a grocery store and a volunteer fire station on the left. Several roads cut through the thick stands of trees to the right, but God only knew where they would take him. He had the option to speed along the sparsely traveled highway, but the big choppers could quickly overtake him on the open road. His best shot was to pull into the grocery store, the La Honda Country Market. At least he'd have witnesses around, which might deter the bikers from getting too ugly.

A paved parking lot bounded the store and afforded little in the way of concealment. The best he could do was to park on the side instead of the front. He listened for the sound of motorcycles as he got out of the car. Nothing. Only distant bird calls out in the forest. Maybe he was overreacting. Maybe paranoia was getting the best of him. He didn't like the thought. One thing he'd never been was a chickenshit.

He went around front and entered the store, setting off the tinkle of a little warning bell mounted atop the door. An older woman wearing a black apron stood behind the counter and looked up through thick bifocals. "Hi, how you doing?" she asked in a pleasant voice. Stone pictured her with permed gray hair at the christening of her third granddaughter.

"I'm not really sure," he said and turned to look out the window at the main road.

"So, what can we do to fix that?" she asked cheerfully.

Before he could think of an answer, the rumble of big bike engines invaded the quiet outside and burbled into the store. Here they came, fully a dozen of them. One of the lead bikers pointed to the side of the store where Stone had parked. They curved on in, formed a semicircle directly in front and started to dismount. Lank hair, dirty jeans, scuffed boots.

Stone turned to the woman. "Stay here." He didn't want to put her in harm's way; and if harm had a way, this was surely it. He opened the door and walked out onto a concrete walkway about a foot above ground level. The bikers had bent into a line around him that precluded any escape. The tall one, the one he'd clubbed at Altamont, occupied the center. An even taller one stood next to him who Stone recognized as one of the leaders on the stage at Altamont. The guy looked like an archetypal composite of every hellish illustration of Satan that Stone had ever seen. Oily obsidian hair down to his shoulders. A black beard trimmed to a sharp point beneath his chin. A prominent hook nose. All with the chronically irritated eyes of a man who never slept.

"Hey wanna know something?" the tall one said to Stone. "I got a headache. Same headache I've had ever since you smacked me. Now what do ya think we oughta do about that?"

It had been dark at Altamont, but here Stone got a good look at the biker's face, with the cruel brown eyes and thin lips curled in a nasty grin. Stone knew his only chance was to stand his ground. "I think you should get back on your bike and ride on outta here before things get out of hand."

"Oh you do, do you?" the tall one said. All the while, Satan stood absolutely still, with eyes carefully assessing Stone. Unless he called for restraint, the entire pack would soon advance and take their revenge. He did no such thing, and the advance began, one step at a time. Stone could only hope to get a few good licks in before he went down for good.

An unmistakable sound came from behind him. The slider on a semi-automatic shotgun pumping a shell into the chamber. The Angels halted their advance and Stone turned to see the old woman from inside now standing in the open door, rifle in hand. She brought it down to waist height and leveled it at the bikers.

"I think you better do just what the man said," she advised in a calm voice. "I think you should just ride on out of here."

The tall one didn't buy it and started forward again. "And what you gonna do if we don't? You gonna shoot us?"

The woman tilted the weapon down slightly, pulled the trigger, and blasted a little crater into the pavement a few feet in front of the biker, who started and jumped back.

To drive home her point, the woman chambered a second shell.

All eyes went to Satan, who remained motionless with his gaze fixed on Stone and the woman. A crow cawed in the distance. Several dogs barked.

Satan said nothing but threw his thumb over his shoulder toward the road.

The Angels retired to their choppers in sullen silence, circled around, and headed back toward Kesey's place.

The woman turned to Stone, who was at a loss for what to say. "You know, they can really be pests sometimes," she remarked.

It was the way she said it that got to Stone. As if the neighbor kids had made too much noise during a squirt gun fight.

They went back in, and he bought twenty-five dollars' worth of snacks before taking off.

11.

GOLDEN GATE PARK

The nighttime rain beat incessantly on the roof of the old pink and white van. It spoke to Carson about the incident at Altamont and filled the gaps in his cratered memory. It told of being hunted by the outlaw bikers and a mad flight through the departing crowd. It revealed the frozen faces around the campfire and the chaos that followed. It replayed the horrible moment of impact. It reprised his sullen journey home in the back of a pickup truck driven by strangers.

But then again, what did the rain really know? It wasn't there that night. What part was true, and what part was fabricated? He would never know and didn't really want to. He already carried more than his share of the weight of the world.

He sat parked in the rear of the Kezar Pavilion and watched the raindrops hit the windshield and twist the night into a distorted abstraction. About a block away, the lights of the Park Police Station curled and danced across his vision. He knew the place well, from almost every angle. About eighteen months ago, he had built a bomb with enough destructive power to level the entire structure. He would have succeeded save for a chance encounter at precisely the wrong moment. To prevent copycat attempts, the event had never reached the media.

Like any good technician, Carson carefully reviewed what had happened and learned from his mistakes. This time would be different, or so he hoped. Once again, he had to contend with the asshole Mahler and his wobbly knowledge of bomb design. But unlike the first episode, he asserted himself to the point where Mahler had to make some concessions. The bomb would be more compact and easily transported. To make up for a smaller destructive radius, it would be surrounded by hundreds of one-inch fence staples, a very wicked form of shrapnel, each with twin daggers to rip and tear.

Like last time, the bomb used a simple alarm clock as a timer; only this time Carson took charge of the ignition circuit, which now included a safety switch for security during transport. His goal was to leave as little to chance as possible.

The weakest link in the scheme was not the bomb itself, it was Alice, who was chosen to deliver it to its final resting place on the ledge of a ground-level window. The leadership decided that a reasonably attractive young woman would be the least suspicious person, and they were right. Alice walked in through an open gate in the back, placed the device and was out in less than a minute. Two cops were cleaning out their patrol car while she did it, but they never even looked up.

Back at Pine Street, her exploit was quickly praised as a great and selfless contribution to the revolution. When all the effusive drama ebbed, Carson took her aside to audit the details. Had she placed it where it would blow through the window glass instead of the wall? Yes, she had. Had she turned off the safety switch before placing it? Yes, she had. Had she checked to make sure that the clock was set precisely for the 11 p.m. shift change?

No, she hadn't.

Carson sighed as the rain kept pounding the car's roof. The clock was probably set reasonably close to the right time, but there was no way to sure. He checked his watch. 10:43 p.m.

. . .

Sergeant Brian McDonnell stood in front of the teletype machine as the typehead chattered its way through line after line of text on a continuous roll of perforated paper. As each message concluded, he would tear it off, scan it, and place it in one of several piles. He had yet to see the message he sought, which would announce the results of the election for the station's union rep.

"Ah yes, the man who would be king," Officer Bob Fogarty observed from a few feet away. "Has it come through yet?"

"Not yet." McDonnell said. He was a strong favorite to win the election.

"I'd say you pretty much got it in the bag," Fogarty said. "Let me offer my congratulations in advance. He gave McDonnell an impish grin. "Of course, I'll be expecting a few favors."

Brian smiled. "Of course."

And those were the last words that Sgt. McDonnell would ever say to anybody.

. . .

The blast wave rolled over Carson's rain-spattered windshield and temporarily swept it clean in a stampede of tiny droplets. A dark stand of trees blocked a direct view of the station, but the shouting and confusion had already started and came pouring in the through his open window.

He checked the time. 10:45. Yet another fuckup. Ignition was supposed to coincide with the 11 p.m. shift change. Once again, their chances of taking out a pig or two were rapidly diminishing. And this time, he had a bigger stake in the outcome. He was largely responsible for the design and execution and therefore largely accountable for the outcome. If he failed, Mahler, the technical wannabe, would be waiting to pounce.

Carson tired of the Weather politics, with their endless conflicts, rivalries and hidden agendas. At the Pine Street and the Geary Street safe houses, there were all these closed-door meetings in the kitchen, where "policy" was hashed out, whatever that was. Ayers and Dohrn seemed to be at the top of the heap. Carson considered Ayers to be a hyper-opinionated loudmouth, while Dohrn came across as utterly confident and in control. So who set this bombing mission in motion? He didn't know for sure and really didn't care. His crusade just happened to coincide with theirs and that's all that mattered.

Outside, the plaintive wail of sirens pierced the night. A good sign.

*

Officer Frank Rath heard a screaming buzz in his ears as he came up off the floor. His left arm throbbed, and he saw a random scatter of large staples protruding through the sleeve of his uniform. A wet pool of blood welled up around each penetration. They were under attack. He drew his pistol and stumbled forward in both shock and confusion. The last thing he remembered was standing on the far side of the business office, where Fogarty was joking around with McDonnell over by the teletype.

Several officers came down the stairs from the squad room up above. Dust, glass, debris, staples and blood awaited them. "Frank, you're hurt!" Office Ralph Stimson shouted as he reached the bottom of the stairs.

Rath looked at his punctured arm. "Yeah, I know." He stopped, lowered his pistol and rested against the remnants of a desk.

Stimson looked to the right, where the blast damage was most severe. Two people were partially buried in the rubble. The nearest one struggled feebly to shake off the debris. Fogarty. Stimson saw numerous staples embedded in his right arm and leg. Worse yet, blood flowed copiously from a staple wound next to his right eye.

"Fogarty!" Stimson shouted as he reached out to touch the fallen officer. "Can you hear me?"

Fogarty pawed absently at his wounded eye. "Can't see," he said. "Can't see."

"Just stay put," Stimson instructed. "We got help on the way." He continued on to the person nearest the demolished wall and window. He couldn't be sure who it was.

The face was mostly gone, replaced by lumpen mass of red gore. "Oh Jesus," he muttered softly and looked back toward Fogarty. "Who was here with you?"

"McDonnell," Fogarty said weakly. "Is he okay?"

Rhythmic spouts of red gushed out of McDonnell's neck. Mercifully, he appeared to be unconscious.

"Don't think so," Stimson replied.

· · ·

"Yes! We've got ourselves a dead pig!"

One of the Weatherman burst into the kitchen at the Pine Street house, clutching a copy of the *San Francisco Chronicle*. He reached out and shook Carson's hand. "Congratulations, man. You got the first hit. Way to go."

The others clustered around and read the account, which was a follow-up to the story announcing the bombing two days ago. It seemed that the officer died of a severed jugular and a deadly concentration of fencing staples massed in his brain.

Mahler sat among them and remained silent as the group chattered about this being the real start of the revolution. Carson looked over at him occasionally, and Mahler avoided his withering gaze.

The contest was officially over. Carson was now bomber in chief.

. . .

Christine hung her white lab coat on a hook by the open door. Stone could see Kitty outside, waiting for his entitlement. But instead of fetching a treat, Christine closed the door, crossed to the counter and sat down heavily.

"Trouble?" Stone asked.

"That officer from Park Station died today." She stared at the counter with a bemused smile. "He never really had a chance." She looked up at Stone. "Did you know him?"

"Don't think so," Stone replied. It was a more than reasonable question. Sometime back, he'd wound up enmeshed with the Park Station cops in a case involving big-time drug dealing and a couple of homicides. Along the way, he'd made a few enduring friendships. He was also among the few civilians who knew that there had been an earlier bombing attempt on the station.

"You know," Christine said, "I've always believed that things would get better. That's why I became a doctor back when women weren't supposed to do that. I didn't think it was a long shot. Things would get better. And they have, one step at a time." She stopped and sighed. "But now I'm not so sure. It feels like we've turned some kind of corner and things are headed the wrong way."

"And which way might that be?" Stone asked. It disturbed him to see her like this. She'd always served as the counterpoint to his classic cop cynicism.

"I don't know," she said. "But it's definitely not forward."

Stone nodded. "I know what you mean."

He remembered that Kitty had just been stood up because of all this human angst. Not his fault. Stone went over and opened up the door to see if the cat was still there.

It was gone.

12.

SAN FRANCISCO

"I've been thinking about it," Stone announced to Christine. "The thing down in La Honda was my last shot. I'm out."

"For good?" she asked as she rinsed her breakfast plate in the sink.

"For good," Stone confirmed while spooning cream into his coffee. "Truth is, it's a young man's game. More now than ever. If you're an old guy, you pretty much have to move over to the business side and park your ass behind a desk. That's just not gonna work for me. I was in it for the music."

"Yes, you were," she agreed. She picked up her keys and lifted her white lab coat off the hook by the door.

"I read this thing the other day about mid-life crises," Stone went on. "It said one big mistake people make is to plunge into some career where they have absolutely no experience. It's better to stick closer to something you already know. That way, you can capitalize on your prior knowledge."

Christine had her coat on and the door open. She froze in place and stared at him. "You're not thinking of being a cop again, are you?"

"No, I was not thinking that."

She let his reply hang in the air for a meaningful moment.

"Good."

That said, she was out the door and gone.

"Point taken," Stone said to the empty alcove.

*

Stone tried to pretend he wasn't bored and failed.

He sat in the sun on the short embankment next to the three giant casting pools in Golden Gate Park, a half-hour walk from their house. A lone angler in waders whipped his pole around and curved its line snake-like down the length of the nearest pool. It resolved into a perfectly straight trajectory as it neared the surface of the calm water.

Is this what people do when they're unemployed or retired? He wondered. If so, he had no intention of becoming either. He couldn't survive as a passive consumer of the work of others. He needed purpose and direction. Without it, he would begin to corrode and crumble into anonymous dust – long before his time.

He got up and headed back toward the house for one of the biggest events of the day. Lunch. Would it be ham and cheese or tuna mixed in mayo? A momentous decision.

. . .

The doorbell yanked Stone out of a fitful afternoon slumber. He'd dozed off reading an article in *Time* magazine about Nixon's undeclared war in Cambodia. Not good news.

He came up out of his favorite chair and wondered who it might be. In truth, it really didn't matter. Even the Jehovah's Witnesses would be a welcome break. He'd have them come in and start a spirited debate on the mystical relationship between God and man on the surface of the planet Earth.

He opened the door to none other than Detective Sergeant Linehan of the SFPD.

"Stone, how you doing?" the officer asked.

"Probably a lot better than you," Stone said. Linehan worked out of the Park Station, where the final toll in the bombing had come to one dead and seven wounded. "Come on in."

"Have a seat. Want anything to drink?" he asked Linehan, a fit and graying man with pale blue eyes imported straight from Ireland.

"I'd like a good stiff shot of whiskey with a beer back, but somehow I don't think that'd be appropriate."

"Probably not," Stone said as they both sat down. "Did you know McDonnell?"

"It's a small station," Linehan said. "Everybody knows everybody. God rest his soul."

"Amen," Stone concluded. "You got any leads?"

Linehan sighed. "No. And that's why I'm here."

"Explain," Stone asked.

"Couple of reasons. This thing has left us really shorthanded. We need some new people, at least for the time being."

"That's one reason," Stone observed.

"They've made me the lead guy on the investigation, and I need all the help I can get. I want to bring you in on it."

"Really," Stone said in partial disbelief.

"Yeah, really. You made a lot of friends on the force when you helped us out a couple of years back."

"So, you want me to join the SFPD?"

"Just for now," Linehan explained. "We get it done, you can do whatever." He paused. "I know you got your music stuff, but that doesn't really count right now. I think you know that."

Stone did know that. A fellow officer had been killed, an innocent one. Anything he could do to make it right was damn near obligatory. He'd carry that burden with him all his life.

"Understand," Stone said. "I've got to talk to Christine about it."

"Of course you do," Linehan said. "This isn't an easy deal. Not for any of us. Let me know how it goes, okay?"

"I will," Stone promised. Linehan knew the score. There was no simple way out, especially with Christine.

Stone walked out with Linehan and watched him descend the steps. When he reached the bottom, he turned back toward Stone.

"They blew his fucking face off. You know that?"

Before Stone could reply, he turned and walked off down the sidewalk.

Stone spent the balance of the afternoon rehearsing what he would tell Christine. No matter how he shaped it, it had a really ugly feel. Why, on this morning of all mornings, had she asked if he was considering being a cop again? It was just plain bad luck. But then again, so was the bombing, and so was a dozen fencing staples lodged in someone's brain. And so was the whole nasty business at Altamont. Taken all together, it formed a black vortex looking for the perfect place to touch down. Which just happened to be right here on this otherwise beautiful day.

. . .

The hour of reckoning had arrived. He waited until she settled in at the kitchen counter and had a sip or two of wine before starting. Fortunately, Kitty had the good sense to stay away today.

Christine led off the evening by describing some kind of goof that a young resident had made during an examination. He let it play out before launching.

"You remember Sgt. Linehan?" he asked her.

"Wasn't he one of the guys that helped you with Rhonda?" she asked.

"Yeah, he was. He came by today."

"He came here? How come?"

"He wanted to talk about the bombing at the station."

"Was he there when it happened?"

"Don't think so. He works the day shift."

"Well, I'm curious then. What did he have to say?"

"They've put him in charge of the investigation, and he wants me to help."

Here it came. "Wants you to help? What's that mean?"

"He'd like me to come on board for a while, at least until they catch the guy."

"Am I hearing this right? He wants you to join the San Francisco Police Department?"

"Yeah. You heard right. He wants to bring me in. At least for now."

"And what did you tell him?"

"I told him I'd talk to you."

She put down her wine, straightened up, crossed her arms and gave him the coldest of stares. All bad omens.

"We're talking," she said.

Stone sighed and looked down at the counter. "I've got to do it. I don't have any choice."

"On this very same morning, you told me you weren't interested in being a cop anymore. Now what's so different on this very same evening?"

He saw that coming, but it didn't do him a damn bit of good. It was time for his closing statement.

"Truth is, you can quit the force, like I did in LA and Bakersfield. But in the end, you never quit being a cop. If you're a good one, you're part of the tribe forever. And now someone's killed a fellow cop and you're being asked to help track him down. You can't refuse."

"I guess not," she said.

"Sorry."

"Yeah, well, you gotta do what you gotta do."

They spoke no further for the rest of the evening. It was the worst it had ever been.

13.

GREENWICH VILLAGE

Carson crossed Sixth Avenue and headed east down West 11th Street in the cool night air of early spring. Long rows of four-story townhouses dominated the street. Each had a red brick face and a stoop with a wrought iron railing inevitably painted black. An occasional tree rose from the sidewalk, still leafless from winter. To Carson, who came from El Paso, it all looked like the surface of some distant planet. But here he was, loaned out to the New York Weatherman cell to consult on a mission of great strategic importance, or so he was told. He'd earned the privilege through his success with the Park Station bombing. He knew the leadership considered him politically dubious, but strategically valuable as they prepared to move their struggle out onto the streets.

Carson had flown in carrying a forged driver's license that reflected the pseudonym on his reservation and ticket. The logistics behind his trip remained murky. He suspected it was set up and paid for by a trendy San Francisco law firm friendly to Ayers and Dohrn. Many attorneys here and elsewhere were trying to have their radical cake and eat it too. They saw themselves as prime movers in a new ideological movement based on longstanding liberal principals. They also saw a profound romanticism in the life of the underground activists, those risking all for the sake of lofty principles. However, they weren't quite willing to give up lucrative practices, late-model cars and comfortable homes to join in. To assuage their guilt, they made up the difference with a quiet yet steady stream of covert money.

Midnight was near when he arrived at the townhouse on 11th, and it took some time before someone answered the door. It was a young woman who identified herself only as Cathy to conform to the new norms of secrecy imposed by the leadership. He learned that her parents owned the place and were due back from St. Kitts on Friday. She seemed quite concerned about getting everything cleaned up and everyone out before they arrived. More like a spoiled sorority girl than a seasoned revolutionary.

Carson crashed on the couch, and in the morning, the cell convened at the dining room table, where Carson met several other members, including a troubled woman named Diana and an intense young man named Terry, who came off as the de facto leader.

Carson learned that the designated target was a dance at the non-commissioned officers' club at Fort Dix, about 75 miles south in New Jersey. They had procured 50 pounds of dynamite, which offered the opportunity for a slaughter of colossal proportion. Terry expressed a kind of maniacal glee about the operation. "We're going to take the war right back to the war-makers," he declared. The others appeared committed but hesitant. All the talk about violent revolution had coalesced into a plan of real action, a plan that offered no retreat. Many in the outside world would look upon them not as freedom fighters, but as terrorists. It might be countless years before the sweep of history vindicated their exploits.

Terry thought otherwise. He seemed oblivious to the political currents and believed they would probably all die in service to the cause, and so be it. Carson agreed with much of what he heard from Terry. It was a position of violent retribution not that different from his own, except for the willful self-destruction. Carson could imagine a world where, after a horrific and pitiless struggle, the beast had been defanged, but Terry could not.

When the meeting ended, the two of them immersed themselves in the technical side of bomb making. They descended to a sub-basement where Terry had set up a workshop devoted exclusively to fabricating the device. Two crates held the 50 pounds of dynamite. Loose wires, blasting caps and batteries, and various schematics littered the workbench along with several cardboard boxes of roofing nails.

One look told Carson that Terry had no idea what he was doing. As they talked, he learned that the man was an English major and poet with a real aversion to science and engineering. To construct the bomb, he was simply trying to interpret instructions given to him by other sources. He had no clue what the destructive radius of a stick of dynamite might be. Nor did he know how to build a safety switch to test the ignition circuit prior to arming the bomb.

At one point, the woman named Diana came down the stairs to visit Terry. Carson soon realized that she was Terry's assistant and that she knew even less than he did about bomb making.

Carson sensed that the internal politics here were even worse than his confrontation with Mahler in San Francisco. He was an outsider with no real mandate to take over construction of the device, and this Terry guy was highly strung and ego-driven. Nevertheless, he had to give it a try. At one point, he tactfully suggested a minor modification to the circuitry and got an instant and visceral reaction from the poet-turned-technician, who took it as a personal insult to the integrity of his work and saw no reason why it should be tampered with.

By early afternoon, Carson had decided that he'd been dealt completely out of the deck and went back upstairs, where the mood was tense and sullen among the other cell members. The brutal reality of what they'd set in motion had now settled in completely. In effect, these sons and daughters of the privileged class were putting themselves in mortal jeopardy for the first time in their sheltered lives. Carson had no sympathy. In the war, he'd been in mortal jeopardy twenty-four hours a day for months on end, with no well-placed parents to deliver salvation from on high.

He took off and rode the subway up to midtown and got off near Central Park. He felt edgy and deprived because he didn't have any amphetamines, which would have landed him in serious trouble when paired with his fake ID. Up ahead, an older couple rode by in an open horse-driven carriage piloted by a stoic driver in a ridiculously antiquated costume. For no good reason, he wondered if perhaps the couple would invite the driver to have dinner with them at the Plaza tonight. Maybe they'd find they had much in common.

Probably not.

14.

GOLDEN GATE PARK

Stone looked up from his newly minted desk at the painters and glaziers as they went about restoring some semblance of order to the interior of Park Station. He wished they could also repair the wounded soul of the place, but that was definitely outside their scope of work. The ghost of Sgt. McDonnell would roam the halls for quite some time to come.

Detective Sgt. Stone of SFPD. It felt kind of like slipping into an old shoe. On the work front at least, but not on the home front. Christine continued to be cool and distant. To her credit, there had been no angry outburst over his decision. Even if there had been, it wouldn't have made any difference. As she tersely said at the time, you gotta do what you gotta do. What made it doubly difficult for him was that he had no way to gauge the volume of the anger that must surely bubble within her. He kept trying to console himself with the notion that it was all born out of love and concern for his wellbeing, at least he hoped so. For now, all he could do was batten down the hatches and hope for the best.

"Hey, Stone. You ready?"

Detective Joe Burke pulled up a chair opposite Stone across the desk. He looked thinner than Stone remembered him. Same broad face, flat top and blue eyes, but a lot less tummy. Obviously doing penance for the heart attack he'd suffered back in '67.

"Ready as I'll ever be." Stone looked down at the stack of reports piled all over his desk. A couple of dozen people had been in the building when the bomb went off, and all had been interviewed in detail.

"So where do you want to start?" Burke asked.

"I want to start with last time," Stone said.

"You think it's the same guy?" Burke asked. He knew that Stone was referring to the bombing attempt two years ago, the aborted one that had never gone public.

"Can't be sure, but I think it's a pretty good bet. Anyway, you were a key player, so you're a good place to start."

Burke shrugged. "You read the report, right? I'm not sure what else I can tell you. It was dark. The guy ran. I gave chase. My heart went boom and that was that."

"When you first spotted him, he was crouched under the second window down from the front. Correct?"

"You got it."

"That's right where the new bomb was placed." Stone observed. "Could be coincidence, but maybe not. Anyway, it's worth taking a second look."

"Definitely," Burke said. "While you're at it, you should talk to Bevans over in the bomb squad. He's the one who handled it."

"Thanks, I'll do that." Stone looked down at Burke's original report. "It says here the guy was wearing an army field jacket. That right?"

"Yeah, an old ratty one. We see a lot of that around here. Vietnam vets. You fight the war, you come back, you wind up out on the street. Bad deal."

"Yeah, bad deal," Stone agreed. "But why take it out on the cops?"

Burke sighed. "You figure that out, you let me know."

· · ·

The bomb squad's official title traded drama for formality – the Explosives Ordinance Disposal unit. It resided over in the Central District, so Stone had to tangle with the late afternoon traffic to make his meeting with its commander, a Lieutenant Bevans.

"So, how much do you know about what we do here?" Bevans asked Stone. The man had a very close-cropped military look about him, and Stone guessed that was probably his point of origin.

"Not a lot," Stone admitted. "I'm a vice and homicide guy. We don't blow things up."

"Neither do we," Bevans said. "Our whole mission is to make sure things *don't* blow up. And over the years, we've gotten pretty damned good at it."

"I'm sure you have," Stone agreed.

"But there's a catch."

"What's that?"

Bevans leaned forward. "We can't stop something from blowing up if we don't know it's there in the first place."

"Like at Park Station," Stone suggested.

"Yeah," Bevans said grimly. "Like at Park Station."

"We've had two bombings there," Stone said. "One that killed and one that fizzled. I'd like to start with the fizzle. I was told you headed that up."

"I did. And I've gotta tell you, we're lucky that's the one that didn't go off. It would've wiped out damn near everyone in the station. As I'm sure you know, we retrieved the device intact, and found it was full of an explosive called Semtex. Its main ingredient is this plasticized stuff called pentaerythritol tetranitrate, which is just about as nasty as it gets. It has a detonation velocity of eighty-four hundred meters per second."

"How does that compare with dynamite?" Stone asked.

"Dynamite is about seven thousand. Also, you can a pack a lot more Semtex into smaller space."

"And so why didn't the thing go off?"

"Good question," Bevans said. "We don't know for sure, but I can give you a pretty good guess. The triggering mechanism was radio controlled, which points toward someone with technical skills. Most likely, your Sgt. Burke saved the day by chasing the guy out of range. Simple as that."

"Do you still have the device?" Stone asked.

"As a matter of fact, we do. Minus the Semtex of course. We blew that up. You want to take a look at it?"

"Not right now. Let's move on to the new bombing. Obviously, it wasn't as powerful."

"Tell that to Sergeant McDonnell," Bevans said. "The guys at the FBI lab reconstructed the device by examining the fragments. Turns out it's a classic pipe bomb with a clock for a timer. It's the shrapnel, the fence staples that made it so bad. That and the placement right outside the window."

"Do you think it might be the same bomber in both cases?"

Bevans leaned back in a thoughtful pose. "I do. The devices are very different, but I think the guy learned from his mistakes. He realized he'd been way too ambitious the first time around and failed because of it. He knew his ultimate objective was to kill some cops and that a much simpler approach would get him there with a lot less risk of failure. Unfortunately, he was right."

"Unfortunately," Stone repeated. He was sure that all who'd known the departed McDonnell would agree.

15.

GREENWICH VILLAGE
MARCH 6, 1970

When daylight expired, Carson left Central Park and rode the subway back to the townhouse, where he learned that Terry and Diana had taken a break and gone out. It gave him chance to go down to the workshop in the sub-basement and inspect their progress.

He shook his head at what he encountered. They had fashioned a large globe of gray clay studded with roofing nails and shoved in dozens of sticks of dynamite with blasting caps protruding from the exposed ends. A rat's nest of wires connected the leads from the caps in some incomprehensible pattern. The bomb's ignition circuitry sat off to one side and had yet to be connected. Carson couldn't figure out the details, but it seemed to be centered on a pocket watch. He thought it better to be somewhere else during final assembly.

He went back upstairs and found two other cell members in the kitchen nibbling on Chinese takeout food. One was Teddy, the other was a woman who went by Kathryn. He'd heard vague references to them while on the West Coast but had no idea how they fit into the organization. Both appeared distracted and lost in some kind of dank introspection. Carson was curious about how the remainder of the plan would roll out. Kathryn reluctantly gave him a cryptic overview. They had to be out of here by noon tomorrow when her parents returned from their vacation in the Caribbean.

The bomb would be loaded onto a rented delivery truck and parked at a secure location close to Fort Dix. The area around the targeted club was open to public access, and the package would be part of a bogus food service delivery on Saturday afternoon. Once inside, it would be placed under the stage for maximum effect. Carson wondered who would be driving the truck and making the final placement but decided it better not to ask.

Terry and Diana showed up, both looking pale and drained. Teddy asked them if the bomb was done, and Terry said they were too tired to finish it right now. Bomb making left no room for fatigue and mistakes, he said.

He had no idea how right he would be.

. . .

Carson smelled the omnipresent overlay of engine exhaust in the morning air as he started up 11th Street. He'd risen early and found Terry in the kitchen brewing a cup of tea while Diana poured cornflakes into a couple of bowls on the counter. Both looked far from rested. When he asked about their progress, Terry made vague references to final adjustments of the wiring. He'd become clearly defensive with Carson about the quality of his work.

A little later, the guy named Teddy recommended a small pastry and coffee shop in the middle of the Village, and Carson lingered there, reading the *New York Times*. It spoke of wars, rioting, corruption, bigotry and crime, along with the Dow Jones Industrial Average.

Carson checked his watch. It was getting close to noon, so the cell should be packing up and sending the bomb off to its momentous destination. He'd be flying out this afternoon from La Guardia and would leave this entire fiasco to sort itself out. If this was the heart and soul of the revolution, those in power had little to worry about.

The shock wave caught him off guard, as did the thunderous report of the exploding dynamite.

Up ahead, an angry avalanche of smoke and dust shot out into the street. He staggered under the force of the compressed wave front and grabbed a parking meter to keep his balance. The sound of shattered glass reverberated in brilliant sparkles all up and down the block.

The fool had gone and done it. He'd botched the bomb. Carson crossed to the far side of the street and moved forward to get a better view. Just then, a second even bigger explosion went off, knocking him back against a parked car. Smoke and flame billowed from all the windows and formed an ominous column that ascended into the overcast sky.

When the haze thinned, it became clear that the front wall of the building was largely gone. The exposed inner floors sagged on the verge of total collapse. Soon, the whole interior would pancake all the way down to the street, leaving a yawning gap in the once solid row of buildings.

A frantic chorus of sirens welled up in the background. Neighbors poured out onto their stoops to witness the calamity. Somewhere a small dog issued an endless stream of terrified barks.

Carson wondered how many of them were still in there when the bomb went off. He guessed that both Terry and Diana had been reduced to a gory mixture of shredded flesh and roofing nails. He couldn't be sure about the others and couldn't afford to stick around and find out. He wove his way past a rising tide of fire trucks, fire hoses and fireman. A third explosion sounded from somewhere in the back of the building as he cleared the block.

So much for the revolution.

16.

GOLDEN GATE PARK

"I was in Vietnam," Officer James Pera told Stone. "You expected stuff like this to happen. But not here. What else can I say?"

"Not much," Stone said. Pera was his last interview out of the two dozen men present when the bomb went off. Most were patrolmen located upstairs in the locker room and changing into civilian clothes. Stone suspected that the timing was no coincidence. The detonation occurred just fifteen minutes before the 11 p.m. shift change, which would have put a lot more people on the first floor in the line of fire. Whoever made the bomb had probably screwed up the timer, causing it to go off prematurely.

Stone thanked Pera, who headed out to his patrol car. He stared at the stacks of reports that formed a miniature city atop his desk. He'd been through the whole lot without unearthing even the thinnest of leads. It didn't help that there had been a steady rain that night, which left no one outside. An infiltrator could have walked in the rear gate by Kezar Stadium, planted the bomb and left without anyone noticing. Of course, the gate was now locked, but it wasn't on the night in question.

The only civilian witness was a grounds worker unloading athletic line markers at an equipment shed behind Kezar Stadium. He had a vague memory of a pink and white van pulling out of the rear stadium parking lot around the time of the explosion. He said it was an older model, but that's all he could recall.

His only other source of information was an Army bomb squad that had rushed over from the Presidio and swept the area looking for other devices. It found nothing else of interest. The follow-up by SFPD's bomb squad was a little more helpful. Its analysis confirmed that the device was a timer-driven pipe bomb but revealed nothing about who built it or why.

Finally, there was the matter of the Berkeley police station bombing, which had occurred just a week earlier. Were the two related? Both were pipe bombs and appeared to be timed to detonate during a shift change. Stone figured that they probably were connected, but it did him little good in the short run. A few phone calls to Berkeley told him that the cops over there were about as stumped as he was when it came to nailing a perpetrator. Since it was Berkeley, the radical center of the universe, they suspected it was politically motivated, but had no idea how. The best they could do was agree to share information if and when it became available.

That left Stone with one officer dead and seven wounded and very little else to go on. He sighed. Now the long grind began. Every detective knew the feeling. At the outset, you hoped to quickly dig up a few key pieces of evidence that pointed in the right direction. Witnesses, smoking guns, damning documentation. When it didn't happen, you knew you were going to have to take the long way around.

He decided he would start with the fence staples. They weren't an everyday hardware item, like roofing nails or finishing nails, especially in an urban setting where there weren't a lot of wooden fence posts. Hardware stores were the most likely source, so how many hardware stores were there in the Bay Area? Dozens? A hundred? He'd have to contact every one and ask to see their sales records over the past couple of months. The very thought made him want to curl up and take a nap. And even if he found a few leads, he was still gambling that the store clerks would at least be able to give a physical description of the buyer.

Stone looked up at the wall clock. Christine would be home pretty soon. There was a time when that would have been a source of comfort, but not lately. Although there had been a partial thaw, things were still pretty edgy. Her side of the bed had definitely become private property. The cute stories from the ER over dinnertime wine had all but evaporated.

Oh well. He picked up the thick Yellow Pages volume of the San Francisco phone directory and started to search for hardware stores.

17.

GOLDEN GATE PARK

"I think I've found an angle," Stone told Sgt. Linehan.

"Oh yeah? Like what?" Linehan asked. At this time in the morning his desk was clear. By afternoon, the entire top would be buried in a chaotic sea of paper, save for his phone.

"Semtex," Stone said.

"Semtex? That's some kind of explosive, right?"

"Right." The thought had come to Stone while he was having a nightcap whiskey watching Johnny Carson on The Tonight Show. "It's what was in the first bomb, the one that didn't go off."

"But where does that get us?" Linehan asked.

"Semtex packs a really serious wallop. You want some dynamite; you just walk in and show a driver's license. You want some Semtex, you have to have a blasting license and a clean criminal record. Otherwise, you risk getting busted by the feds. And if you do get pinched, it's probably by the ATF people, so we check their arrest records and see what pops up. It'll be a pain in the ass, but it just might pay off."

Linehan nodded thoughtfully. "Makes sense. Of course, we're assuming that the first bomb and the second are the work of the same guy."

"True," Stone replied. "That makes it a crap shoot, but right now, we're rolling snake eyes every time out, so why not?"

Linehan gave a weary shrug. "Yeah, why not."

. . .

The clerk at the Bureau of Alcohol Tobacco and Firearms in downtown reminded Stone of his third-grade teacher, Mrs. Reynolds. Her hair reflected the practicalities of late middle age, done in a close-cropped perm. A long green cord left her reading glasses dangling beneath her bosom, and her face had a look of perpetual irritation, which she kept in check only because her job required it.

She stood with Stone in the records room, with its rows of steel-framed storage shelves filled with cardboard containers. A ledger rested on a small table near the entrance and she picked it up. "Before we start, I'll need to see your official identification and sign you in."

"Of course," Stone said as he pulled out his newly issued ID and signed the ledger. "What I'm looking for are convictions and fines involving illegal explosives in the last half of 1966 and the first half of 1967."

"Over here," she said and walked to one of the rows between the shelves. "All the explosives violations. They're arranged by date. The period you're talking about should be pretty close to the front."

Stone took a closer look and saw labels with dates on the front of the containers. Each container covered a particular year. "Is there someplace where I can sort through this stuff?"

"If you go on through to the back, you'll find a worktable and a couple of chairs," she replied. "Just one box at a time, and please return it before you move to another one."

"Got it," Stone said.

"And when you're done, please sign out and check back with me before you leave."

"Will do," Stone assured her.

"We close at 5:30," she warned him.

"I'll keep that in mind," he told her but didn't guarantee it. He couldn't resist playing her a little bit. In fact, he hoped to get lucky and be out of here way before then.

She left, and Stone quickly found a big carton labeled 1967 Explosives Incidents. He pulled it out and carried it to the table she'd mentioned. Dozens of file folders lined its interior, each bearing an ID number of some kind. Stone pulled out the first one, which contained a score of documents all related to a case concerning the transport of fireworks in violation of certain safety regulations. The nature of the violation was meticulously described and accompanied by the related statutes. The fireworks vendor declined to challenge the resulting fine in court and paid up. Boring.

The next file proved slightly more interesting. A mining operation with an expired blasting license went around the system because they didn't want to impede their production. They purchased some high explosives from another mining outfit and paid a premium to get what they needed, all done off the books. Both companies declined to contest the charges in court and paid a whopping fine for their misdeeds.

And so it went. Each case demanded careful scanning of the documents to see if Semtex was involved. Along the way, Stone caught a bad case of the yawns. Too bad they didn't have coffee in here.

Finally, on the twenty-first file, he hit a potential winner. The company in question went by the innocuous name of Excavation Equipment & Services and was located in the East Bay. They were a licensed supplier of Semtex and had gotten a little loose in terms of security and inventory control. A police report involving one of their employees triggered an audit that revealed that an entire pound of Semtex was unaccounted for. The company suffered a hefty fine and a temporary suspension of their license.

Stone put the file aside and continued on through the remaining seventeen. None involved Semtex, or anything close. Some bikers out in San Bernardino got busted for a case of dynamite in their clubhouse, but that was about it. Nobody blew anything up.

Stone returned to the file of interest. It generated all kinds of interesting questions. Who was the company employee? What was in the police report? What ultimately happened to the Semtex? Was it recovered and disposed of? Was it still out there somewhere?

He checked his watch. 5:15. He put the file aside and returned the container to its place in the shelving. That done, he took the file in question out to the office area, where the clerk was typing up a memo of some kind.

"I need to make a copy of these documents," he told her. "How would I go about that?"

She sighed and looked up at the clock. "Come with me," she instructed. They walked a short distance into a room with a bulky machine that had a glass top. "What's this?" Stone asked.

"It's a Xerox copy machine," she told him. "It's new here. There's an administrative fee of one dollar per copy." She said it as if it might be the coup de grace.

Stone felt buoyed by his victory in the file room and was quick to counter. "Do we have an account with you? I bet we do."

"San Francisco Police? Yes, I believe so."

"Well then, let's charge it."

She gave it one last shot. "I should inform that if they decline the charges, you will be held personally responsible."

Stone shrugged in mock resignation. "That's just a chance I'll have to take."

. . .

With copies of the file's contents in hand, Stone decided to bypass the station and head directly home. He wanted to make his arrival as close to Christine's as possible. Their time in the kitchen before dinner was a big focal point in their relationship, which right now was at its nadir. Any reconstruction effort would likely start here. At some point, they were going to have it out about his return to police work. He was sure she understood how he had a tribal obligation to find the bomber, but that didn't mean she was emotionally aligned with it. There had to be a workaround, but he knew the only way to get there was to let all the bad stuff erupt into plain sight, where they could work with it. As in any relationship, it would be a very messy but necessary business.

He always felt at a disadvantage in these kinds of conflicts. She was a doctor, he was just a cop. Her family was educated and progressive, his were Okie immigrants fresh off the plains. She was financially flush, he was not. Of course, you could argue that none of that really mattered, but of course it really did. The one thing they did have in common was a previous failed marriage, which ironically turned out to be a good thing because it gave them both a basis for comparison with their current situation.

He turned back to the matter at hand. Excavation Equipment & Services. They were located in an industrial district next to Oakland International Airport. With the morning traffic, it would take at least an hour to get there. He decided it was better to just show up than to phone ahead. The last thing he wanted was a carefully prepared response based on the advice of their attorney.

. . .

Excavation Equipment & Services occupied an utterly anonymous warehouse constructed of tilt-up concrete walls with a small office front and twin loading docks off to the side. A rugged assortment of old pickups and vans dominated the parking lot, along with a new Mercedes that probably belonged to the owner. Inside, a bare counter separated the office from a waiting area composed of two cheap chairs and a hanging fern in desperate need of water. A young woman looked up from her typing as Stone approached the counter. He guessed it was her first job out of high school.

"Can I help you?" she asked.

"Yes, I need to speak to the owner or the general manager," Stone answered.

A little cloud of confusion settled over her modestly pretty face. Apparently, there was no established protocol for this kind of situation. "Did he know you were coming?" she asked.

"Probably not, but I'm pretty sure he'll want to see me," Stone volunteered.

"Can I tell him who you're with?"

"Absolutely. My name is James Stone. I'm with the San Francisco Police Department."

"Oh." The cloud grew ever more opaque. "Let me see if he's available."

"Thank you." He took a seat while she trailed off into the back somewhere. A little stand between the chairs held some trade magazines, and he picked one up. It was called the *Engineering and*

Mining Journal and was thoroughly incomprehensible to anyone outside the business.

"Mr. Stone?"

Stone looked up to a thickly built man dead center in middle age. His broad face and bald head featured a mouth creased into a permanent scowl. "Jim Fowler. What can I do for you?" he asked.

No invitation to take a seat. No offer of coffee. Not a good start. The man might be good at blowing things up and digging them out of the ground, but public relations was definitely not part of his skill set.

Stone stood up. "Mr. Fowler, thanks for taking the time to see me. This isn't an official call. I'm just looking for a little information if you could spare a moment or two."

"What kind of information?" Fowler asked warily. Behind him, the young woman stared at the two of them, her face drowning in curiosity.

"It's about a former employee. Could we talk in private? At this point, I'd like to protect his identity."

Fowler pointed to a door off to his right. "In here."

Stone followed him into a meeting room full of dreary furniture and framed pictures of various mining operations, all done in glorious black and white. "Let me say right off, this had nothing to do directly with you or your company."

"Then what *does* it have to do with?" Fowler threaded his sausage-size fingers and leaned forward as he said it. "What employee are you talking about?"

"I'm not sure, and that's why I'm here. We have an investigation going on that involves ATF records. I found out that you guys were fined a couple of years back over some missing Semtex."

"That's a done deal," Fowler shot back. "We had a problem, we paid a fine. It's over."

"I'm sure it is, and I could care less. What interests me is it referred to a police report that apparently triggered the whole thing."

"We got fucked," Fowler said. "And there wasn't a damned thing we could do about it. That Simmons asshole ripped us off, and we took the hit for it."

"Simmons?"

"Yeah, Bobby Simmons. You know what the guys out in the warehouse used to call him? Pig Eye. I should've let him go the minute I heard that."

"Interesting," Stone commented. "Every bit helps. Right now, I'm just following a paper trail. Did they ever catch him?"

"Yeah, but it didn't matter because they didn't have any evidence. You can't prove somebody stole something if you can't prove they ever had it."

"The Semtex?"

Fowler looked at Stone like he was an idiot. "Yeah, the Semtex."

"Sorry, I'm getting a little confused," Stone apologized. "How did you ever figure out that he stole it in the first place?"

"The ATF wound up arresting him for something else and found out that he worked here. We had to do an audit and we came up short."

"Did they say what he was arrested for?"

"Dunno. Didn't even bother to ask. By that time, we were totally fucked, so who cares? He was a real sleaze bag. Coulda been anything."

Stone paused. "Simmons, huh?"

"Yeah, Robert Simmons. You find him, you tell him I got a blasting cap I'm going to shove up his ass."

Stone had to smile. "Will do."

. . .

The U.S. District Court occupied several floors of the nearly new Federal Building on the edge of downtown. It featured underground parking for the chosen few, but unfortunately Stone didn't yet have the SFPD sticker that would have let him park for free. He didn't mind the setback because he found himself in a very optimistic frame of mind. The discovery in Oakland of one Robert Simmons came as a real breakthrough in his pursuit of the Park Station bomber. Armed with the name, he had a solid navigation point as he navigated through the intricacies of whatever bureau-cracies he might encounter.

He caught yet another break when he reached the Clerk's office on the 16th floor. The staff proved friendly and helpful in his pursuit of Robert Simmons. When he said he was looking at potential cases within the past couple of years, they told him it was probably still on file at this location rather at an archives site down in San Bruno. Better yet, they had a library-like system of indexed file cards, including cross references by defendant name, date, violation type, and so on.

Ten minutes later, a clerk opened a long drawer in a big matrix containing all cases of record. She sorted alphabetically under 'S', and sure enough, up came Robert Simmons, attached to case number USDC-N-17473A.

Five minutes later, he was sitting at a reading table with a thick folder the clerk had fetched from a long row of tall metal file cabinets. Could it really be this easy?

No, it could not.

Just a few pages in, he discovered that Robert Simmons had been tried and convicted, all right. But not because of explosives. He'd been charged with illegal possession of a combat weapon capable of firing on full automatic. His sentence came to five years in the Federal Penitentiary at Lompoc, which indicated that the judge considered him a somewhat less than sterling character.

Stone made a quick guess. Simmons had traded the Semtex for the weapon. When he was busted, he told his attorney, a public defender no doubt, about the trade. But the attorney, clever devil that he was, realized that since the weapon's owner had disappeared with the Semtex, the government had no evidence to prosecute Simmons on that charge, which would have been substantial. His advice to Simmons: Clam up. Deny any knowledge. That Fowler guy at Excavation Equipment & Services had figured it mostly right. No wonder he drove the Mercedes.

The court record showed that two SFPD officers had testified. They had obtained a warrant based on a tip from a gun store owner and searched Simmons' apartment when they took him into custody. There was no mention of finding any explosives. Shortly thereafter, they handed him off to the ATF, who probably weren't happy they weren't called in in the first place.

Stone sighed. He plowed on through the rest of the documents and found little else of immediate use, except for a description of the weapon itself, a U.S. Army issue M16. For some reason, it didn't include the serial number. He'd have to follow up with the ATF, but first he'd talk to the two SF cops and get their take on Mr. Simmons.

The material in file was way too voluminous to copy, so he borrowed a legal pad and wrote down a summary of what he'd found. He checked his watch as he finished. The two detectives that testified in the case were out of Hunters Point. Just enough time to get there before traffic picked up.

. . .

"Pig Eye," Detective Sgt. Bigelow said with a contemptuous grin. "He might have been smart enough to use the kick stand on his bike, but I doubt it."

"He was a biker?" Stone asked as he sipped some bad coffee.

"At least he thought he was," Detective Sgt. Foster added. "Claimed he rode with the Angels. If he did, it was right at the back of the pack."

Both men had the weathered look of veterans who had seen a little too much in their time and packed on the pounds in the process. The Hunters Point posting didn't help. It covered some mean territory.

"When you searched his place, did you see anything that had to do with explosives?" Stone asked.

"Nope," Bigelow said. "Just a lot of beer, porno, paraphernalia, and engine tools. Why you ask?"

"It looks like he stole some explosives from his employer, and I'm willing to bet he traded them for the rifle," Stone said. "Anyway, why didn't you just let the ATF people handle the bust?"

"Because it was our lead, not theirs, that set the whole thing in motion," Foster explained. "The gun store owner owed us some favors and set up the sting that busted him. The ATF would've never got even close to the guy if it wasn't for us."

"I guess we did hang onto him a little longer than normal," Bigelow admitted. "It turned out he had some information about a capital murder case we were into at the time. We needed to make sure we pumped him dry before we turned him over."

Stone thought he recalled the case in question but had better things to do at the moment. "Thanks guys. I owe you one."

"Good luck with ATF," Bigelow said, and broke into a sardonic grin. "Tell 'em we said hi."

"Yeah, sure. I'll do that," Stone said. "You remember the agent over there that handled this thing?"

"A good Irish lad named Bannon," Foster said. "Not a bad sort, really."

"I'll keep that in mind," Stone said.

. . .

While he browned the stew meat, Stone put out a peace feeler.

"I finally got a break in the bomber case today," he announced to Christine, who sat at the dining table reading a magazine. She no longer cozied up on the stool by the kitchen counter, which was a statement in and of itself.

"Good," she said in a tone devoid of all color.

Stone gave her a moment for an addendum, but none came. If she had, it would have signaled a willingness to engage. No deal. He briefly considered turning off the heat, putting the pan aside, and dumping all their relationship's cards out on the table. Bad idea. The timing just didn't feel right.

He wondered how much of this behavior you inherited from your parents, either through nurture or nature or both. Were we all just drifting about at the whim of our genes and childhood memories?

Stone cut his rumination short and flipped the chunks of beef. It was his best move under the circumstances.

18.

SAN FRANCISCO

The dining room table in the Pine Street apartment also served as the social focal point for the residents. Somebody had scrounged some extra chairs so up to ten people could gather around it. And it was here that Carson had to listen to their endless exchanges about the townhouse explosion in New York, as if they could somehow talk it out of existence. Worse yet, he was frequently called on to testify, like a witness in some kind of criminal proceeding. And worst of all, they were often offended by his interpretations.

"Yeah, well I met Terry Robbins, and the guy was a real righteous dude, man," a young man said.

"Yeah, maybe so, but that doesn't mean that he knew how to build a bomb," Carson replied.

"He was the poet of the revolution. His words were beautiful things," a young woman in Birkenstocks added.

"But his bombs weren't," Carson retorted. "I was there, I saw them. They were a mess. He fucked up and blew them all into little pieces."

"Yeah, but he did it in the service of the revolution," another resident chimed in. "And that's what counts."

"Did you see Cathy and Kathryn in the nude?" someone with a prurient streak asked.

"No, I did not," Carson answered. The question irritated him. They had been over it a hundred times. Incredibly, the two women had walked out of the collapsed wreckage, both completely naked. A neighbor woman had scooped them up and given them shelter, which bought them time to go on the run before the police closed in. All after Carson had prudently left the scene.

"I've heard they're coming here," someone else said. "They've got wigs and fake ID so they can move underground."

"I think they were doing a lesbian thing when the bomb went off," another resident said. "That's why they were naked."

"Fuck you. The revolution isn't about passing bourgeois moral judgements on other people's sexual behavior. It's about room to move wherever your body wants to take you."

"Right on."

"Did you read what the pigs said about Diana? She was blown into a bunch of pieces that were stuffed with roofing nails."

"Oh yeah? Well what about Terry? All they found was some skin and smashed bone wrapped around a sewer pipe. Not a good way to go."

"Hey, let's get real: Are we supposed to believe the pigs about our people? Don't think so. There's a good chance they're being held in secret, so they can be tortured and interrogated without any interference."

And on it went. Carson left them and went upstairs to one of the communal bedrooms with foam rubber mattresses flung across the floor. Alice reclined on one, reading Che Guevara's book on the true nature of popular uprisings. "Am I missing anything?" she asked Carson.

"Nothing," he said flatly. "Absolutely nothing."

"You seem really cynical since you got back," she commented.

"I was really cynical before I ever left," he said.

"How come?"

His eye went to the famous photo of Che on the back of the book. "Would you fuck Che if you got the chance?"

"Of course I would," she said without hesitation. "He's the heart and soul of the entire movement."

"Well, I would fuck Bernadine Dohrn," he countered. "But she doesn't seem to be around much anymore. And why is that?"

Alice hesitated. "I think she and Will have a lot to work out. This is not a good time for them, or for us."

"Ah, so that's why they moved into that nice little pad over in Tiburon? Never been there, but I hear it's all tricked out. You think it would be okay if we just stopped by for a little visit?"

"Well maybe not," Alice admitted.

"Know what else?" Carson went on. "They've been spotted out and about at upscale restaurants all over the city. Wining and dining with their trendy attorney pals while we live on canned soup and noodles. Somehow that just doesn't seem right, doesn't seem like a revolution at all, seems more like business as usual in the land of pigdom."

"That's a really ugly thing to say," Alice responded. "I mean, someone has to provide leadership and they've stepped up to it."

"Stepped up," Carson repeated. "Yeah, good choice of words."

"I'd like you to leave now," Alice said, and went back to her book.

"You got it." Carson could feel the inexorable tug of the Benzedrine he'd taken a little earlier. It had a mind of its own and ignored all pretense of civilized discourse. If Carson was a movie, the dope was the director, and it was looking more and more like a real flop.

19.

SAN FRANCISCO

Agent Bannon of the ATF clasped his hands behind his head and leaned back in his chair as if to appraise Stone from the proper distance. "So, what can I do for you, detective?"

"They told me out front you handled a case involving a Robert Simmons," Stone said.

Bannon broke into an amused smile. "Ah yes. Pig Eye. A real master criminal. And what would you like to know about Mr. Pig Eye?"

"You guys put him away on a weapons charge, right?"

"A genuine U.S. Army M16 combat rifle. Seven hundred rounds per minute on full automatic," Bannon answered. "A real collector's item."

"I gathered that," Stone said. "But that's not why I came over. After talking to a few people and looking at the files, it looks like he might have also been dabbling in explosives. But I don't see that showing up anywhere."

Bannon brought his chair forward and folded his hands on the desktop. "No you don't." He looked at his watch. "You're in luck. I've got just enough time to tell you a little story."

"And how does it go?"

"It starts with me getting a buzz from a couple of cops out of Hunters Point. They've pinched this Simmons guy who was dumb enough to try to peddle an M16 to a licensed gun dealer. They hand him off to us and by then, of course, he's lawyered up, so we don't get much. We do, however, get his place of employment, where he spent considerable time in the proximity of high explosives."

"And it gets you to thinking…" Stone contributed.

"If a guy was dabbling in contraband weapons, why stop there? Why not move on to some real blasting power? So we require his employer to do an audit, and guess what? They come up a pound short of a plastic explosive called Semtex."

"And then?"

"Two things," Bannon replied. "First, we lean on Pig Eye, but by now he's learned to clam up completely. Second, we lean on his employer for failing to secure high explosives."

"And that's the end of it?"

"Not quite. I had a chat with the U.S. Attorney, who pointed out this little problem. We don't have any evidence. The stuff has vanished. The only place it exists is on the debit side of an audit report. So there you go. We stick with the weapons case and get the conviction. End of story."

"Interesting," Stone said. "You don't suppose he stole the Semtex to get the gun, do you?"

"It crossed my mind," Bannon said with twinkle. "And then it ran off."

. . .

A vertical vapor trail, a harbinger of apocalypse. It jabbed its way needle-like into the sky and curved seaward. Clearly a missile of some kind.

Stone pulled off the road just north of Lompoc, some 250 miles south of San Francisco, to get a better look. It might make him late arriving at the Federal Corrections Facility, but who cared? In an hour, the place might well be a burning pile of radioactive rubble. If he was witnessing Act One of The End of the World, he didn't want to miss a beat.

The missile continued its skyward arc and disappeared into the upper reaches of the stratosphere. And just as it slipped from view, Stone made the critical connection. The vast sprawl of Vandenberg Air Force Base started just a few miles north of the penitentiary and extended for miles along the coast. He'd heard that they tested missiles here, and now he knew for sure. It wasn't the apocalypse. Just a dress rehearsal.

Several vehicles passed as he got back in his car. He felt slightly humiliated. Just another rube suckered by the government fireworks. He wondered if Pig Eye had a cell with a view of the launchings. Of course not. He had to stop calling him Pig Eye, even in his inner dialogue. Their scheduled meeting was diplomatic in nature, and Stone had no cop-like leverage to back the biker into a cooperative corner. Simmons undoubtedly agreed to this talk to see if he could extract same kind of trade out of the deal. A better cell. Advanced canteen privileges. Stone would then do the usual, and promise "to see what he could do." For Simmons, it left a thin strand of hope that it just might really happen, which was better than none at all. And so went the dance.

"Mr. Simmons, thanks for taking the time to see me," Stone led off. "They treating you right?"

Simmons shrugged. "Maybe. I don't know." He scratched his right nostril. "But I do know you." He had a round face, flat nose and slit-like eyes beneath oily brown hair. The origin of his nickname was obvious.

"Really?" Stone said. "I don't think we've ever met."

"You're Stone the record guy. You tangled with the brothers up at Altamont. So now you're a cop, huh?"

"Now I'm a cop," Stone admitted.

"How'd that happen?"

"It's a long story. Pretty boring, really. I started out as a cop and now I've gone back to it. Not much else to tell you."

"And what's all this got to do with me?" Simmons wanted to know.

Stone knew he couldn't lead with the stolen Semtex. For one thing, it was pure speculation on his part. And the minute he did so, Simmons would walk out. Besides, the explosive itself wasn't the point. It was the identity of the guy who wound up with it.

He needed to take the long way around. "Look," he said. "You did what you did with the rifle and that's ancient history. None of my business. What I'm interested in is the guy you got it from."

"Oh yeah. That guy." Simmons switched gears into barter mode. "You know, life in here can be a bitch. Maybe there's some way to make it a little more comfy."

"Could be," Stone said. "I'm supposed to meet with the warden on the way out," he lied. "We have a good talk here, and I'll see what I can do."

Simmons took that as a go and launched. "The guy was a vet. Really crazy. I mean they're all crazy, but this guy was way over the top. A really sick fuck."

"Did he have a name?"

"Not that he ever said."

"How'd you meet him?"

"You know Chocolate George?"

"No but I've heard of him," Stone said. Simmons was referring to a Hells Angel who hung out in the Haight and gained a certain amount of notoriety as the biker lion who lay down among the hippy lambs.

"Yeah, anyway, George knows this guy from the street. The three of us trip over to a joint in Hunters Point called The Ball and Chain for a few beers. After that, the guy would show up now and then and get wasted. Wouldn't say a word. Really weird. Then one night in the parking lot he hits me up for this rifle deal." Simmons leaned back. "Any more than that, you'll have to talk to my lawyer."

"I don't think that'll be necessary," Stone said and stood up. "Thanks and have a nice stay."

"You'll talk to the warden?"

"Yeah, I'll talk the warden."

. . .

Stone sat at the tiny desk in his budget-level motel room on H Street in Lompoc. He'd just scribbled a few notes on a legal pad when the heartburn came on. No wonder. He'd made the mistake of ordering chicken-fried steak at the restaurant down the street, something nearly alien to his digestive system, thanks to Christine. Luckily, he had some antacid tablets in his shaving kit, and he chewed a few before plopping down on the bed.

He looked at his watch. 7:30. He couldn't put it off any longer. Time to call Christine. It was the first time they'd been apart overnight in quite some time. He missed her; and because of the prolonged spat they were having, he missed her even more.

He had to wade through the phone instructions to figure out how to place the call and reverse the charges. She answered on the third ring and accepted the call from the operator.

"Just checking in," he said. "I'm at a cheap-ass motel in downtown Lompoc. Doesn't even have a TV. Looks like the Bible's going to be my entertainment tonight."

That was the best he could do, and she couldn't do much better. The conversation shuffled along like a walk through a cool drizzle in late fall. Eventually, it lost whatever meager thread was holding it together and an anxious silence followed.

Stone finally broke it. "Time for me to sign off. I'll see you tomorrow."

"Okay, see you then," she replied.

He was a split second from hanging up when she came back on.

"James?"

"Yes?"

"I love you."

"And I love you too. Goodnight."

"Goodnight."

Not surprisingly, he slept quite well that night.

The Sleeper stood alone and watched the waves explode off the rocks. He lived nearby in the Outer Richmond District and sometimes walked to this spot where the Pacific met the Golden Gate. The marine breeze took him back several decades to Cape Cruz in Cuba, where his unit was first set upon by government forces. They had just endured a brutal sea voyage and lost most of their gear trudging through the steaming swamps. He was half starved, and a fungal infection had plunged his feet into agony.

Their guide had betrayed them and disappeared into the night. They had yet to learn whom to trust in these remote regions. Their answer came mid-morning, when several small planes started to circle the sugar cane field where they were hidden. The firing commenced soon after. The Sleeper's only defense being an aging rifle and little ammunition. The man next to him gasped as a bullet ripped through his lungs. The Sleeper hunkered down and fired blindly until one of the leaders grabbed him, and they crawled into the safety of some dense woods. They had no time to render aid to the wounded man.

The brutality of it all settled in. Miami became a distant dream, and the politics of revolution took on an entirely new meaning. There was no turning back.

The Sleeper looked over to where the Golden Gate Bridge made its timeless march across the deep blue bay. Nine years had passed since he hunkered down in the cane. America had tried its best to seduce him with all its glitter and charm. America had failed. He'd watched the parade of history, and it repeatedly validated his conviction about where this country was headed.

The masses had loved JFK and worshiped him as a king, and thus overlooked the colossal blunders on his watch. He'd tried to invade the Cuban homeland at the Bay of Pigs and had not only failed but had betrayed those loyal to him. He went on to light the fuse of military intervention in Vietnam, which eventually exploded into a full-scale war of imperialism. When he discovered the Cuban missile bases, he didn't hesitate to bring the country to the brink of nuclear war.

His successor, Lyndon Johnson, dabbled in socialism with his Great Society but wound up obsessed and distracted by the communist presence in Southeast Asia. He poured a half million men into Vietnam and got fifty thousand of them killed in a pointless struggle.

And now Nixon, who appeared more adroit at foreign affairs but was building a fascist police state behind the scenes.

He kept all these observations private and steered clear of political opinions of any sort. He had become a ghost, even to himself. He couldn't risk marriage because it would eventually expose him through a slip-up of some kind. He'd had a series of girlfriends, but never brought them into his confidence. His entire identity depended on his devotion to the cause and what it required of him. A lonely proposition, until considered from a global perspective. Ultimately, it placed him near the very center of history as defined in these tumultuous times. While others wallowed in the mundane, he ascended to heights they could scarcely imagine.

20.

SAN FRANCISCO

It took Stone only a single conversation with a solitary hippy to realize he'd screwed up in a most humiliating way.

The hippy in question was the proprietor of a psychedelic poster shop on Haight Street in the heart of the district. Dozens of posters lined the walls and screamed out in mad whorls, brilliant colors and seasick type. The summer of love was long gone, and the customers were all tourists at this point. The proprietor sported a foot-long ponytail, droopy mustache and tinted wire-frame glasses with quarter-sized lens. It came off more like a costume than anything else.

"Chocolate George? Yeah, I know where you can find George. He's smokin' a big fat J way up high in the sky," the proprietor informed him with a leering grin.

It turned out that Chocolate George was dead and had been for some time. Buried with two quarts of his beloved chocolate milk stuffed in his coffin. The biker, who had a big fan base among the district's original denizens, had been turning a corner right here on Haight Street when Mr. Death showed up. Somehow, his front wheel caught the bumper of a car in front of him. It flung him to the pavement in a most vicious manner and he died shortly thereafter at the hospital. A massive funeral followed. He remembered seeing it on the news but had spaced out the details.

Stone retreated back out onto the sidewalk, now the province of junkies and homeless hustlers. He'd just lost his last direct link to the nameless vet and his readily fungible combat weapon. Time to mount back up and head down the paper trail once more.

. . .

"Back so soon?" Agent Bannon of the ATF asked Stone, who had just phoned him.

"Yes, I am," Stone said. "I went down to Lompoc and had a visit with your friend, Mr. Simmons."

"Did you come away enlightened?"

"Well, yes and no. I limited our conversation to the individual who provided the rifle. I didn't come away with a name, but I did get a lead on someone who might have known him. Unfortunately, that someone is no longer with us."

"So there you go," Bannon said. "Now what?"

"I'd like to know a little more about the weapon itself. I assume that information is a matter of record somewhere. Serial number, fingerprints, that kind of thing."

"Not a problem. I can have it sent over to you."

"Appreciate it. Would it be possible to get a look at the rifle itself? What happens to stuff like that?"

"Here's how it works," Bannon explained. "It all comes under our forfeiture policy. Any evidence we seize in a criminal matter is held in a storage vault until the case is settled. If there's a conviction, it's considered forfeited by the offending party, and it's ours to keep."

"Then what happens?"

"One of three things, depending on what it is. We can destroy it. We can sell it at auction. Or we can place it into official use, which is what usually happens with something like a combat rifle."

"In other words, you gave it back to the Army."

"In other words, yes, we gave it back to the Army."

"Would you have a record of that transaction?"

"Yes, we would. I'll include it."

"Thanks. Anything else I should know?"

"At this point, you know as much as I do. You find out anything more, you let me know, okay?"

"Fair enough."

. . .

They knew they were the last of their kind. Stone could see it in their faces as they did calisthenics, assembled for instruction, jogged toward the rifle range and did all the other things expected of new recruits in the course of basic training. They sensed that after eight fruitless years, the U.S. war in Vietnam was on the verge of collapse, and that they would be called upon to supply the terminal punctuation mark. A thankless and potentially fatal task.

Stone parked at Fort Ord's main command center and looked out toward the nearby Pacific Ocean. It struck him as ironic in the extreme that this ancient and brutal enterprise occupied such a beautiful landscape. He shrugged it off and went inside to attend to the business at hand. In the alcove, a graphic display directed him to the desired office, where he would meet with the U.S. Army Materiel Command.

After a brief trek down several gray halls with green linoleum tile floors, he found himself sitting across from a Major William Petrosini, a sad-eyed man who looked like his personal war had ended some time ago.

"Now let me get this straight," the major was saying. "The ATF had a weapon, an M16, which they originally held as evidence and then returned to the Army through their forfeiture program."

"That's correct," Stone said and pushed a sheet across the metal desk between them. "I have their record of the transaction and the weapon's serial number."

The major held up both his hands. "Hold on. Let's back up here. What's driving all this?"

"I know for a fact that the weapon's original owner was a Vietnam veteran. And I strongly suspect he traded it in exchange for some high explosives. What I'm trying to do is use the serial number so you can trace it back to whoever it was issued to."

The major closed his eyes and nodded with a sickly smile. "Yes, yes," he said softly before his eyes reopened. "Do you know how many M16s are currently in circulation?"

"No, I don't." Stone sensed that he should cut this short and head for home, which was two and a half hours north. But protocol demanded he stay on to the bitter end.

"I can't give you an exact number, but it's now somewhere over a million. So that would leave us with a lot of searching, now, wouldn't it? Plus, in any combat zone, anarchy creeps in and records get fuzzy. And to complicate things even further, we've had numerous instances of people disassembling rifles and shipping them home in pieces. Now if you put all that together, I think you'll agree that we've got a bit of a problem."

"Yeah, maybe so," Stone said.

"Now what I *can* do is generate a request and submit it to Central Command. Want to know how long you'll have to wait for a reply?"

"The twelfth of never?" Stone suggested.

"And how long is that?"

"It's a long, long time," Stone said. "Like, maybe forever." He considered telling the major it was in a song by Johnny Mathis, but he doubted that would make much of an impression.

"Well then, there you have it," the major said as he pushed the sheet back in Stone's direction. "Good luck."

21.

BAY AREA

"Over a million, huh?" Linehan said as he poured some standard cop-issue coffee into his mug. Outside, a colorful bird of some kind perched on the window ledge at the Park Station and cocked its head to one side as it stared at them with no small measure of curiosity.

"That's what the man said," Stone replied. "I guess he had a point. I mean, how do you keep track of a million of anything, especially in the middle of a war?"

"Seems like we've reached the end of the paper trail," Linehan said. "What do you think?"

"I think you're right."

"Got any nifty ideas about what's next?"

"Unfortunately, I do," Stone said. "And it's something I should have done in the first place, but I put it off because it may be a real pain in the ass."

"Let me guess. Berkeley," Linehan said, in an obvious reference to the bombing in their police parking lot.

"Berkeley it is," Stone said. "Which takes us into the wonderful world of dueling investigations."

Linehan grinned knowingly. "You forgot to throw the FBI into the mix, which will make it a three-way pissing match."

"Yep, it's only matter of time. But there's no way around the fact that they were bombed within a week of us. Coincidence? Maybe, but probably not. The only way to know is to line up the facts and see what matches. Truth is, they may have close to nothing, which means it'll look like they've been caught with their dicks down. Otherwise we would have heard from them."

"That it will," Linehan agreed. "Tell you what, let's try a little diplomacy. Before you go, I'm going to call the chief and see if he can talk to the head guy over there. Might help grease the skids."

"Let's hope so," Stone said.

The bird on the ledge had heard enough and launched into flight.

. . .

It was a cease fire and not the outset of peace. Stone knew as much but decided that it was at least progress in the right direction. Christine had quietly returned to her position at the kitchen counter and sporadically engaged in bits of conversation. Still, the underlying issue remained unresolved: He'd become a cop again, and she didn't like it. It always hovered close by, waiting for an opportunity to descend.

But not tonight. Stone ran the spaghetti through the strainer in the sink and deposited it in a bowl on the counter, where it produced a soft cloud of steam. He turned the sizzling ground beef around the pan, gave it one last chop and mixed in the tomato sauce.

"I'm going over to Berkeley tomorrow," he informed her.

"To see the police?" she asked.

"Yeah, but I should be back by dinnertime. Unless there's a jam on the Bay Bridge."

"You never know," she said.

"No, you don't."

Keep it light. That was the way of it right now. If you didn't, it might be like taking a Band-Aid off a cut before it healed.

. . .

The Berkeley chief of police made a sweeping gesture out his office window toward the sprawling campus. "You know how many students we've got here? I'll tell you. Damn near thirty thousand. Now you tell me, how many of 'em are communists or sexual deviates or both?"

"Don't know," Stone said.

"Fact is, neither do I. But what I do know is that it's a lot more than you'd find on your average campus. So, let's make a guess. Let's say two thousand. That's a lot of suspects, Detective Stone. A lot."

"I'd say so."

The chief leaned in close from across the desk. "I've got one officer with a permanently mangled arm and a couple more that are close to stone deaf. If it's one of those kids out there, there's going to be hell to pay. I guarantee it."

He leaned back and took a deep breath to collect himself. "I'm sorry about your guy over there. McDonnell, right? It's a really ugly way to go."

"Yes, it is," Stone said. "Obviously, we need find out if there's a connection with what happened to you. That's why I'm here."

"A connection," the chief said. "Truth is, we don't have shit. Just a little physical evidence from the remains of the bombs. That's it."

"At least, it's someplace to start. I'd like to talk to your bomb guy and compare notes with what we've got from Park Station."

"Done deal," the chief said. "He's out right now, but I'll have him give you a call. We sent all the fragments and residue samples to the FBI labs. What they came back with was pretty generic. Pipe bombs with stopwatch timers and nine-volt batteries. Not exactly genius stuff. Nothing that would ID any particular person or group."

Which prompted Stone to think of the anonymous vet and the rifle and the Semtex. "One more question. You made a rough guess about the radical population here on campus. What kind of people wind up involved in that kind of thing?"

"It's a mixed bag," the chief said. "You've got rich kids, you've got social misfits, you've got perverts, you've got show-offs, you name it."

"Do you see any Vietnam vets?"

"Oh yeah," the chief affirmed. "Big time. And you know what? In my book, they're the only ones that have a genuine beef. They go over there and get shot to shit and they come back here, and nobody gives a shit. I'd be a little pissed off, too."

"Yeah," Stone said. "I guess I would, too."

In fact, more than just a little pissed off. More like in a prolonged murderous rage. It might just be time for Stone's investigation to undergo a change of venue.

22.

SAN FRANCISCO

The office of Chief Alfred Nelder occupied one corner of the Hall of Justice on Bryant Street, and it more than met Stone's expectations. Walnut paneling, historical photos, massive desk flanked by U.S. and California flags. Not surprisingly, its owner turned out to be as much politician as commanding officer. When Stone entered, Nelder took the initiative by coming around the desk and shaking Stone's hand.

"Good to have you on board, Detective. As you've probably figured out, we need all the help we can get. So, what can I do for you?"

"It's about the Park Station bombing," Stone said as they sat down on opposing sides. "I think the investigation needs a new direction. And what I have in mind requires some high-level policy decisions."

"High-level policy decisions," the chief repeated with a very sober demeanor that collapsed into a smile at the end. "I guess that's what this office is all about now, isn't it? So what do you have in mind?"

Stone had learned some time back that when dealing with the top people, you best not ramble. He delivered a concise summary of the investigation to date. The seized weapon, the Semtex, the anonymous vet, the dead-end paper trail, and his visit to Berkeley.

"Okay then, where's that leave us?" the chief asked.

"It's pretty much agreed that there's a large radical population around the campus. What I learned from the Berkeley cops is that it includes lot of Vietnam vets. From past experience, we know that when radical groups turn violent, they favor things like bombing."

"You think your veteran bomber is dwelling among them?" Nelder asked.

"I can't be sure, but right now I think it's the best shot we've got."

"And how might we do it?"

"I go undercover over in Berkeley. I pose as a rogue academic who lost his job somewhere in the Midwest. I start attending political discussion groups and see who shows up. If we're lucky, we get our guy, or at least get close to him."

The chief gave a single nod. "Now I see why we're talking. You want to go undercover in the backyard of the Berkeley police, which also happens to be the playground of the FBI."

"That's it."

Nelder darkened. "Did you know McDonnell?"

"No sir, I didn't."

"You've been around a while, so you know that there's good cops and bad cops. Sergeant Brian McDonnell was a good cop, a very good cop. And even more to the point, he was one of our own. So, you know what I say to the Berkeley people and the FBI? Fuck 'em. Go do it."

Before Stone could reply, Nelder stood to terminate the meeting with a handshake. "Good luck."

"Thank you, sir." Stone had now come to understand that you didn't get to be the San Francisco Chief of Police by backing down from difficult decisions.

. . .

"I'm going to be on kind of a weird schedule," Stone announced to Christine as he chopped the parsley to garnish the chicken carbonara. "I'll be doing a lot of work over in Berkeley for a while."

"Berkeley?" she asked. "Why Berkeley?"

"I think that maybe the guy that we're looking for is part of the campus radical scene. I'm going to see if I can mix in and flush him out."

Christine put down her wine glass. "What you're trying to tell me is that you're going to go undercover."

"I suppose you could look at it that way," Stone said. "But that's not really accurate. When people think of undercover, they think of super risky stuff with drugs and guns and homicide, like in the movies. But here we're talking about a bunch of college kids dabbling in politics before they enroll in dental school. Not the same."

"Right," she said, and then no more.

23.

SAN FRANCISCO

Mr. Fear was back. For the first time since the war.

Carson had given the nameless dread a name to flush it out of the shadows. In the jungle, it hovered over you like a vicious insect, ready to summon the bullet that would kill you or the shrapnel that would shred you. Its relentless presence left you vaguely sick and eternally edgy.

Mr. Fear had shown up here on Pine Street in a deep dream, one that yanked Carson back to wakefulness after nearly eleven hours of sleep. In it, Mr. Fear stalked him through endless mounds of wrecked cars baking in the desert sun. They radiated waves of heat that contorted the air and spoke of burnt and roasted flesh. He sought respite in the shadows but found none. The heat dilated his pores and coated him in an oily sweat that followed him back into a waking state.

He rolled over on the futon where he slept and checked his watch. It registered late morning. A shaft of sunlight shone in through the stained gossamer curtains and planted a cheerful rect-angle on the far wall, but it brought him no comfort. Mr. Fear had hitched a ride out of the dream and left him with that sick and edgy feeling. Only this time, Carson knew precisely from whence it came. He'd run out of speed several days back and now paid the price. He flew on like an airplane with its fuel tanks bone dry, its engines starved of substance and the ground coming up fast. Exhaustion had set in and held him firmly in its suffocating grip.

More dope. That was the answer. That was always the answer. Anything with an "ine" on the end. Benzedrine, Dexedrine, any amphetamine. It all lit the same boiler inside him. He'd learned that in the dry desert wastes around El Paso while still in his teens, along with his buddies in old pickups one step away from the wrecking yard owned by his stepfather. You got the pills over in Juarez, just a quick trolley ride across the Rio Grande. A few bennies and case of beer did the trick. You were off to somewhere in the Great Forever, where no one cared that you came from the wrong side of the proverbial tracks. Or that the school staff cheerfully reported that you were "average," as if that was a major achievement for the likes of you.

On one such excursion, he got his first lesson about people in uniform and the true meaning of justice out on life's highway at the onset of adulthood. A cop pulled them over and spotted the case of beer in the bed of their pickup. He ordered them to remove it and place it in the trunk of his patrol car as "evidence." Even at sixteen, Carson knew it was a shakedown, and thirty milligrams of ingested Dexedrine prompted him to protest. The cop came over with a smile and put his hand on Carson's shoulder as if to give him some fatherly advice. "Son," he said, "you got a few things still to learn." That said, he gut-punched Carson hard enough to fold him up like a jackknife. Before he could recover, the cop cuffed him and threw him in the back of the patrol car while his buddies cowered in silence. "Y'all go on home," he told them, "We're gonna take a little ride."

The cop drove for maybe a half an hour out into the great void to the east, where coyotes stalked jackrabbits through the darkness. He said nothing until they stopped, and he yanked Carson out of the back. "I'd say you got a little walk ahead of you," he remarked while he took the cuffs off. "And know what? It's gonna give you a little time to think about what happens when you fuck with the cops. And if you're a smart boy, it's gonna stick. Now get the hell outta here."

And Carson did think about it as he trudged back toward the urban sky glow to the west. The asshole cop was a stooge, doing the bidding of others to keep the little people in line. There was no such thing as justice, there was only the exercise of power. Later on, when he was drafted, sergeants, lieutenants, captains, and so on joined the ranks of the asshole cop. All stooges in the preservation of power for those so very far above. People who sailed yachts on Sundays and skied their winters away.

And now here he was on Pine Street with their sons and daughters who were on a political thrill ride, the ultimate expression of youthful rebellion. There was going to be a "revolution," they said, but no one talked much about the aftermath, except that the "people" would take over. And which people would they be? People just like them, of course, the natural inheritors of the power so fastidiously accumulated by their parents. Only they would yield it in benign ways, of course.

No, they wouldn't. Carson knew better. They would simply trade economic power for political power and keep their feet squarely on the necks of people like himself. He had a better idea, the utter destruction and dissolution of the ruling class. He had no idea what might replace it, and really didn't care. The conflagration itself would serve as suitable vengeance.

As if on cue, Alice walked in, holding a book of Chairman Mao's most notable quotes. "You've been asleep a long time," she commented.

"I need a hundred bucks," he said bluntly.

"What for?" she asked.

For the first time, he wanted to hit her. With a tightly clenched fist, right in the face. The suddenness of the impulse startled him. For all that ailed him, violence toward women had never been an issue. He stifled the urge but felt it simmer in his gut. The dope, or the lack of it, now had a permanent toe hold.

"I've got to get a refill," he told her.

She knew precisely what he meant. "You know, you might be able to find a higher purpose if you read some of the literature..."

"Fuck the literature," he said. "I need a hundred bucks. Right now."

She sighed. "Okay, but next time, you need to..."

"You want a revolution, you need bombs. You want bombs, you need me. A hundred dollars. Now."

. . .

Carson could feel them back there, somewhere along Stanyan Street. They kept their distance like real pros and didn't close the gap. They had him nailed and they knew it. One of the rich kids back at the safe house was behind it. Had to be. They'd complained to daddy about him. That bad bomb guy is bullying us, and we're afraid. So daddy opened the money spigots to take care of it, just like daddy always did. Attorneys were consulted, and they reached into the shadows and brought in the contractors, the kind that specialized in surgery that would circumvent the need for more complex and lengthy legal maneuvers.

Mr. Fear came in tight and rode him piggyback to the southern corner of Golden Gate Park. A bar caught his eye in mid-block, and he made straight for the entrance. With a little luck, he could evade his pursuers. He picked up the pace and found himself in a little pub where the TV spewed a basketball game to empty tables. After positioning himself so he could see out front, he ordered a beer from a sleepy-eyed barmaid. He watched out the window for some sign of his hunters. None came. The cold beer went down nicely and chased away Mr. Fear. Maybe no one was out there. Maybe it was all in his mind. He couldn't be sure. He drained the beer down and left.

Twenty minutes later, he reached the house on Ashbury Street rented by the Hells Angels. Done in the Stick style, it strongly resembled its neighbors, save for its occupants. After knocking, he suddenly realized he had no legitimacy here. You couldn't just show up on the bikers' doorstep and say you wanted to buy some speed. It didn't work that way. As the door swung open, he desperately searched for a connection.

"Yeah?" the biker said. A denim vest hung on his broad shoulders and sported numerous patches, including several swastikas.

"Pig Eye told me to check in with you guys," Carson said. It was the best he could do in the exigency of the moment.

The biker's scowl collapsed into a grin. "Pig Eye, huh? He still down in Lompoc?"

"Yep," Carson answered, hoping to God that he was right.

"Come on in."

A bizarre assortment of furniture populated the living room. A couple of lawn chairs, a couch spattered with burn marks, a coffee table improvised from a cargo hatch. In the dining room, a beer keg perched on a table scarred with inscribed initials.

"So who are you?" the biker inquired.

"Name's Carson."

"How you know Pig Eye?"

"Did some business with him before he went up."

The biker lit up in a flash of cognition. "Wait a minute. You're not the guy he swapped with to get the M16, are you?"

Carson had no choice. He really needed the speed, and this was his chance to close the deal. "Yep, that was me."

"No shit?" The biker looked up the nearby staircase. "Hey Lenny!"

"Yeah?" a voice answered from upstairs.

"Come on down and meet the guy who laid the M16 on Pig Eye." He turned to Carson. "This calls for a beer, man."

Carson followed the biker into the dining room, where he slid a few paper cups off a big stack resting on the table. He primed the keg with a few pumps and poured them each a full cup.

"You fought in the war, huh?" he asked.

"Yep, I did."

The biker raised his cup in salute. "Well here's to you, buddy."

Carson found it comically absurd that this outlaw hoodlum would respect his war record when the general public would do nothing of the sort. The world had come to rotate on an extremely wobbly axis.

While they spoke, the biker named Lenny came down, poured himself a cup and turned to Carson. "Good old Pig Eye. Did you give him a good deal on the rifle?"

"A very good deal," Carson said.

"I hope so," Lenny said. "Because you may have a real problem."

"How's that?" Carson asked.

"I was just down there and saw him. He said that this cop from San Fran showed up out of nowhere and started pumping him about the rifle deal. He wanted to know more about the guy that gave him the gun."

Carson felt a stab of fear shoot through him. "A cop? What did he tell the cop?"

"The guy really pressed him, but old Pig Eye didn't say shit because he didn't know shit. You guys must have not been very tight."

"Did he say who the cop was?"

"Yeah, it was a detective named Stone, James Stone. Turns out this same guy had a beef with a couple of the bros over at Altamont. Weird dude. Used to be in the record business. Better watch your back, man."

"I guess so," Carson said in the calmest voice he could muster. "Hey, you guys got any crank for sale?"

"Could be," Lenny replied. "How much?"

"Not much," Carson said. "How about a hundred bucks worth?"

"No problem," Lenny said. "Sounds like you're going to need it."

"Could be," Carson said. In fact, he was thinking the very same thing.

24.

BERKELEY

Stone recognized Alan Ginsberg right off. The poet sat alone at a small table near the back replete with pen, legal tablet and a cup of espresso. His work consumed him, and he scribbled furiously without ever looking up. The Caffe Mediterraneum, located a few blocks south of the Berkeley campus, suited the poet well. It served as a big mixing bowl for those living out on the fringe of things. Artists, intellectuals and activists of every stripe mingled here and engaged in spirited verbal combat while consuming caffeine by the gallon. Their audience consisted of students who sought a different path than that dictated by their parents and peers.

Stone found himself standing, coffee in hand, listening to an exchange about the vacuous nature of life among those inhabiting the American suburbs and pursuing blatant materialism. Jeans, corduroy sport coats and tweed flat caps carried the day.

Stone absorbed phrases like the pecuniary society, dialectical materialism, and so on.

Interesting, but not what he was here for. He moved across a tiled floor of black and white squares to another cluster, this one with younger participants. It proved to be a much better bet, with talk of American imperialism, embedded racism and the endless war in Vietnam. They had commandeered one of the few available tables. Half a dozen people sat around it, with a gallery of another half dozen looking on from behind them. A few were Black, most were White. Fully half were women.

"Fuck the Constitution," a young woman was saying. "I don't care what it says. It was written by a bunch of old white guys looking to cement their power. And guess what? It worked! They're still in the driver's seat two hundred years later. Just ask the Blacks, just ask us women. It's a pig's world. Always has been."

"So how do you run a democracy that's not a pigs' convention?" A young man asked. "That's the real question here, now, isn't it?"

And so it went, a verbal dingy adrift on an endless speculative sea. It brought Stone a certain measure of relief. He'd invented a cover identity that had him come from a small private college in Missouri where he'd taught political science. He claimed they let him go before he reached tenure because of his unconventional views that promoted a socialist utopia of sorts. So here he was in Berkeley, the great Vatican of the left, where he planned to sequester himself while writing his "book."

His anxiety centered on someone calling this academic bluff, someone seeking an opinion on some esoteric theory, or a specific historical incident: Did Trotsky predict the collapse of the Weimar Republic? What did Mao eat on The Long March? How are resources allocated in the absence of free markets?

But now he saw a way out. A half hour of this group's meandering dialogue presented him with one very salient observation: Nobody listened. The minute somebody launched into a monologue, the others were mentally constructing their response without hearing the speaker out. No one would ever probe Stone in depth. Whatever the query to him, his response would be sidelined only moments later by an intervention of some kind.

He tested his theory by striking up a conversation with a youngish guy standing next to him. It worked. He managed to get across that he was a rogue professor from the Midwest, but that was about it. The guy, with a big tangle of curly hair and a minimal beard, started to rave about this band he was going to start and how they would devote themselves to "social consciousness."

Stone's plan was to steer these kinds of conversations around to the general subject of revolution, which would hopefully put him in the proximity of more extreme political attitudes, such as taking to the streets or war with the pigs. He was about to do so right now, but a pair of new arrivals drifted into his peripheral vision, a couple in their early twenties. The man immediately grabbed his attention. He'd seen him before, at Altamont, in the psych tent. The guy called Matt. The crazy guy sobbing with rage.

What was he doing here? He appeared quiet, withdrawn even, with no interest in the great debate swirling around him. Stringy long hair, patchy beard, hollow cheeks and distant eyes. He obviously didn't recognize Stone, but why would he? At Altamont, he'd been in the grip of an episode of acid-induced psychosis.

None of which explained his presence at a politicized, cerebral coffeehouse in the middle of downtown Berkeley. Stone suspected the answer had something to do with his female friend, his companion from Altamont. Tonight, she looked like a sorority girl gone wrong. Severe straight hair parted in the middle, makeup nearly absent, yet still vaguely attractive.

Stone could only hope she didn't recognize him, which might greatly complicate things. His concern evaporated when she promptly waded into the verbal free for all, which utterly consumed her.

"So are we all just going to stand on the sidelines and let the revolution try to start itself?" she asked.

There it was. The key word. Revolution. She now had Stone's full attention. Over the next half hour, she waded in and out of the dialog with similar expressions, but none denoting violence. Her companion, Matt, said nothing but regarded her with a kind of piteous dismay.

The dialectic droned on, darkness descended outside, and the group began to disassemble of its own accord. The couple headed toward the doorway and Stone decided to tail them at a discrete distance. The warm air of early spring prevailed out on the sidewalk where he set a pace about half block behind them. They turned the corner up ahead, and he sped up to ensure he didn't lose visual contact. It put him on a quiet street with all the shops closed and foot traffic nearly absent. Ahead, the couple came to an intersection and waited for the light.

He slowed to keep his distance and suddenly felt two hands grip his arms on either side. Turning to one side, he saw a young man in conservative casual dress with close cropped hair. Turning to the other, he saw much the same.

"Hi there," the first man said to him. "We need to have a little talk."

"About what?" Stone said. The pair was sizable and athletic. A physical struggle was not advised. Besides, they smelled like cops of some kind.

"About national security," the other one said.

"Let me guess," Stone said. "You're FBI."

"Something like that," the first one said with a smart-ass grin. Out on the street, a generic sedan roared up beside them.

The second one pulled out his ID with his free hand and held it up in front of Stone. "Got the picture?" he asked.

"Yeah, I got the picture," Stone replied. He held his temper. They had no reason to hold him and no legal right to do so.

"We're gonna take a little ride, have a little talk, and then you're on your way."

"Suppose I told you I'm a cop working undercover," Stone said as they towed him toward the waiting car.

"Oh yeah? Suppose I told you that you're a rogue poly-sci professor from a little college in Missouri looking to get in on the radical action here in the big time."

Stone immediately knew the score. Audio surveillance. The café had a mezzanine above the main floor, and they'd posted someone up there with a tape machine and highly directional microphone.

The three of them filed into the back seat, with Stone in the middle. The driver put the car in gear, turned the corner at College Avenue and headed south.

"Where we going?" Stone asked.

"Not far," the first agent said cryptically.

Stone decided to stay mum for the time being. There was no use sparring with them under the present circumstances. Until they were somewhere with a phone, they had no way to verify his identity. Besides, the only thing he had to communicate was his contempt for what they were doing. When Chief Nelder found out, there would be hell to pay. His position as the chief of police of the City of San Francisco positioned him way up there in the country's law enforcement community. He would have direct access to FBI Director Edgar J. Hoover and would undoubtedly use it.

They rolled on out of Berkeley and into North Oakland, where they pulled up in front of a nondescript two-story office building.

"Never seen an FBI field office that looked like this," Stone commented as they got out of the car.

"Yeah, well, it does the job," the second agent said.

The first agent unlocked the entrance, and they went into a meeting room right off the alcove. The first agent flipped a switch, and the overhead fluorescents came on to reveal folding metal chairs around a collapsible worktable.

The first agent gestured toward a chair. "Have a seat."

"Don't mind if I do," Stone said with just a sprinkle of arrogance.

"Undercover cop, huh?" the first agent said as he sank down into a chair and put his feet up on the table.

"Undercover cop," Stone verified. As he sat, he matched the agent's flippant feet-up pose just to irritate him.

"You wouldn't have ID, would you?" the agent asked.

"You probably should have asked me that before you ever laid a hand on me," Stone said.

"Well, we didn't," the agent said. "So do you, or don't you?"

"Of course I do," Stone taunted. "Like all undercover cops I keep it with me all the time in case the bad guys might want to see it."

"Don't be a smartass," the agent said. "We're just doing our job."

"Oh yeah? In that case, I think the very next part of your job is going to be to have your buddy here get on the phone to the San Francisco police and inquire about one Detective James Stone working out of the Park Station."

The two agents exchanged a glance, and the second left the room. The first took his feet off the table and assumed a more reasonable pose, with his self-assurance backed into reverse.

"Okay," he said, "let's assume you check out. Why the hell is a city cop from across the Bay schmoozing in a radical hangout and posing as a pinko professor from the Midwest? Doesn't make much sense."

"Makes about as much sense as bugging private conversations and apprehending private citizens on the street without any cause."

"Who said anything about bugging?" the agent asked suspiciously.

"Nobody." Stone said. "Didn't have to. How'd you know about the professor and the Midwest? You caught it on tape."

The agent sensed imminent defeat and took the conversation up into the conceptual stratosphere. "We've got a war here, friend. Just as real as the one in Asia. And ultimately, just as dangerous. It's up to us to keep a lid on it. If we don't, you'll wake up one morning and see the likes of Castro or Mao Tse-tung on TV addressing the nation as our new great leader."

"So what?" Stone mocked. "That'll make your job a lot simpler. You can walk down the street and detain anybody you want any time you want for any reason you want."

"Sometimes you've got to bend the rules a little to keep them from breaking. We do what we have to. No more."

The second agent appeared in doorway and motioned to the first. "Hold that thought," he told Stone and the two disappeared out into the hallway.

Stone looked at his watch. If this didn't wind up soon, he'd be in trouble at home. Christine was clearly freaked about his undercover work, and his coming home late wouldn't help the cause one bit.

The first agent returned with a slightly sheepish look. "My apologies, detective. You check out."

"Surprise, surprise," Stone said.

"Yeah, sorry. Park Station, huh?"

"Yeah, Park Station."

"So, you're over here trying to run down the bomber, right?"

"Something like that," Stone replied. There was no use issuing an outright denial, especially after the twin bombing in Berkeley. They'd obviously been tracking the case and knew all about the fence staples lodged in Officer McDonnell's brain.

"You track what's moving through Congress?" the agent asked.

"Not really," Stone said.

"Well, you probably missed the Organized Crime Control Act. Just signed into law. Gives us and the ATF a broad mandate to hunt down bombers of every stripe. Including whoever bombed your station."

"And?" Stone asked.

"We've got the brain power and fire power to make it happen, so it's time for you to share whatever you've got and step aside."

"And let the big boys take over?" Stone asked. You couldn't miss the venom in his voice.

"And let the big boys take over," the agent confirmed. "This thing goes way beyond a bombing or two. We think it's part of a broad conspiracy to bring down the entire government, and I don't think you're quite ready to take that on."

"And you are?" Stone challenged.

"You better hope so," the agent said. "The whole country better hope so."

"Really now," Stone said. "You know, I don't think I got your name."

"Trobe," the agent answered. "Agent Peter Trobe."

Stone stood up. "I think you owe me a ride back to where you found me, Agent Trobe."

"Okay," Trobe said. "And with a little luck, we'll never see you there again."

"You never know," Stone said.

25.

SAN FRANCISCO

"Okay, let me get this straight," Chief Nelder said. "You're doing your thing at this radical hangout in downtown Berkeley. You leave and these FBI guys show up out on the street. They forcibly detain you but don't formally arrest you. They take you over to a location in Oakland where they hold you while they check out your story. Is that about it?"

"One more thing," Stone said. "They said to butt out of the bombing case, that it belongs to them and the ATF. Something about new legislation from Congress."

Nelder sighed and stared off into the great beyond. The morning sunlight shone into his office at a severe angle that amplified every crack and wrinkle in his aging face.

"That's insane," the chief said. "But you know what? We live in insane times, so what do you expect?" He paused, picked up a pen and rocked it between his fingers. "No way they'd do this without a green light. Someone higher up let them off their leash. They know we can't go public about this because it would blow our whole operation. It's complete bullshit. I'll take this all the way up to Hoover if I have to."

"Why stop there?" Stone said in partial jest. "What about Nixon?"

A sick smile came across Nelder. "I'll tell you why. Hoover's a real piece of work, but I've got a pretty good idea where he stands on things. But Nixon? The guy's as sneaky as he is crooked. No telling what's going on."

"I see your point," Stone said. "So where does that leave us for now?"

Nelder ditched the pen, brought his forearms to rest and folded his hands in very authoritative manner. "You go ahead. You do your thing. You owe it to Officer McDonnell and the whole department. I'll handle the politics. There's nothing in the constitution that says we have to piss off just because we're the local guys."

"Good to hear," Stone said. He'd already come up with a Plan B and was ready to go.

. . .

The golden bear struck a prowling pose atop its pedestal and glittered in the spring sun that fell across Sproul Plaza. The metal beast gazed down on the cluster of wooden picnic tables outside the Bear's Lair, a campus watering hole. The bear had listened to countless beer-fueled conversations that wafted up off these tables. Talk of the evils of capitalism, the compassion of socialism, the decline of empire, the specter of racism, the clash of the sexes, the lure of psychedelics, the rule of law, the curse of anarchy, the fall of religion, the rise of secularism.

The bear had heard it all and took no sides. Nor did it today as Stone, the rogue professor, nursed a glass of Pabst and chatted with a student couple that sat opposite him. The girl's long blonde hair fell down over a flannel shirt of male origin. The boy stroked a wispy beard that failed to hide his pale skin. Stone learned that she pursued a major in English literature, he in Architecture.

"We're in crisis," she pronounced. "The American Century is over, thirty years ahead of schedule. Macho stupidity has peaked. We're fighting a war of imperialism halfway around the world, just to prove we've got the biggest dick. I mean, why else? The fucking domino theory? I mean, come on!"

"Interesting," Stone commented. "So what do we do about it? Or is it just too late? Should we all be putting our life jackets on?"

"Maybe so," the boy said. "Maybe the whole thing has to crash, and we build a new thing out of the rubble."

Stone took notice. The conversation had just vectored in an opportune direction.

"So that raises an interesting question," he ventured. "Do we just sit around and wait for it all to fall down and suffer to the maximum, or do we bring it all down right now while we can still avoid the worst of the fallout?"

The girl shrugged. "There's a lot of people around here who think it needs to happen as we speak. And they just might be right."

"That means political action, maybe in the extreme," Stone observed. "And you know what? It always comes down to the individual. Are you personally committed? That's the big question."

"And the big answer is hell, yeah," the boy said. "We gotta do what we gotta do."

"So, you'd be willing to take to the streets if that's what was called for?"

"I'm not a violent person," the girl said. "All that seems to do is set off more violence. We need to find alternatives."

"And you?" Stone said to the boy.

"I think we've got a way to go before it gets that bad," he said. "So check back with me then."

"I'll do that," Stone promised, and raised his glass. "Cheers."

Dead end. Oh well. Many other opportunities awaited, and this setting had several advantages over the Caffe Mediterraneum. Most of all, its outdoor location on the broad plaza offered no place to set up unidirectional microphones.

The man sitting to the right of Stone watched as the three glasses came up. He appeared to be engaged in a separate conversation, but he wasn't. All the time, he'd had his ear cocked to the dialogue between this man in early middle age and the pair of students. Radical professor exiled from the Great Plains. Working on book about the "new socialism." Interesting. He would pass it on.

The eavesdropper was just a few years older than the student pair. Graduate level vs. undergraduate. He was also living proof that not everyone on campus veered sharply to the left. His politics trended in the opposite direction, although not that far. What truly set him apart was that he loved being a spy. His academic performance was mediocre, as was his social life. Spying gave him a sense of empowerment that he found nowhere else.

He drained his glass and left. He wanted to go and jot down some notes while the dialogue was still fresh.

. . .

"He's at it again," Agent Trobe told Aaron Andrews.

"Already?"

"Already. One of our inside people caught him at the Bear's Lair. Same guy, same schtick. Claims he's a poli sci professor with a radical bent from the Midwest. Got to be him."

"Jesus," Andrews sighed. Agent Andrews was more than just an Agent. He was a Special Agent. Better yet, he was a Special Agent in Charge, in charge of the FBI's San Francisco office. "Know what?" he said. "I got a call this morning from Chief Nelder. He was more than a little pissed that you busted one of his boys without cause over in Berkeley. Says he'll take it all the way up to Hoover."

"You think he will?" Trobe asked.

"Depends," Andrews said. "I think we just had our first test. There's no way this guy – what's his name? Stone? – would be back at it without Nelder's express consent. If we take him down again, the chief's going to make good on his threat."

"Then what do we do?" Trobe asked. "Are we just going to roll over? I mean, this guy could do some serious damage to our informant network."

"We can't let that happen," Andrews asserted. "We've had two bombs go off right in the laps of the cops, with one dead and dozens injured. These guys are screaming for blood, and I can't blame them. We need every asset we can muster to get the people who did this."

"Agreed," Trobe said.

"At the same time," Andrews cautioned, "we can't let this Stone thing blow up into plain sight, where the press gets a shot at it. If it goes all the way up to the Director, there's a good chance it'll get leaked. We've got to figure out a way to contain the damage and also keep the SF cops out of our swimming pool."

"Understand," Trobe said. "Let me work on it."

"You better work really fast," Andrews warned. "That's all I can say."

"That's all you need to say," Trobe responded. He already had an idea.

. . .

Every major FBI office had one lurking in the shadows, a director of the local counterintelligence program, cryptically known as COINTELPRO. The program dated from the mid-fifties and had repeatedly proved its worth by deploying barrages of lies, half-truths, and insinuations against target groups to sow internal dissension, doubts and confusion. Its operations often required great ingenuity to construct and execute. It was one thing to shoot someone in the head, and quite another to render them paralyzed without ever touching them.

The local director, an Agent Wallace, listened with great interest as Special Agent Peter Trobe described what he had in mind. As far as COINTELPRO went, it was a novel situation and would require an equally novel solution.

"You really think they'll authorize this?" Wallace asked Trobe.

"It's all about how it's presented," Trobe said. "I'll write the memo. It'll be on me, not you."

The Bureau kept strict tabs on counterintelligence operations to prevent them from getting out of hand. You had to submit a formal request and get a formal green light. But Trobe was a master of the system and knew precisely how to keep the request free of red flags.

"Let's assume we're getting a green light and move ahead," Trobe said. "Got any ideas how you might pull this off?"

"As a matter of fact, I do," Wallace replied with a malicious smile that came with the trade.

. . .

The offices of the *Berkeley Barb* on University Avenue operated continually on the verge of chaos. Cluttered desks, constant chatter, clacking typewriters, random imagery thumbtacked to the walls, deadlines always looming. Privacy was unthinkable.

When Lisa Vaught's phone rang, she thought it might be her boyfriend phoning to apologize for what an ass he'd been last evening. It wasn't, not even close.

"I've got someone that wants to talk to a reporter," the receptionist told her.

Lisa inwardly groaned. The *Barb* was at its peak, with a weekly circulation of 90,000 worldwide and a legendary status among alternative newspapers. Not surprisingly, this made it a powerful magnet for crank calls from the dispossessed, the disaffected and the certifiably insane.

"Put 'em on through," Lisa said. You never knew, that was the problem. It might be from someone who just started World War Three.

"Vaught here," she announced. "To whom am I speaking?"

"My name is Karen Richter," the caller said. "And I saw something really strange last week at the Caffe Mediterraneum."

Here we go, Lisa thought. She saw aliens disguised as literature professors.

"Oh yeah, and what was that?" she asked.

"There was this guy there. He was telling people he's a professor from out of town somewhere. But he's not. I'm sure of it. He's a cop from San Francisco. He's a detective and his name is James Stone."

"So wait a minute. How do you know all this?" Lisa asked. The woman now had her attention. Covert operations by law enforcement were a hot ticket for the *Barb*. The bad guys were almost always the feds, with no city cops in the mix. The addition of a local detective would definitely make it newsworthy. But only if it checked out.

"I'm going to the University of San Francisco and I'm majoring in performing arts," Ms. Richter responded. "I work part-time at this bar over by Golden Gate Park. He comes in now and then with his cop buddies, so I've got a pretty good idea who he is."

"What brought you across the bay to a place like the Med?" Lisa asked.

"Politics," Ms. Richter said. "Some of us in the department lean pretty far to the left and we like to go places where they speak our language."

"I'm sure you do," Lisa said. That done, she went over the facts once again, and included the name of the bar where the putative Stone and his friends had an occasional beer. The girl didn't have a phone but gave Lisa a number where she could leave a message.

She would run this by the editor when he got loose to make sure it was worth chasing. But right now he was in a heated discussion with their art director about tomorrow's cover, which featured a nude, interracial couple flashing twin peace signs while they embraced in front of Sproul Hall.

. . .

Stone marveled at Kitty's unshakable sense of entitlement. It meowed only once when he opened the door with the tuna, a solitary and reluctant meow. He put the food down and slid it in the animal's direction, expecting it to scamper forward and greedily consume it in a feline display of gratitude. No such luck. It glared at him and waited until he shut the door before approaching the dish.

He went back to the kitchen counter and cut up some tomatoes, cucumbers, mushrooms, and lettuce to make a shrimp salad. Christine sat in the living room and watched the evening news on TV. It spoke of a wildcat strike against the U.S. Postal Service. Stone considered remarking about how it might cause a real mess but thought the better of it. Things were still not right between them, and they both knew it. But neither wanted to confront it directly and spark a major domestic conflagration.

It couldn't go on this way forever. Something had to give. He could only hope that it gave in the right direction.

. . .

The phone rang incessantly at the *Barb*'s front desk. Lisa Vaught felt sorry for their receptionist who was their first line of defense. Last week's cover with the interracial nudity had sparked a colossal outrage.

Lisa also felt sorry for herself. She didn't need any additional distractions while she wrote her piece about this Stone guy working undercover among the local radicals. She was still fiddling with the headline but thought that something like "City Cop Caught Spying" worked pretty well.

She'd done all her fact checking and the girl's story came back clean. Karen Richter was indeed enrolled at the University of San Francisco in the performing arts department. The bar where she worked verified her employment there. Finally, the SFPD really did a have a Detective James Stone among their ranks. She'd called Richter back and left a message at the number she'd been given. Within the hour, the woman phoned back, and they went over the details one last time. Everything remained consistent with her original account.

The story was good to go. After dropping the copy in her editor's inbox, she headed out onto University Avenue, where she found relative peace and quiet.

. . .

"Hey Stone, guess what?" Sgt. Burke said as he approached Stone's desk with a tabloid of some kind. "Congratulations! You're a media star."

The *Berkeley Barb*. Burke laid the paper flat across Stone's desktop and opened it to the second spread. A headline in bold capitals ran across three of five columns and announced **CITY COP CAUGHT SPYING**. Stone quickly skimmed the underlying article and got the gist. Someone was onto him.

"The Berkeley cops sent this over. I guess maybe politics isn't going to be your thing," Burke teased him. "At least not in California – unless maybe you want to run for governor."

"Don't think so," Stone said. "Mind if I keep this?"

"Be my guest," Burke said and wandered off.

Stone gave the story a closer look. The byline was by an L. Vaught. He needed to have a talk with this person. A phone call didn't seem appropriate. It could be ignored. Best to meet L. Vaught in the office in the flesh.

He checked his watch. It was still early, and he could be over there by mid-morning. But before he went, he needed to make a quick stop at the coroner's office.

. . .

As Stone took in the offices of the *Berkeley Barb*, he wondered how they ever managed to get a paper out, especially once a week. The place was a master class in total chaos. Fortunately, the receptionist was the exception to the rule.

"Can I help you?" she asked.

"Yes, my name is Stone. I believe you have someone named Vaught on your staff. Are they available?"

"Oh, you mean Lisa. Let me check and see if she's in." She punched some buttons on her phone console. "Lisa, there's a gentleman named Stone here to see you." She frowned. "Oh, I see." She lowered the phone. "Unfortunately, she's on deadline right now."

Stone smiled. "Tell her I bear her no ill will. I'll only take a couple of minutes of her time."

The receptionist relayed his request, nodded and looked up. "She says okay, but only for a minute or two."

"That'll be fine."

When Lisa Vaught came into view, Stone's intuition painted a picture of her background based on many similar encounters over the years. A rich girl getting down for the cause. Father an industrial executive, mother the perfect hostess. Freshman year in a sorority until she saw the light and went bohemian. Now a dedicated servant of the unvarnished truth. And what was wrong with that?

He held to a statesman-like course and offered his hand as she approached. "Ms. Vaught, thanks for taking the time to see me. I appreciate it."

"Detective Stone, right?" she said as she took his hand. Hers was cool and dry. Not a trace of apprehension.

"Right," Stone replied. "Is there somewhere we could talk for a minute or two?"

"Not here, but there's a coffee place right down the block."

"That'll be just fine."

"You still in school?" he asked as they covered the block down University Avenue.

"I graduated a year ago."

"Let me guess: With a degree in journalism."

"That would be right."

Stone took note of her tailored jeans, the tight weave of her cotton blouse, and the hand-tooled sandals. Definitely subsidized. For Lisa Vaught, economic necessity was a distant planet. They took a table in the corner of the coffeehouse, right under a poster of Che Guevara.

"I want to say straight off that I don't doubt your competence as a journalist," Stone said. "What you said in the story is essentially true. Yes, I am indeed a detective with the San Francisco police. And yes, I did present myself as an out-of-town political science professor."

"Then why are we having this conversation?" she asked.

"A reasonable question," Stone replied. "And to answer it, we'll have to go off the record. Agreed?"

"Agreed."

"Your story begs one simple question: What was I doing there in the first place? Was it radical politics? No. That's not the kind of thing that motivates me."

"Then what was it?"

"This." Stone pulled out a photograph and handed it to her. A picture of the shredded face of Officer McDonnell taken by the coroner.

The carefully cultivated professional poise of Lisa Vaught evaporated. "Oh my God!" She shut her eyes after just a brief glance and slid the photo back across to Stone. "What is this?"

"It's the face of the officer killed a few weeks back in the Park Station bombing. My job is to find whoever murdered him. I suspect the bomber is somehow tied to the radical community here in the Bay Area. I went underground to see if I could dig up some leads. But then I was the one who got dug up. Now who do you suppose would want to do a thing like that?"

"I don't know," Lisa said. "You tell me."

"It all points back toward your source, whoever that is. I think you might want to take a second look at their credibility." He pointed to the photo lying face down on the table. "And so does this man's family."

Lisa felt slightly sick but kept her composure. "Okay, we just went off record so let's keep it that way, agreed?"

"Fair enough."

"I had a single source. I'm going to tell as much as I can without actually identifying them. I was contacted by a person attending the University of San Francisco who told me about you being undercover over here. They said they recognized you from a bar you hang out at with some other cops."

"And what bar was that?"

"The Golden Rooster."

"Never been there." He paused and put the photo away. "Here's what I suggest. Phone up the University and tell them there's an emergency and you need your source to phone you back immediately. You've got two possible outcomes. One is that you get your source on the line. The other is that it's someone who has no idea why you called."

"This person also gave me a number where I could contact them," Lisa volunteered. "But I can't give it you without compromising them."

"Then don't," Stone said. "If this person's story doesn't hold up, I can always check that out later. One last thing. I know everyone around here is knee deep in politics. I'm not. In this country, anyway, politics is about people yelling at each other. That's not me. I deal with people killing each other."

"I believe you," she told him. "And just to be on the safe side, I'll go back over this whole thing one more time. Let's say for a minute that I got it all wrong. Do you want me fired? Do you want us to print a retraction? Just what is it that you want?"

"No, I don't want you fired. And I don't expect a retraction. All I want is the person who did this. Fair enough?"

"Fair enough." Stone found her to be on the attractive side, with bright green eyes, flawless skin and generous lips of a soft pink. He wondered if this inclination was born out of his current difficulties with Christine.

"Let me know how it goes," he said and pulled out his wallet. "Coffee is compliments of the San Francisco Police Department."

She smiled. "Tell them that on behalf of the nation's underground press, I'm quite grateful."

. . .

The call came in the late afternoon. A lot sooner than he expected. He'd just finished typing an investigative update when his phone rang.

"Stone here."

"This is Lisa Vaught. I'm afraid I owe you a big fat apology."

"And how's that?"

"I got hold of The University of San Francisco and explained that there was an emergency, that I needed to speak with Karen Richter as soon as possible."

"And how did that go?" Stone smiled to himself. Vaught had just revealed the name of her source, which meant that her source wasn't her source after all. It wasn't a slip. She was too smart for that.

"I was expecting a hassle, but I didn't get one. They were very nice. They had her schedule on file and sent someone to yank her out of class. I had her on the phone in half an hour."

"Let me guess: She had no idea who you were."

"You got it. And she's never set foot in the Caffe Mediterraneum. She does work at the bar, the Golden Goose, but she's never seen a cop in there. And she's never heard of James Stone."

Stone chuckled in amusement. "That's a lot of nevers right in a row. I guess we can pronounce me falsely accused."

"I guess we can. I owe you, detective. Let me start by suggesting an alternative explanation to what's going down. It might sound a little strange, but I think it's worth checking on."

"Go ahead."

"As you know, we here at the paper are not exactly buddies with the FBI. From time to time, we've run investigative articles on one of their operations called COINTELPRO, which stands for counterintelligence program. Ever heard of it?"

"Only by name." Alarms bells were already sounding. She was onto something, even if she didn't know why.

"It started in the fifties, and basically generates false information to create chaos and hostility among groups opposed to various U.S. policies, like the war in Vietnam. At times, it's gotten really ugly and destroyed reputations and marriages and even gotten a few people killed. It's all dirty tricks done in the shadows. They just pick their target and blast away, with no trail of accountability. One of their favorite ploys is to feed disinformation to the mainstream media, which is always a sucker for anything that will raise their ratings. But as far as I know, they've never used the underground press. That's why I didn't pick up on it from the get-go."

"Time to go off the record again," Stone said. "Okay?"

"Of course."

"We're not the only ones investigating the Park Station bombing. So is the FBI, and it's turned into a turf war. They want us to step aside and let the big boys take over."

"I can't imagine you're okay with that," Lisa said. "Not after what you've told me."

"No, I'm not okay with that. And neither is anybody else around here, from the chief on down. So that leaves the FBI with a big problem. There's no way that they can legally prevent us from staying on the case. So what do they do about it? I think we just got our answer."

"Maybe so," Lisa said. "It sure points in that direction."

"You told me that your bogus source gave you a phone number to contact her. Right?"

"Right. I used it a couple of times. It always went to a message machine and then she phoned me back."

"Why don't you let me have it? I'll see what I can do with it."

"There are things you can do? Of course there are," she added cynically.

"As a sign of good faith, I'll share whatever I find. When this all plays out, you might have a pretty good follow-up story. A close-up and personal look at FBI counterintelligence in action."

"Could be," she said.

"Look, I know this might sound kind of weird, but I'd like to stay in touch with you as this case moves along. I know we're probably not on the same page politically, but we might not be as far apart as you think. You don't strike me as the kind of person who thinks that extreme violence against others is an acceptable solution to anything. Am I wrong?"

"No, you're not."

"Good, because neither do I. So let's work together until we have some good reason not to." He grinned. "I've always heard that politics makes strange bedfellows and I guess this is a case in point."

"That it is." Cop or not, she couldn't help but like this James Stone. He had a ring of truth about him that you seldom encountered. "Talk to you later."

"Later," Stone replied and hung up. He rummaged in his top desk drawer, pulled a departmental directory, located the number he was looking for, and dialed.

"Pacific Bell Special Services," the operator said. "How can I help you?"

"Hello, I'm Detective James Stone of the San Francisco Police Department. Badge number 1762."

"Thank you, detective. Please hold while I verify."

"Will do."

Stone twirled a yellow pencil through his fingers while he waited. As always, he wondered why it had its hexagonal shape. Recently, he'd concluded that it was the closest thing to a circle that felt comfortable in people's hands.

"Thanks for your patience," the operator said. "And what can we do for you?"

"I need a reverse lookup on the following number," Stone said, and gave her the number Lisa had given him.

"One moment please."

Stone quit twirling and played a game of tic-tac-toe. The X's won.

"The number is part of a block of numbers assigned to the U.S. Department of Justice. I don't have any information beyond that. Sorry."

"That'll do. Thanks for your time."

Stone hung up. Of course, she didn't have any information. Because the number was being used by the FBI for highly questionable practices. He phoned Lisa back at the *Barb*.

"I checked the number you gave me," he told her. "It's assigned to the Department of Justice.

"How about that," she said. "No surprise, right?"

"None at all. I'll talk to you soon."

"I'm sure you will. Goodbye."

Stone grinned as he cradled the phone. She was a bit of a smartass, but somehow he found that appealing. Thanks in part to her, he now had a solid case against Agent Peter Trobe and his pals in the COINTELPRO business. But he needed to consider it in a larger frame of reference. If he pulled the trigger, it would undoubtedly set off a major ruckus. But it would do little or nothing to get him any closer to hunting down the bomber. It might even become a major distraction. He needed to put it aside, at least for the time being.

Oh well. At any rate, he'd gained a useful, albeit reluctant contact in the heart of liberal Berkeley.

26.

SAN FRANCISCO

"Hey check this out!" Hostler said as he waved a copy of the *Berkeley Barb* at Carson. "They caught a pig with his pants down. A San Francisco cop. Pretending like he was some kind of spy. Pretty fucking dumb."

Carson sat hunched over the kitchen table in the Pine Street house. He spooned a bowl containing a small measure of corn flakes and a half dozen tablespoons of sugar. His hand shot out impulsively and tore the paper out of Hostler's grip.

"Hey man, I wasn't done with that," Hostler said in weak protest.

"Well now you are," Carson countered and scanned the headlines on the first two pages. Hostler, a freshman dropout on the dole from his family, was afraid of him. They were all afraid of him. For all the talk of revolution, physical confrontation was not part of their vocabulary.

Hostler sighed. "Yeah, okay, whatever." He stalked on out of the kitchen while throwing up his hands in exasperation.

Carson ignored him and continued to scan the inner pages of the *Barb*. His teeth hurt, as well they should. He fed them a poisonous combination of sugar and amphetamines and never brushed. A swarm of bacteria invaded and caused them to crack and crumble while turning brown then black. Lesions and abscesses lined his gums and inner cheeks. However, it wasn't difficult to hide the damage. He no longer smiled or even grinned.

There it was, on the third page. "CITY COP CAUGHT SPYING." It had all happened at a coffee place over in Berkeley, where the guy was posing as some kind of professor. But he was really a San Francisco cop, a detective, and his name was James Stone.

James Stone.

Carson's pulse shot up. His left eyelid sporadically twitched. His breath turned shallow and rapid.

James Stone.

The cop who was stalking him because of Pig Eye and the rifle. The cop who smelled something a lot bigger. The cop who was going to hunt him down and take him out.

And now that same cop had caught a new scent that brought him even closer. He'd somehow sniffed out Carson's link to the radical community, probably through the bombings. Worse yet, Stone was probably hooked up with the FBI, so he now had a whole herd of pigs to help him.

Carson looked down at his cereal bowl where the milk, cereal and abundance of sugar had coalesced into a lumpy slush. He pushed it away.

When they caught him, they weren't going to arrest him. They were going to take him out. With a solitary round from a skilled marksman. He knew the shot by heart. He'd seen it over and over in the jungle. The entry point right below the cover of the helmet. The exit point on the far side, delivering a big red ball of brains and gore.

Mr. Fear knew all about it. Mr. Fear was now along for the ride. And most importantly, Mr. Fear knew how to deal with an assailant of this type.

You took them out before they took you out.

· · ·

And there the target was, centered in the merged circle of the field glasses. Medium height, athletic build, early forties by the look of it. A somewhat handsome face that might have landed him in the movies if he hadn't gone the pig route.

Carson watched intently from the old sedan that was the safe house's sole source of transportation. He lowered the glasses as Detective James Stone left the sidewalk and ascended the stairs to his residence on 43rd Avenue. It wasn't hard to find his home address, which was listed in the 170-page San Francisco phone directory, along with his phone number. Most cops shunned this kind of exposure, but for some reason Stone hadn't bothered. He'd been in the music business, so maybe he felt he needed to be accessible. No matter. What counted was that Carson now had a firm image of James Stone's personal appearance, which was central to what he had in mind.

. . .

Carson pulled out his sketch book as he took a seat on a bench bordering Peacock Meadow at the west end of the park. In the chaos of the last few years, he'd lost the schematics of his original bomb design for Park Station. It would have been truly spectacular. Powered by the Semtex from Pig Eye, the entire structure would have collapsed, killing everyone within. No shrapnel necessary.

His new design was more focused and modest in scale but employed the same trigger mechanism found in the original. It was activated remotely through a wireless signal, meaning you could position yourself at a safe distance and detonate the device on demand. The key technology was a pair of walkie-talkies commercially available through Radio Shack stores. You generated a signal with one of them in the transmitter mode, and it was picked out of the air by the other in the receiver mode. Some additional wiring turned the receiver circuitry into a switch which was connected to a nine-volt battery and blasting cap. For an explosive, Carson chose a classic pipe bomb design using dynamite placed inside. For shrapnel, he would use gaffer's tape to wrap the pipe with several layers of one-inch roofing nails.

The aggressive tactics of the Radio Shack salesclerk elevated Carson's state of agitation to just short of real trouble. First, the guy kept trying to sell him ancillary products, like rechargeable batteries and the like. Then he gave the impression that he couldn't complete the sale without officially adding Carson to their mailing list, whatever that was. In the end, he backed down and accepted cash, along with a bogus name that Carson gave him to put on the receipt. At some point in the transaction, he'd come to realize that he might be putting himself in genuine physical peril.

Back at the Pine Street house, Carson stashed all the bomb's components in a grocery bag which he stored under the stairwell. He waited until 3 a.m. to fetch the bag and begin the assembly process at the kitchen table. The oddness of the hour had no impact on him. The amphetamines had shattered his sleep cycle and left him feeling jumpy yet exhausted at the same time. He spread the parts out on the empty table along with his minimal tool set and hand-drawn schematic.

"Whoa, dude!"

Carson came bolt upright, knocking his chair over onto the linoleum floor. Of all people, it was Hostler, the privileged dropout idiot.

Hostler surveyed the contents on the table with jaw slack and eyes wide. "You're making a fucking bomb! Far out, man!"

"Get the fuck out," Carson commanded. "Now."

"I didn't know we had any plans for bombs right now," Hostler said. "Where's this gonna go?"

"It's going right up your ass unless you get the fuck out of here."

Hostler was apparently too dumb to know that he was teetering on the precipice of disaster. A sheltered life could do that to you. "Hey man, we're all in this together," he informed Carson. "I think you should share what you…"

In a shot, Carson came around the table, grabbed Hostler by the throat and pinned him up against the refrigerator door. The kid's eyes bulged in horror as he looked out upon a world he'd never known.

Carson came in nose to nose and clutched Hostler's throat tight enough to nearly seal off his windpipe. All that remained were tiny little gasps of desperation. His face turned a frantic pink.

Carson fought off the urge to finish the job and crush the trachea. It would be quite satisfying but would cause more problems than it would solve. He spoke to Hostler in a deliberate and measured fashion. "If anyone hears a word about this – and I mean anyone – you won't live to see the sun come up. Understand?"

He relaxed his grip, and Hostler emitted a series of laborious gasps with his mouth wide open and his eyes still bulging.

"Understand?" Carson repeated and bore down on his grip enough to demonstrate his intent if he didn't get an answer.

Hostler managed an urgent nod. His vocal cords had yet to recover.

Carson took his hand away and stepped back. Hostler slid down the refrigerator door into a deflated heap on the kitchen floor. He'd wet his pants and labored desperately to draw air in though his compromised windpipe. His terrified eyes never left Carson.

"Now where were we?" Carson said. "Oh yeah, get the fuck out."

Hostler struggled to his feet, backed toward the kitchen entrance and stumbled off into the darkness, where he crawled up the stairs.

Carson shook his head and went back to work. The guy wouldn't have lasted five minutes in combat. Welcome to the revolution.

The Sleeper walked his dog down Clement Street past an open-air market filled with the pinks, yellows, reds and greens of tropical fruits. The proprietor was slicing open a grapefruit to display its succulence to a potential buyer.

It took him back into the jungle, to the traitor and the gravity knife.

He'd taken it off a dead government soldier and learned how you launched the blade out of the handle to lock it in place. In idle moments, he practiced the motion until it became second nature. The size of the handle limited the length of the blade and dictated that it was best used for slashing and not stabbing.

Not long after, a traitor was detected among their ranks. Several times the man had reported their location to Batista's troops in exchange for generous amounts of cash. They had suffered numerous casualties as a result. The leadership marked him for execution and deliberated on how it should be done. The enemy was present in force nearby, and a gunshot would reveal their location.

It fell upon The Sleeper to execute him with the knife. He followed the traitor down a remote trail and clicked the blade into place. The traitor turned at the sound, and The Sleeper slashed his throat before he could react. The man staggered backward with eyes bulging, mouth gaping, and blood spurting from the severed arteries in his neck. He crashed to the ground and his jaws opened wide in a silent scream before he went limp.

The Sleeper found the traitor's death disturbing but not overwhelming. Ultimately, it equated to social justice for crimes against this most righteous of causes. The man's horrified face flashed before him as he teetered on the brink of sleep, but it gave way to cheering crowds of victorious workers. Just before he drifted off, he wondered what his father would think of what he had done. In a strange twist, he was sure the old man would approve. The savagery of it all would trump the politics and prevail.

In the following months, his gravitas among the leadership grew steadily. He'd proven himself both utterly devoted and ruthlessly efficient, a combination highly valued in the insurgent hierarchy and one that would endure well into new order. One of Che's lieutenants took him under his wing and mentored him on the dynamics of radical politics as practiced on the battlefield. He proved an apt student and rapidly rose in rank. It guaranteed that if he survived the war, he would most certainly survive the peace.

Many others would be a lot less fortunate.

The Sleeper felt a tug on the leash as his dog, a German Shepard, signaled him it was time to head home. He took in the happy bustle along the street, the smiling people, the fashionable dress, the sleek new automobiles. Privileged, indulgent, self-satisfied. All an illusion, built on the backs of the workers of the world.

But not for long, he reckoned.

27.

GOLDEN GATE PARK

Stone thumbed through the latest issue of the *Berkeley Barb* while sipping on some coffee at his desk. It had made him a satirical media star around the office and earned him the title of Spy Man Stone, so he thought he owed it at least a little attention.

The inside front page featured a photo of an enraged feminist taking a swing at some guy who had jumped on stage during a rally and kissed her. At the bottom, a cartoon presented a heavily stylized male character telling a female character, "I'm a good anti-racist and a good anti-imperialist and I expect as much from all the broads I screw." The female held a big stick behind her back with a nail protruding. Stone thumbed on and found some provocative speculation on page 7 entitled "Was Jesus Gay?"

He had just moved on to page 8 when the phone rang. "Stone here."

"Yes, Detective Stone. I, uh, have some information that maybe I could share with you." The male voice had a definite edge to it.

"Oh yeah? What kind of information."

"I saw that thing about you in the *Barb*. It makes me think you're trying to learn more about the police bombings."

"I see. What's your name?"

"Sandler. Jerome Sandler."

"And what makes you think I'm working on the bombings?"

"You're a city cop. You work at Park Station, where the guy was killed. You show up in Berkeley, trying to get into the radical underground, where people make bombs. I could be wrong, but I don't think so."

"Okay then, just what kind of information are we talking about?"

"It's not something I want to discuss over the phone. You never know who's listening."

"No you don't. So why don't you come over to the station and we'll meet in person?"

"I've gotta tell you, I'm not really comfortable being around that many cops."

"Well then, Mr. Sandler, just what did you have in mind?"

"You know where Peacock Meadow is?"

"In the park?"

"Yeah, in the park. There's a bench in the middle along the far edge, right off the path. It's a safe place. We can talk."

"And just when do you want to do this?" Stone asked.

"Let's say one 'o clock. You're only ten minutes away on foot. Should be easy."

Stone caught himself just as he was about to agree. What if the guy was one of the bombers? What if Stone was the next target? He made a rapid mental calculation and came up with a solution that bought him some insurance.

"I'm a busy man, Mr. Sandler. The best I can do is to be there sometime between one and one thirty." Stone knew that the bombings all involved timers. If the bomber didn't know the exact moment he would arrive, he couldn't time the detonation to take him out.

"Okay," the voice said without hesitation. "See you then. Only you, right?"

"Only me," Stone promised.

. . .

Carson situated himself in the shade on a wooded slope just above the green expanse of Peacock Meadow. If afforded him a clear line of sight to the park bench below. He'd concealed the device in a stand of shrubs about 30 feet down the path from the bench, where it waited to do its awful business.

He checked his watch: 1:10 p.m. Traffic rolled by on the opposite side of the meadow, where JFK Drive threaded its way through the park. The detective would take the path along the meadow's edge, the shortest route to the bench, the one that would take him right past the bomb.

Stone crossed JFK Drive at the crosswalk nearest the meadow and walked down the paved path to where the grass started. A mild spring had rendered it a luxuriant green. He looked over and saw the park bench across the meadow, just as the caller described. Empty. He had to assume that the caller was playing it safe and wouldn't expose himself until he was sure that Stone was alone. Stone continued on and turned onto the curved path that led to bench.

There he was, coming down the path. Carson executed a mental checklist. Safety switch off. Red LED indicator on. Antenna extended. Subject entering blast radius.

His thumb hovered over the transmit button.

"Hi. What are you doing with that?"

His pulse leaped and he whirled to face the voice. A child. A girl maybe four years old, with a round face and pigtails. Where had she come from?

"Sorry, I'm busy right now," he said with all the restraint he could muster.

She didn't get the hint and pointed at the walkie-talkie. "Is that a toy? What's it do?"

He shifted his vision down to the path. Stone had just walked past the center of the blast radius.

"It's not a toy," Carson said in an ugly tone. "You've got to go. Right now."

"Sarah!" A female voice called from up above. "Come on. We've got to get going."

"Oh, all right," the girl yelled peevishly. She waved at Carson. "Have a nice day."

She started up the slope, but it took a few moments before she was out of sight.

Carson yanked his gaze back to the detective down on the path, who had reached the far end of the lethal blast radius.

He jammed his thumb down on the transmit button.

The blast's solidified wave of compressed air hit Stone from behind at several hundred miles per hour. It flung him forward several meters and deposited him on the pavement, where he bounced several times before coming to a stop. The force of it rendered him temporarily deaf and threw him into a state of shock. From a great mental distance, he felt a series of muted stings in his back. Still, the core of him carried on.

I fucked up. It wasn't a timer. It was something else.

An atavistic compulsion came over him to get to his feet. If he didn't, he became easy prey for every predacious beast that had ever stalked the earth.

He rose on wobbly legs but could only stagger a short distance. A vicious ringing saturated his hearing. The mild stings on his back erupted into burning fires.

I should have known. He caught me cold. Why am I not dead?

Voices from far off. Shouting and confusion. Hands grasping his arms, bringing him down to a sitting position. Faces, fearful faces.

"Momma, what was that?"

Carson heard the little girl's question drift down from above as he watched the smoke from the blast quickly dissipate. It didn't look good. Stone was staggering to his feet, wounded but not expired. Onlookers were already converging on him.

Carson shoved the walkie-talkie in his pocket. He couldn't leave it here because they would eventually figure out that the bomb was remotely detonated and search the area looking for evidence. He'd toss it in a trash can once he made it over to Haight-Ashbury.

"What made the big bang?" the little girl was asking her mother on the path above.

"I don't know, sweetheart, but we have to go. Right now," came the mother's anxious reply.

Carson looked down below where several onlookers had placed Stone in a sitting position, and he knew he couldn't linger here any longer. The little girl was sure to tell her mother about the man with the toy down in the bushes. The mother would then relay this information to police, who would promptly seal off the area. He made his way along the side of the slope for some distance, then descended to the path bordering the meadow. Sirens now pierced the afternoon, and he could see the cluster of people now surrounding Stone. He considered posing as a passerby to get closer and appraise the extent of Stone's injuries. Too risky. He turned and started down the path that led back into the Haight.

. . .

"Dr. Harmon?"

Christine turned from the X-ray she'd been examining and faced one of the ER admissions people who worked out front. The woman appeared quite anxious, which was unusual given her occupation.

"We, uh, just had an admission that may be related to you." She looked down at a clipboard she was carrying. "His name is James Stone. Does that sound familiar?"

Christine's heart headed for the moon. "What happened? Where is he?"

"They just put him in Bay 5. I don't know the details, but he was conscious when they rolled him through."

Christine felt the world shrink as she left the X-ray room and hurried down the hall. What happened to him? At least he was conscious. A good sign. A great many people who came here unconscious stayed that way. Forever. What were his injuries? Would they kill him? Would they cause him permanent damage? She was right. He shouldn't have gone back to being a cop.

She tried to stem her rampant speculation, but her anxiety won the standoff. A hint of tears formed in the corners of her eyes.

She burst into the ER's main room and headed toward Bay 5, where the curtain was pushed shut. As she closed the distance, one of her fellow ER doctors opened it and stepped out. "Christine, he's going to be okay. He's conscious, he's lucid, and the wounds are superficial."

Christine pushed past him and into the curtained bay, where Stone lay on a portable bed. "James, oh James. What happened?" Tears flooded her eyes and her professional composure crumbled.

"It's okay, babe," he said. "Got knocked a little silly. I'll be fine. Just need a few stitches."

"What happened? Tell me what happened," she demanded.

The attending doctor came in behind her. "There was an explosion. It was at the east end of the park. That's about all we know."

"A bomb?" she asked.

"Maybe. Don't know," the doctor said. "We're going to take him over to X-ray and see if he broke anything, but it doesn't look like it. Then we'll take care of his back."

"His back?" The panic had receded enough that Christine noticed the bandages wrapped around his upper torso.

"Take a look." He reached over to a plastic bowl and held up a blood-stained roofing nail. "We found five of these embedded in his back. Those wounds are all going to need stitches."

Stone reached out and grasped Christine's hand. "Don't worry," he said dreamily. "It's going to be okay."

"They gave him 15 milligrams of morphine on the way in," the doctor commented. "He may not be so optimistic when it wears off."

Christine sighed. "It's hard to say. He's not your average guy."

And that's why she loved him.

28.

SAN FRANCISCO

Stone sat on a straight-back chair at the kitchen table to keep the pressure off his wounded back, which still hurt to the touch. At the hospital yesterday they had cleaned and stitched the five indentations and bandaged each separately. The nails had all impacted at shallow angles, so each left a T-shaped impression in his skin. He wanted them as evidence, so they bagged the nails up and he brought them along when Christine drove him home. She spent the morning with him, still fretting about possible head injuries, and left after lunch to finish her shift.

He pondered the nails, which he'd put in a saucer on the table next to his notebook and pen. They were absolutely generic in appearance and almost certainly untraceable. He turned to the notebook, where he was meticulously recording every detail he could summon up, from the time the phone rang on his desk until the bomb exploded in the meadow.

He still felt angry and humiliated that the caller had outwitted him about the detonation mechanism. He'd made the stupid assumption that it would be a timer of some kind. The moment the caller so readily agreed to a random meeting time should have sent up a warning flag, but it didn't.

To put things in order, he'd written up a carefully constructed timeline. That done, he picked the pen up to record questions that as of yet had no answers. For starters, were the caller and bomber the same person? He strongly suspected that they were but had no definitive answer. Also, was the call part of a conspiracy involving multiple people? Maybe. And was it connected to the two police station bombings? Probably, but how?

And then there was the matter of the ill-timed detonation. Without a doubt, the bomber had situated himself on the slope above the meadow, so he had a clear view of Stone's proximity to the device's location. Burke had called this morning and informed him that the bomb squad guys had been all over the scene and taken measurements and made calculations. It seemed that if Stone had been five or six feet closer to the detonation, he would have had roofing nails firmly embedded in his heart, lungs and liver. So why had the guy waited until Stone was almost home free? No telling.

The phone rang. "Stone here."

"Hi. It's Lisa Vaught from the *Barb*. Are you okay?"

"And why wouldn't I be?" he asked. There had been no official statement that he'd been injured by the blast yesterday. What was going on?

"I'm a journalist. I have sources. You got hurt in the park."

"Well this time, your sources got it right," he responded with obvious irritation.

"I'm so sorry. I feel terrible about this. It's pretty much all my fault. None of this would have happened if I'd gotten it right. I just had to know if you were okay."

He could hear the quiver in her voice. She was speaking from the heart. It softened him considerably. "Yeah, I'll be alright. And it wasn't all your fault. You got suckered by the pros. You're not the first. They've been doing stuff like this a long time and they're really good at it. So give yourself a break."

"Thank you," she said softly. "Is there anything I can do to help?"

"As a matter of fact, there is," he told her. "You hear anything more about bombs – even firecrackers – you let me know. Same thing goes for killing cops."

"I will. I promise."

"And from now on, double-check your sources, okay?"

"Absolutely. I promise."

"Good. Talk to you later."

Stone heard the latch click as Christine opened the front door and hung up her lab coat. She'd brought in a big plastic bag full of Chinese takeout and put it on the kitchen counter, where she methodically removed the cartons. All without a word to Stone. She appeared tired and distracted, but a bad day in the emergency room could easily bring that on.

"So how were things in the ER today?" he asked.

"I wasn't in the ER today," she said.

"Oh yeah? So where were you?"

She removed two plates from the cupboard before answering. "I took a walk. A long walk."

"Where did you go?"

"I'm not really sure. I wasn't paying much attention."

Stone had a bad feeling. This was getting really creepy. She started opening the cartons. "You want fried rice or white rice?"

"Neither," he told her. "I want to know what's going on with you."

She pulled out a serving spoon and started dishing portions onto the plates. "No, let's start with you. How are you feeling? How's your back?"

"Still pretty sore," he admitted.

"Are you taking the antibiotic?"

"Yes ma'am."

"And what about the Percodan?"

"Nope."

"Why not?"

"I need to keep my head straight while I work things out."

"Work what things out?"

"I'm trying to account for everything that happened between the time I got the call and when the bomb went off."

She gave him an incredulous stare that went off the charts. "You're not thinking of going back to work, are you?"

Uh oh. He thought they had reached an accommodation on the subject, but maybe not. Apparently, nearly getting blown to bits was not part of the deal. He had to do his best to hedge.

"I don't know," he said. "I'm just trying to put some things together, that's all."

"Let me be more specific. After everything that just happened, you're not going to continue working for the San Francisco Police Department, are you?"

"I hadn't really thought about it," he said. "I..."

"Well maybe it's time you *did* really think about it. And maybe it's time to think about a little more than taking one for the team. Maybe you should think about the damage to our relationship and more specifically the damage to me." She closed her eyes and breathed deeply. "Don't you get it?" she asked. "Don't you understand what it would do to me if I lost you?"

No, he didn't. And for the first time since this conflict began, the potential damage came into hard focus for him. He'd always felt the presence of her love but also saw her as fundamentally independent and self-contained. That he might dwell so very close to the center of her had escaped him. But now, in this moment of truth, it became inescapable.

"I'm sorry," he told her. "I didn't think about it that way."

"Well maybe it's time you did," she replied.

And so it went. Salvo after salvo, late into the evening. Several times, he approached the threshold of acquiescence but backed off. The takeout Chinese food cooled on the plates and in the cartons and went untouched. Collateral damage in an unwinnable war.

29.

GOLDEN GATE PARK

"So here's ground zero," Findley said. "Truth is, you came really close to getting wasted."

"So it would seem," Stone commented.

The two of them looked at a blackened patch of tall grass about five feet off the paved path. Findley was the SFPD bomb squad guy assigned to the case. He struck Stone as both intelligent and competent.

"If it had been a little later in the season, we would have had a grass fire on top of everything else," Findley added. "But there you go."

"Yeah, there I went," Stone added. Overhead, the morning sun engaged in a brilliant struggle to penetrate the thin cloud layer. Its intense light saturated the ground cover, turning the grass in Peacock Meadow a brilliant, liquid green. "Mind if we sit down?"

"Oh, yeah," Findley said, slightly embarrassed. "You're probably not one hundred percent yet, right?"

"I'm getting there," Stone said as they walked over to the park bench, the very same one where he agreed to meet the bomber. "Let's talk about what you've found so far."

"Lotta nails," Findley said. "But you know all about the nails."

"Yes, I do," Stone said laconically. "Anything else?"

"Just one thing worth talking about." He reached in a leather satchel he was carrying and pulled out a baggie containing a roughly rectangular piece of black plastic. He offered it to Stone. "Be my guest."

Stone peered at the object, which was about an inch and half wide and two inches long. At one end the letters "REA" ran across its scorched surface, done in a futuristic typestyle with letters spelling "The Spor" visible below in a cursive rendering. At the very bottom was a small circular hole.

"You got a pad and pencil?" Stone asked. "I want to make a sketch of this."

"Here you go," Findley said as he produced the materials. "I'll get you a picture as soon we photograph it for evidence."

"Thanks," Stone said as he started a careful sketch. "Let's talk about the trigger. I'm betting it wasn't a clock because he didn't know exactly when I'd show. That leaves some kind of wireless thing. What do you think?"

"I agree, and I'd go a step further. If it was radio-controlled, there had to be a power source for both the bomb and controlling device. Since there's no AC power out here in this part of the park, it was probably battery-powered. That narrows it down to portable things like CB radios and walkie-talkies... Uh oh."

Stone looked up from his sketch. Two suited figures were making their way across the meadow and closing in on the yellow crime scene tape that staked out the far reaches of the blast.

"Here come the feds," Findley said. "Better stash all this for right now."

Stone pocketed his sketch and gave the rest back to Findley.

"One guy's ATF for sure," Findley observed. "The other guy I don't know."

Stone did know. Special Agent Peter Trobe of the FBI ducked under the yellow tape and waved at them. Just as if nothing had happened. Just as if their COINTELPRO program hadn't publicly exposed him. Just as if they hadn't pinned a target on his back and damn near got him killed.

"Good morning, gentlemen," Trobe said as he approached the bench. "You had a really close call, detective," he said to Stone with an unctuous smile. "How're you feeling?"

"Pissed," Stone shot back. "Really pissed."

"I see," Trobe said with a thoughtful nod. "Maybe we should put that aside for a moment and get down to business. This is Agent Tom Edgars of the ATF. And I assume you're Detective Findley from the city bomb squad, correct?"

"Correct."

"I'm Special Agent Peter Trobe. As you probably know, recent federal legislation has given us and the ATF a broad mandate to investigate bombings of precisely the type we have right here." He spoke directly to Findley and ignored Stone. "Now I know you and your people have already put serious work into this case and that's greatly appreciated. Of course, we'll need to be copied on everything you've done up to this point. As we move forward, it's critical that there be a single agency in charge of the investigation. Otherwise, we have a body without a head and things start to slip through the cracks. Agreed?"

"Agreed," Findley said.

Trobe brightened. "Good!"

"The SFPD is both ready and able to take charge of this thing," Findley declared. "Any assistance you can render will be greatly appreciated."

Trobe's face fell. "I'm afraid that doesn't make a lot of sense, detective. We have resources on tap that transcend anything a local police department can bring to bear. No offense, but we're the logical choice here."

Findley held off for a moment while composing a response. Stone filled the gap.

"Fuck you."

"What?" Trobe asked, as if he hadn't heard right.

"I said fuck you," Stone repeated. He'd strayed far from his usual state of composure. He surprised even himself. His anger had reached a full boil and was spilling out unchecked.

Trobe gave the other two men an apologetic expression, as if he understood the core of Stone's discontent. After all, the man had just survived an extraordinarily violent attempt on his life. "Would you excuse us a moment, gentleman?" he asked them, and turned to Stone. "If you don't mind, I'd like to have a word in private. Okay?"

Stone pointed out into the meadow toward the crime scene boundary. "Let's go."

The ATF agent and Findley looked on anxiously, both worried that the confrontation might become physical. "You going to be alright?" Findley asked.

"I'm going to be just fine," Stone said through clenched teeth. He spun and headed out over the grass, with Trobe a few steps behind. When they reached the yellow tape, Stone whirled to face him.

"You goddam near got me killed, motherfucker," Stone hissed. "You know that?"

"No, I don't know that," Trobe said calmly. "I'm not sure what you mean. What's the problem?"

"Can you spell COINTELPRO?" Stone asked. "I bet you can. I bet you can do even better. I bet you can explain how you used it to try to get me off the bombing cases. You blew my cover and pinned a target on my back."

"Look," Trobe said. "You've just been through a really bad episode, so it's not surprising you're a little on edge. But you've got to understand it's really coloring your thinking. You don't want to be rushing to judgement right now."

"Alright then, let's talk about Karen Richter who ratted on me to the *Berkeley Barb*. Or did she now? It turns out that the real Karen Richter never heard of me. And she's never set foot in the Caffe Mediterraneum. It also turns out that the contact number she gave the reporter belongs to none other than the U.S. Department of Justice. Now you know what that all adds up to? Counterintelligence on steroids. You fucked me, Trobe. You used your program against a fellow law enforcement officer, which qualifies you to be the asshole of the century."

Trobe fell into visible dismay as Stone spoke. But not for long. He quickly recomposed himself and started off with a repentant sigh.

"We're talking about a very complicated situation," he explained. There's a lot I can't tell you. You just have to understand that it's all a matter of national security at the highest levels. Sorry, that's about as much as I can say."

"That's plenty," Stone shot back. "I got the general idea. Bullshit at the highest levels rolling downhill. Now you hear me: I'm not going away. I'm going to track down whoever tried to kill me, and your best bet is to just stay the fuck out of the way."

"I think that's a very poor decision," Trobe said. "One that you'll live to regret."

"Are you threatening me?" Stone demanded.

"Physically no," Trobe said. "Professionally, yes."

"Oh yeah? Well try this on for size: The *Berkeley Barb* would love to do an expose about how the local FBI office ran a COINTELPRO scam on a local police officer and duped the *Barb* into running with it. Cops rat out fellow cop, who damn near gets killed. Very ugly. Now if they chose to do so, I'm sure I could be a big help. Got the picture?"

"Just what is it you want?" Trobe asked, with a notable touch of anxiety.

"Like I said before," Stone replied. "Stay out of my way. Way out of my way."

. . .

Kitty sat at the top of the stairs with its outrageous sense of entitlement when Stone returned from the park. He desperately needed a distraction, and Kitty delivered magnificently. If for only a moment, he was able to put aside his attempted murder, his battle with the FBI and his domestic conflict with Christine. He'd done a quick personal inventory and decided that things were worse than they had ever been, worse even than his exile from the LAPD and subsequent divorce.

Stone looked at the kitchen counter and sighed. All the Chinese takeout from the previous night was still out and wasting away at room temperature, a casualty of last night's blowup. He considered giving some of it to Kitty, but the cat was way too uppity to accept second-hand takeout. Instead, he fetched a can of tuna from the cupboard, opened it, and set it out in front of the expectant beast.

"Premium fresh chunk," he told Kitty. "The best there is."

Without even a hint of gratitude, the cat started in on the tuna. "You can thank me later," he said, and went back inside. He wondered if the animal knew anything about sarcastic humor.

He sat down heavily at the dining room table with its straight-back chairs that spared his back, which still hurt to the touch. Various notes and diagrams littered the tabletop but so far hadn't produced much. He pulled the sketch of the bomb fragment out of his shirt pocket and added it to the pile. It was trying to give him a hint, but he had yet to recognize it.

It occurred to him that maybe he was working in the wrong direction. Maybe he should start at the top of what they knew and work his way down. Fact: The device was a dynamite-powered pipe bomb, easy to make and easy to source the explosive. Fact: It was almost certainly detonated by remote control by someone observing his approach. Fact: It had to be powered by batteries, which also implied that it was highly portable. Fact: The fragment looked like it came from something mass-produced.

Stone sat upright and stretched. Back in the park, Findley had said it might come from the something like a CB radio or a walkie-talkie and his speculation jived neatly with all the facts. So where would one go to purchase such an item?

Stone looked back down at the table and smiled for the first time all day. There it was, right in front of him, a leftover from last week's mail. A Radio Shack catalog, all 136 pages of it, from the undisputed king of low-cost electronics. Once you got on their mailing list, it was more or less a life sentence. A few years back in Los Angeles, Stone had an urgent need for a cassette deck and Radio Shack came through. In his haste, he signed on to their mailing list and now lived with an endless stream of their marketing publications. For all he knew, they might even follow you into the afterlife.

He placed his sketch of the fragment next to the catalog, so he had a reference, and started thumbing through the product sections until he reached walkie-talkies. And there it was, beyond any doubt. Page 63 featured three different models, all built from the same plastic casing with the word REALISTIC emblazoned across the upper portion. Its futuristic typeface matched the REA on the fragment sketch, with electrified serifs done in silver against a black background. The second piece of type from the sketch, the "Spor," narrowed the field even further. Only one of three models had "The Sportsman" printed on it.

So there he had it, the Realistic 2-watt Sportsman walkie-talkie, with "single channel operation" and "powerful long range." An unintentional accomplice in a murderous scheme to kill him. He went to the catalog's final few pages and found an index listing all the store locations in California. It included ten outlets in the Bay Area, from San Rafael down through San Jose.

He immediately began to outline a plan to canvas them. He'd start with the two right here in the city and then move further afield. At each location, he had one additional card to play when talking to the clerks. Most likely, the bomber had picked up his trail after the publication of the *Barb* article, which was only a few days ago. All he needed was a list of purchases of this particular product from the *Barb*'s publication date until very recently.

He briefly considered starting his search immediately but was simply too tired. He'd been continually awakened by a burning jab every time he tried to roll onto his back last night, which left him with an acute case of sleep deprivation. Right now, he needed a nap more than anything, so he went into the bedroom and plopped face down on the mattress. Warmth and quiet quickly descended. A bird chirped from somewhere out back, a swallow by the sound of it. The pillowcase's soft cotton caressed his cheek. A bed spring issued a muffled sound as he shifted his weight. He'd left one thing undone, but it could wait until he woke up. He needed to mentally prepare for the next round of domestic skirmishes with Christine. The very thought drove him even deeper into exhaustion and he promptly slipped away into a dreamless void.

· · ·

Stone awoke to the baritone rumble of a passing streetcar over on Judah Street. The waning light told him he'd slept longer than expected, and the bedside clock confirmed it. Nearly six-thirty. He gingerly got up and expected to find Christine in the living room or kitchen, but they were empty. Slightly after five was her usual time of arrival, but her ER gig made it highly variable. You couldn't leave someone gasping, bleeding or choking just because it was quitting time. In any case, she shouldn't be much longer, so he started thinking about dinner. All the recent chaos meant he hadn't made it to the grocery store, so he'd have to improvise.

The phone rang just as he put his hand on the refrigerator handle. He lifted it off the wall mount and answered. "Hello?"

"Hi, it's me," Christine answered. She seemed quiet and somehow reticent.

"You're running late," he said. "Someone die on you?"

"No, nothing like that," she said. "I'm not coming home tonight."

"You're what?"

"I've got a room at a hotel downtown. The Charlton. I'm not trying to hide. I want you to know that."

"Then what *are* you doing?" he asked with a rising pulse.

"I've given it a lot of thought. We've got a big problem and we're not getting anywhere with it. We're just grinding each other up. We need some distance. We need a new take on it. I'm way too young to become a widow, especially when it can be so easily avoided."

"Okay then, where do we go from here?"

"You spend some time on your own and see where it takes you. You can weigh all the pros and cons of what we have. Then we can talk."

"Are you really sure this is the best thing to do?" he asked.

"Yes, I'm really sure. Like I said, I've given it a lot of thought. I'm sorry. I don't see any other way."

"I don't know what to say to that," Stone said. "I just don't know."

"You don't have to say anything. I've got to go now. We're going to start fighting again if we stay on the line, and that won't help anything. Anyway, you know where to find me if you need me. Goodnight."

She hung up before he could respond. He cradled the phone and stared absently out the front window. Deep down he wasn't surprised by what she'd done. He'd just not wanted to face the possibility. Now he had no choice but to come to terms with it.

So here he was, alone in a lifeless shell of a home. It dredged up ugly memories of the final innings in his marriage to Grace, now ten years past. It wasn't a phone call that time; it was a brief note, written in her carefully constructed cursive, announcing that she was moving in with her sister so she could "think things through." He'd never know the nature of that thought process, only that it swiftly terminated their union and left him financially and emotionally devastated.

When he went in the bathroom, he suddenly noticed that all Christine's things were gone: The soaps, creams, conditioners, shampoos, and colorful vials holding various aspects of female arcana. He'd been here all day and their absence had failed to register. It told him more than he wanted to know about his obsession with the bomber case.

He walked out and looked at the bits and pieces of the evidence strewn across the dining table. The bastard had nearly killed him. Now he was doing the same to the one and only relationship he had that really mattered.

Forget about being a cop. What he really wanted to do was find this guy and kill him.

30.

OUTER SUNSET DISTRICT

Stone finally caught a break, albeit of modest dimension. The nearest Radio Shack turned out to be on Irving Street near 20th, a twenty-minute walk from his house. He found it wedged between a Chinese restaurant and Pakistani one, neither open at ten o'clock in the morning. His entry triggered an audible alarm comparable to a wounded duck. The clerk, a young man barely out of acne, looked up from behind black-framed glasses and saw opportunity. He came around from behind the counter.

"Yes sir, can I help you?" he asked.

Stone considered telling him that it was better to wait and pounce after the customer did a bit of browsing. He declined, and pulled out his ID. "Hi, I'm with the San Francisco police. Do you have one of your catalogs handy?"

"Yessir, I do," the clerk responded eagerly. "Right over here." He led them to a pile stacked at one end of the counter. "Anything in particular you're looking for?"

"As a matter of fact, yes," Stone said while opening the top catalog to page sixty-three. He pointed to the product in question. "A 2-watt Sportsman walkie-talkie."

"Ah yes," the clerk said. "Good choice. And I do believe we have that model in stock. Let me check."

"No need," Stone said. The clerk looked puzzled. "It's part of an investigation." The clerk lit up. No surprise. Bad guys aside, almost everybody likes to be part of an investigation.

"Really? How can I help?" the clerk asked.

"I need to know if you've sold one of these things in the last couple of weeks. Can you check your sales records?"

"Don't have to."

"Oh yeah?"

"I don't sell a lot of these," the clerk explained. "Most people spend a little more and step up to the 2-watt or 3-watt model. An extra thirty bucks doubles your power. So it tends to stick with me when I sell one. And especially this time."

"Why is that?"

"The guy was seriously weird. I mean, we get some really geeky and nerdy people in here, but this guy was different. He seemed super nervous and got pissed off when I tried to put him on our mailing list."

"How did he pay?" Stone asked.

"Cash. I can look up the transaction, but there's nothing there. He wouldn't give me a name to put on the receipt. I told him that might screw up the warranty, but he didn't care. Like I said, totally weird."

"You really want to help?" Stone asked.

"Absolutely."

"Two things. First, I'd like to arrange for you to come down and work with our sketch artist to see if you can reconstruct this guy's face. Second, I'd like you to phone your other stores in the Bay Area and see if any of them have sold one of these things recently. Can you do that?"

"I'm on it," the clerk said with an enthusiastic nod.

"Good." Stone handed him one of his SFPD cards. "Let me know what you find, okay?"

"You got it."

He asked for the clerk's card and thanked him for his help.

Now, at last, he was getting somewhere.

. . .

They came by in ones and twos. Everybody from the station captain down to the dispatcher. They inquired about his health, his healing, his spirits. They pledged their loyalty and support. They expressed their confidence in his work.

This afternoon marked Stone's first official appearance back at Park Station since the bombing, and the show of solidarity genuinely touched him. He could have stayed home on medical leave, but the empty house was simply too oppressive. Better to be here, where the company of others kept his soul from sliding too far down into the depths.

The phone rang and yanked him out of this pleasant rumination. "Stone here."

"Hello, my name is Janice Keyes," the caller said. "I was told you're the person in charge of the bombing in the park."

Stone instinctively went on guard. The last stranger who phoned him about a bombing incident went on to try to kill him. "Yes, that would be me," he replied. "And what can I do for you?"

"I was there," Keyes said. "I didn't see it happen, but I was there. With my daughter."

"That's good to know… I'm sorry, is it miss or missus?"

"Missus. I'm sure you're really busy and I wouldn't bother you, but I think my daughter saw something that might be important."

"I see. And just what was it that she saw?"

"We'd just left the Camellia Garden. You know where that is?"

"Yes, I do." Like most cops at Park Station, Stone had gradually acquired a mental map of Golden Gate Park, from Haight-Ashbury all the way down to the Pacific. The garden in question sat on the high ground overlooking Peacock Meadow.

"We were walking on the trail right above. My daughter went ahead a little way and kept ducking down into the bushes. Then I heard her talking with someone and got worried. I called for her and she came back up onto the trail. I asked her who she was talking to, and she said it was a man who was playing with a toy. She'd only been out of my sight for maybe a minute, so I wasn't too worried. We walked a little farther down the path, and I heard the explosion. We couldn't see it and just kept going until we got to the Conservatory of Flowers, where I was parked."

The moment Keyes mentioned the man with the toy, an image of the Realistic Sportsman walkie-talkie saturated his inner vision.

"How old is your daughter, Mrs. Keyes?"

"She's five. Her name's Carmen. She just started kindergarten this year."

The girl's age was a double-edged sword. She was old enough to give a lucid account of her experience, but not to be a credible witness in any legal proceeding. It also explained her mother's hesitance in contacting the police.

"Would it be possible for me to talk with Carmen for a few minutes?" Stone asked.

"Okay, but that's as far as I want it to go. She's a five-year-old girl, so that's the end of it."

"I absolutely agree," Stone said. "If you give me your address, I can be there within the hour. Does that work for you?"

"That works fine," Keyes said, and gave Stone the address.

. . .

Stone felt slightly guilty for verifying Janice Keyes' identity as if she were part of a conspiracy of some sort, but it seemed justified under all the recent circumstances. In any case, she came up clean, and he headed out to the family home over in Pacific Heights.

They lived in a townhouse on Octavia Street that hinted at a certain level of prosperity. The doorbell responded with a synthesized bit of Bach when he pressed it. Janice, an attractive woman in her early thirties, answered in a casual yet stylish dress.

"Mrs. Keyes, I'm Detective Stone," he said as he showed his badge. "Thanks for seeing me on such short notice."

"Not a problem," she said. "Come in."

Stone had pegged it right. Contemporary furniture done in soft leather. Original art, mostly abstractions. Large bookcase full of hardcover editions.

"Would you like something to drink?" she asked.

"No thank you," Stone said.

"Before we start, I want to make sure you're not going to say anything that's going to upset her," Mrs. Keyes said. "She's just a five-year-old little girl."

Stone gave her a reassuring smile. "You have my word."

"Okay, then. Please have a seat. I'll get her."

Mrs. Keyes went up the stairs and came back down with Carmen in tow. Stone stood politely to greet her. She couldn't have been any cuter, with a round face flanked by pigtails, a tiny nose, and eyes brimming with curiosity. An undercurrent of sadness flowed through Stone. She was the kind of child he'd always hoped for but would never have.

Carmen didn't wait for an introduction. "Are you a real policeman?" she asked as she looked up at him.

"Yes, I'm a real policeman," Stone said. "And I'm very pleased to meet you."

"My mom says you want to know about the man in the park."

"If that's okay with you," Stone said. He noticed that Carmen's mom visibly relaxed as he lived up to his promise. All of them sat down, with the girl on a hassock in front of Stone.

"So can you tell me what you were doing when you saw this man?"

"I was following a bird, a really funny bird. It hopped down into the bushes, and I went to find it."

"And that's when you saw the man?"

"He was playing with a toy. He said it wasn't a toy, but it sure looked like one. Then my mom called, and I left."

"Good girl." Stone reached into his coat pocket and pulled out the page in question from Radio Shack. "I'm trying to figure out what that toy was. Let's look at a picture I brought and see if you can pick it out. Okay?"

"Okay."

He put the page with the three walkie-talkie models down on the hassock beside her. Without the least hesitation, her index finger shot out and landed on the 2-watt Sportsman model. "It's *that* one," she said.

"Very good! Can you tell me why?"

"It's all black and has a little round knob. That's why."

Stone looked at the page. She'd nailed it. The other two models had a silver panel in the middle and larger knobs. It reminded him that children can be observant in ways that escape most adults. "That's very good, Carmen," he told her. "You've got really sharp eyes. I've got just one other question. Can you tell me what the man looked like, sort of?"

Carmen scrunched her little round face into an exaggerated look of concentration. "Not too much."

"That's okay," Stone said. "Thanks for trying." He turned to mom, but before he could speak, Carmen cut in spontaneously.

"He looked scared," she said. "Like when you see a monster or something."

"Excellent," he told Carmen. "That helps a lot." He turned to the mom again. "Could we have a quick word before I take off?"

"Sure."

"You've been a big help," he told Mrs. Keyes after Carmen went back upstairs. "And don't worry. We're not going to do anything that exposes her. There's just one more thing. We have a sketch artist that can build faces from verbal descriptions. I'd like to make an appointment for her to sit down with him. It's all completely confidential."

"I'd have to talk with her father about that," Mrs. Keyes replied.

"Understand." He pulled out his card and handed it to her. "You can get me any time. Goodbye now."

. . .

Stone paused and leaned back in his seat before starting the car. The late afternoon shadows gave the sidewalk a bluish cast on the west side of the street.

First the clerk and then the kid. Two big steps in the right direction. It put enough fuel in his tank to power him forward, at least for the time being. He spotted a payphone at the far end of the block, at the intersection with Union. Why not go for three? He climbed out, locked the door and headed down the sidewalk.

"Hotel Charlton," the clerk answered, just as a truck roared by on Union. The noise irritated Stone. It was hardly the right background for what might be a very delicate conversation. "Yes, could you connect me with one of your guests, a Christine Harmon?"

"Yes sir." She picked it up on the fourth ring. Good timing. One more ring and he would have fled back into anonymity. "Hello."

"It's me," he answered.

An appropriate pause followed, which he'd expected. She wouldn't want to present herself as eager to engage. "How are you?" she finally asked.

"I'm doing okay."

"Are you taking the antibiotics?"

"Yes, I am."

"Do you have any pain?"

"Just a little. It's pretty much gone." She was hiding behind her professional persona, which was understandable under the circumstances. "I thought maybe we could have some dinner and talk about things," he suggested.

A bigger pause this time, one loaded with a silent store of doubt and conflict. "I'm not ready for that," she finally said. "Not yet."

Not yet. A two-word semaphore that signaled there was still hope. He knew better than to push it any further.

"Understand," he responded. "I'll be in touch, okay?"

"Okay."

They hung up, and he looked over to an Italian restaurant across the street, where a young couple sat at a table out on the sidewalk. Love in full bloom, with all its rapturous smiles and dreamy eyes. They had no conception of the complex emotional terrain they would eventually have to negotiate. Nor should they. Better to bask in the moment.

He headed back toward his car. Two and a half out of three. Not a bad day.

31.

SAN FRANCISCO

"It was you, I know it was," Alice told Carson.

They sat on a wooden stoop outside the rear of the Pine Street apartment. The surrounding buildings denied it any sunlight and created a canyon of urban solitude. Carson flicked the last of his cigarette out onto a dirty apron of ancient cement. It rolled to a halt and sent up a slender column of bluish smoke.

"What makes you say that?" Carson asked.

"It was all over the papers last week: A bomb goes off in the park, and it nearly kills this pig, who just happens to be there. It was you. Had to be. You ambushed him, but something went wrong, didn't it?"

Carson's arms had gone itchy on him again. He rubbed them vigorously, almost to the point of open abrasion.

"I don't know why you just can't tell me," Alice continued. "You're a hero. You're lighting the fire that'll become the revolution."

"A fire, huh? Well good." He changed the subject. "Did they try to put you on the mailing list?"

"They did and they were kind of pushy about it, but I said no."

"You didn't give them your name, did you?"

"Of course not. But I think they thought it was kind of weird that a girl would be buying this sort of stuff."

"Maybe." He'd sent her to a different Radio Shack than the one where he purchased the walkie-talkies. After what was to come, they'd be all over this thing with a microscope. He now had everything he needed to pull it off.

Last time, Stone the pig got lucky. But this time would be different. This time, he would encounter Carson's masterpiece.

. . .

"We drew pictures!" Carmen informed Stone. The little girl beamed at him as she stood with her mother in a hallway on the third floor of police headquarters downtown.

"You did, huh?" Stone asked her with an affectionate smile. "I bet they're really good. What do you think? Are they?"

"I think they're really, really good," she said proudly.

"Of course, they are," Stone said and turned to Carmen's mother. "Thanks for all your help with this, Mrs. Keyes. We'll take it from here."

"Glad to help, officer," she responded.

Stone squatted down to Carmen's level and pulled out two dollars. "I think you should take your mommy and get a little ice cream."

Carmen switched to high beams as she took the money. "What do you say, Carmen?" her mother asked in that unmistakable parental mode of voice.

"Thank you."

Stone watched them recede down the hallway. He felt a little wave of sadness for what he would never have but put it aside as he entered the office of the sketch artist.

"So, what have you got?" he asked Charlie Severs. Legend had it that Charlie was a portrait artist out on the downtown streets until he impressed a couple of beat cops with the quality of his work and wound up on the city payroll. In any case, he consistently delivered the goods.

"Congratulations," Charlie said. "Looks like you hit the jackpot." He pointed to two sketches pinned side by side on a bulletin board near his worktable. "The one on the left is from the girl. The one on the right is from the store clerk."

They weren't exactly the same, but they never were. They were built up by patiently showing witnesses alternative feature sets for eyes, mouth, chin, face shape, and so on. These two renderings were well within the margin of error for comparison purposes. Gaunt cheeks, lank hair, recessed eyes, scowling lips, patchy beard.

Stone now had a reasonable facsimile of the man who tried to blow him up.

But it didn't end there. The images had an ethereal subtext to them that he couldn't quite pin down. It drifted just out of reach, out past the far edge of his memory, where substance dissolved to speculation.

"Great work. Can I get copies?" he asked Charlie.

"Comin' right up," he answered. "We got a new machine that does 'em in a heartbeat."

"So I've heard," Stone said.

. . .

"That's your guy?" Burke asked as he looked over Stone's shoulder at the renderings laid out on his desk.

"Sure looks like it," Stone replied. "Two witnesses, same description."

Burke picked one up and scrutinized it. "Too bad they didn't have his name, address and telephone number. You gonna try to get these into the *Chronicle*?"

"I've got a call into our public information guy, but I haven't heard back yet."

"Well good luck if you do. Problem is, the *Chronicle*'s got a huge circulation. You'll get hundreds of call-ins, then you've got to figure which ones aren't the usual nut cases. And then you've got to follow up on everything that's left."

"Thanks," Stone said with a grimace.

Burke put the rendering back down. "Don't mention it. Just trying to save you a little grief, that's all."

Stone's attention went back to the pictures as Burke wandered off. The sheer inertia of the case was slowly blunting his primal urge to flat-out murder this guy. Given enough time, it would burn out entirely. He smiled to himself. Given enough time, everything would burn out. Cities would grow and die. Nations would rise and fall. Glaciers would advance and melt. All lost to the drum-beat of a clock that couldn't be seen or stopped.

The phone rang. Christine. "Hi. How is your back doing?"

His back. Was she really calling about his back? Not likely. It was an overture.

"It's better. I can sleep on it now."

"Good. Look, I think I'm ready to talk. Can you come down here this evening?"

"I don't see why not. What time?"

"Let's say seven. The food here isn't too bad, and they've got a quiet bar."

"All right, I'll see you then."

"Bye now."

His internal elevator started up toward the penthouse but stopped halfway as he looked once again at the pictures. Even at that, halfway up was a long way from the sub-basement.

. . .

Special Agent Peter Trobe plopped the spiral-bound report onto his clean desktop. He liked the heft of it, which symbolized the massive resources the Bureau could muster to attack a particular issue. This time around that issue was the California membership of the Weather Underground. For an extended and frustrating period, the Bureau had been virtually clueless as to the whereabouts of all the major players. They had quite literally gone underground and left no trace.

But then a single incident had given the FBI the break they needed to turn things around. On the East Coast, they had arrested one of the members on a charge related to so-called days of rage, when they had run amok through downtown Chicago. It turned out she had a bogus driver's license obtained in the name of a long-dead infant. Pow! The Bureau had stumbled onto the scam the underground people were using to mint fake IDs.

In a massive display of clerksmanship, a dozen agents had descended upon the San Francisco Department of Health and gone mining for the names of dead babies who had birth certificates issued during the time the Weather cadre began showing up in the city. The trick was to find infants who, if they had lived, would approximate the age of the suspects.

It took six weeks but in the end produced twenty-seven such certificates. Armed with the resulting list of names, they moved on to the Department of Motor Vehicles where they discovered that eighteen of these long-departed souls had new driver's licenses issued to them. The final trick was to match the photos and signatures on these licenses with all criminal records related to the Weather Underground.

Bingo. They had at least a dozen matches, including some of the big players, like Dohrn, Jones and Ayers. It was just a matter of time until the paper trail led them directly to these people, through things like parking tickets and vehicle registrations.

Trobe brushed an annoying little crumb off his desktop while he contemplated the report in all its bureaucratic glory. It made him think of that city cop, Stone, who thought he could bust these people all by himself. Wrong. Sometimes, might makes right and this was one of them.

. . .

"Well lookee here. It's Pig Eye's pal."

The same biker stood at the door as last time. He opened it wide with a theatrical flourish and gestured toward the interior.

"Come on in, brother. I bet you're lookin' to get cranked."

"Yeah. For starters," Carson said as he nervously took in the scene as Lenny came into view.

"For starters?" Lenny asked derisively. "And then what? A ticket to the moon?"

Carson ignored the jab and got right down to business. "I need three sticks of dynamite and a couple of blasting caps."

The two bikers lost their smirks and looked at each other wordlessly. Finally, Lenny turned to Carson. "And what makes you think we'd have something like that?"

"Just a guess," Carson said. An educated guess. He knew that a number of California chapters had been busted or probed for possessing explosives. If they didn't have it here, they'd know where to get it in a hurry.

"Okay, let's say we did have some," Lenny speculated. "We're not talkin' wholesale. We're not even talkin' store price. We're talkin' about three times that much. Still interested?"

"Still interested," Carson confirmed.

"Okay, because you're a vet and a friend of the club, here's what we can do: A hundred for the crank just like last time – and another hundred for the dyno-mite. What say you?"

"Including the blasting caps?" Carson asked.

"Including the blasting caps," Lenny said with a condescending smile. "I'm gonna throw those in for free."

"Yeah, whatever," Carson said. "Let's do it."

. . .

It felt like a first date. Even after all this time.

When Christine answered Stone's knock on her door at the Charlton, she emerged looking extremely attractive but also slightly reserved. Stone sensed that they both wanted to grab each other in a fervent embrace, but the timing was wrong, and they both knew it. Best to start with a buffer of small talk and wait for the encounter to find its natural course.

"How are you feeling?" she asked as they started down the hall.

"Pretty good," he said.

"No pain?"

"No pain," he confirmed.

"Have you finished the antibiotics?" she asked as they boarded the elevator to the lobby.

"Just took the last one this morning."

"Good."

They lapsed into silence for the rest of the ride down. It seemed the proper thing to do.

"The food here is pretty decent," she said when they entered the lobby. "Unless you want to go someplace else."

"No, it'll do fine," he answered. This whole thing was complex enough without adding yet another venue to it.

Once seated in a booth toward the back, they ordered a bottle of Pinot Grigio before looking at the menu. Their waiter, an older

Asian gentleman, sported a black bow tie perfectly horizontal with respect to his collar. Stone had never been able to achieve anything close.

Their conversation remained at the superficial level when the wine came, and they perused the menu. Frank Sinatra played softly in the background, a Gil Evans arrangement. Cop or not, Stone still had an ear for that kind of thing. He steered the discourse in her direction.

"Are you back at work?" he asked.

"Yeah, back at work. Same old thing."

"Are you taking a cab?"

"No, I brought my car over here. They have a lot right next door," she said.

"Is there anything you need from the house?"

"No, I'm fine. Thank you."

And so it went. The waiter returned and took their orders. He had the sautéed prawns and she the chicken penne. They returned to their wine as he departed. She looked dazzling in a burgundy wrap dress with a cascade of pearls looped around her neck. He'd had the good sense to change into a tan suede blazer and white dress shirt. He could only hope that by the end of the evening, they would feel as good as they looked.

The time had come to shift up a gear. There was no way they could sustain this level of superfluidity for much longer.

"So you're the one that called this meeting," he said with a soft smile.

She stared down into her wine glass as if it might be bottomless. "Yes, I am."

She looked up with a shiny film forming over her eyes. "We have a lot to lose, James. You know that, don't you?"

"Yes, I do," he admitted with a slight lump in his throat. "More than a lot," he added. "More like everything, at least for me."

"For me, too. We need to see this thing through. We need to get to the other side, where we can be ourselves again."

He reached out and put his hand over hers. It felt slightly cool in his palm. "You're right, and we'll just have to take it step by step. I think I know where to start. I'm willing to make a promise."

A hint of doubt settled over her, as he knew it probably would. "What kind of promise?"

"I will promise that the instant we catch this guy, my cop career ends. Forever." He took a sip of wine. "I'd like to do it sooner, but I've gotten myself in too deep to get out on a dime. Which is entirely my fault, and for that I'm deeply sorry. I've put you through a lot. All I can do is ask your forgiveness and spend the rest of my life making it up to you."

Outside of the promise part, he hadn't rehearsed any of what he'd just said. It bypassed the usual filters of reason, discretion and consideration, and simply tumbled on out.

She left his gaze, looked down at her hands on the table and sighed. "I don't know what to say to that. It's a lot. I'm going to have to think it through."

"Of course you are. Like I said, it's just a start. I know that. Maybe we should give it a break for now."

"Good idea," she said and picked up her empty wine glass. "I think I could use a little more if you please."

"Most certainly," he said as he reached for the bottle.

Dinner came, and as they ate their dialogue rotated into the past, into times when she was a woman doctor in a man's world of medicine, when he was an exiled LA cop from Hollywood Vice, when they fell in love during uncertain and perilous times on the streets of Bakersfield, of all places.

When dinner was done, and the bottle empty, she asked him how his back was doing, did he still have the bandages and stitches?

He said yes, he did; and she said it was time to go up to her room and take care of all that.

And possibly, a little more.

32.

SAN FRANCISCO

Stone tried to keep a lid on himself. The evening with Christine had most certainly exceeded his expectations – especially the ending. Right now, it felt like a contract where negotiations were complete and all that was needed was a final signature. At least, that's how it appeared from his perspective. But was his aligned with hers?

The phone on his desk rang and ended his guesswork. "Detective Stone?"

"Speaking."

"Patrolman Jennings. We're just wrapping up an incident over on Ashbury. Thought you might want to be in the loop."

"Depends. What happened?"

"The Hells Angels rent a house over here. You know about that?"

"I've heard about it."

"They try to keep a low profile and fit in, but now and then we'll get a call that they're having a party that spills out onto the street. We got a call from one of the neighbors that they were raising hell yesterday evening and threatened him when he complained."

"Oh yeah? What was going on?"

"That's the part I thought you might want in on. It seems they were sloppy drunk and setting off blasting caps in their driveway."

"You mean blasting caps as in dynamite?" Officer Jennings now had Stone's undiluted attention.

"That's right. When the neighbor guy tells them to cut it out, one of 'em comes back all shitfaced with a couple of sticks of dynamite and threatens to blow up his house if he turns them in."

"I see. Did you follow up with the Angels?"

"We talked with a couple of them this morning. They looked really hung over and said they didn't remember much about what went down. I don't think they want any trouble. They said it wouldn't happen again and offered to apologize to the neighbor. Anyway, I thought you'd want to know about it because of the dynamite."

"I do. How about you drop off your report once you get it written up?"

"No problem."

"Thanks for the tip. Talk to you later."

Stone hung up and quickly parsed what Jennings had told him and what he should do about it. For starters, he'd found no known connection between the Hells Angels and the blast in the park. It wasn't illegal to own dynamite so he couldn't brace them on that account. Under the circumstances, it would be very tough to get a search warrant and see what they were holding. On the other hand, here was a semi-criminal organization very nearby and possessing the very same explosive that had nearly taken him out.

In the end, he decided it warranted his attention but not immediately, because there was no immediate action to take. Probably better to spend time figuring out how to leverage the sketch of the bomber, which was much closer to the heart of the matter.

. . .

Everyone attended. They gathered in the kitchen, around the table and along the walls, the underground faithful come to hear the revolutionary gospel as preached by the most legitimate of its heirs, a black man. All white babies are pigs, it had been said, and most knew it in their hearts to be true. Redemption would come in the form of black rage and purify them with its searing heat. And so it was that they clustered around the rhetorical fire.

"Like each of you," Nyanga told them, "I'm a fugitive. Some would say a fugitive from the law, but I would say a fugitive from the fascist tyranny of the white pigs. And in this, I would be correct."

Nyanga radiated a singularity of purpose that held them transfixed. His eyes had a preternatural gleam to them that played off against his skin of soft brown and a coal black beard trimmed almost to a stubble. Two other black men flanked him, both solid in build and stoic in nature with lips creased into permanent scowls.

"I could tell you a sad story. I could tell you the story of a child who was brutally beaten by this father. And I could go on to tell you how this father was in turn beaten by his father and so on and so on. But then I could go on to tell you what set this chain in motion, how the first of these men was brutally beaten by his white owner. And how this white pig's cruelty was passed on down and visited upon the innocent. Over and over."

Carson stood along the wall at the back and surveyed the audience. They stared at Nyanga in a mixture of anguish, admiration and guilt. Carson himself sensed something else in this man, a deep well of violent intent.

"I am not a bad man now, nor have I ever been," Nyanga continued. "I tried in vain to make a decent life. I worked as a painter and a mechanic and was always tossed aside when I was no longer convenient. And my reward? They put me in Vacaville; but you know what? It gave me time to read, time to think. It washed away all my guilt, all my failure. I came to realize that I was made to fail. I'm a product. A product of the white man's persecution not only of the black man, but of all the black man stands for. They would like to erase us, and the first step is to imprison us and, as you all know, that step is well underway. The prisons bulge with black brothers unjustly jailed for the crime of simply being black. And mark my words, step two is coming, where the gas chambers and electric chairs run day and night to take care of the problem."

Ah yes, thought Carson. The slow curve has ended, and the fast pitch is coming. Good.

"And so just what are we supposed to do?" Nyanga asked the rapt assemblage. "Line up like little sheep and get mowed down?" He leapt to his feet. "Wrong! We're supposed to fight! And keep on fighting till we get the justice we deserve! The revolution is here. It's time to take it to the streets and visit hell upon the pigs until they cower before us. It's time to bring out the guns and the knives and the bombs. Not next month, not next year. Now!"

Having reached a high note with his call to action, Nyanga sat back down and closed his eyes. The audience looked on in stunned silence.

This wasn't like Dohrn exhorting the masses at the Council of War in Michigan. In the end, that scenario turned out to be hollow histrionics. This was for real. And they knew it.

. . .

When the kitchen cleared, after a long string of individual audiences with the black charismatic and his cohort, Nyanga approached Carson.

"They tell me you're the bomb guy, and I hear you're pretty good. That right?"

Carson gave a noncommittal shrug. "Could be."

Nyanga smiled. "I was watching you. You're not like them. I can tell."

"How?" Carson asked.

"It took a while before you bought into what I was saying. My guess is you've heard a lot of revolutionary bullshit slung around here. Am I right?"

"You're right."

"So now I've met 'em, now I know. Never gonna happen with these people. They're a bunch of pussies. All talk, no walk."

"Seems so."

"Way I hear it, you took out the pig in the station. And you damn near took out the pig in the park. Seems like you're the only one around here walkin' the walk. I think maybe it's time you hooked up with some people who take this shit seriously. Dead seriously." He reached in his pocket and handed Carson a slip of paper with a phone number. "You think about it, brother. You let me know."

Before Carson could respond, Nyanga pivoted and strode out of the room, with his two companions right behind.

. . .

Carson pondered Nyanga's offer while he prowled the clothing bins in the Goodwill store on Fillmore. Nyanga was an odd name, most likely an alias, but the man himself had a solid ring of authenticity. His assessment of the Weather Underground aligned quite nicely with Carson's. It had become a political snail retreating into a shell where it would cower and eventually starve.

He pawed through a bin full of used men's shirts and decided that his next move should wait until he completed his current one. Nyanga would have to wait, but not for long.

And there it was, a forest green uniform shirt done in the classic industrial style. Better yet, it had a name patch sewn above the right breast pocket that read "Genco," whatever the hell that was.

He held the shirt draped over his forearm as he waited in line for the cashier. It was the last item on his list. He already had a leather tool belt, and he'd stolen a short stepladder from the maintenance closet at the apartment. All that remained was a final test of the bomb circuitry before arming it when he reached his destination tomorrow afternoon.

A portable radio sat perched on a small shelf behind the cashier and played a recent tune by the Rolling Stones.

"*It's just a shot away*," said Mick Jagger.

33.

SAN FRANCISCO
MARCH 4, 1971

Carson would have preferred a cloudy day or, better yet, a rainy day. Either would have made him less conspicuous. But the morning sun blazed unhindered out of a clear blue sky as he pulled the short stepladder out of the trunk, along with a large gym bag. He glanced quickly up and down 43rd Avenue and saw no one out. Good. He reached in the trunk one last time, pulled out the leather tool belt and buckled it over his jeans. It gave him an air of authenticity when combined with the industrial work shirt he wore. He'd become an electrician, sent to service a faulty porchlight fixture at the residence of one James Stone. It was a solid cover, and might even hold if Stone himself showed up, which was highly unlikely. A little research had revealed that the pig didn't own the place, so the landlord would be handling all the maintenance issues.

The house itself stood above a single-car garage, in much the same style as all the other houses on the block, each with a bay window pushing out toward the street. Off to one side, a flight of cement stairs rose to a recessed porch area with a brief threshold in front of the door. Carson had ventured here one time before, late at night, and discovered that the porch's ceiling included a recessed area with a built-in ledge that must have served some structural purpose. It was invisible from the street if you were entering, which made it ideal for concealing something, like a bomb.

Carson quickly carried the stepladder and gym bag up the stairs into the shade of the porch. He unzipped the bag, which contained a cardboard container shaped in a long rectangle that held the pipe with the explosives surrounded by nails, along with the battery and triggering mechanism. In all, it represented his most sophisticated work to date and made him think of Miguel, his instructor in Cuba, who would most certainly applaud his effort.

The trigger consisted of two parts wired in series to each other. The first was a clock-driven timer which served to activate the second, a proximity sensor which would set off the bomb when it detected motion anywhere on the porch. The timer portion solved two problems. First, you had to have a way to get off the porch without activating the sensor once you'd armed it. Second, you only wanted the device active during a certain time window to minimize the chance – however small – that someone other than Stone would set it off. Carson knew that the pig normally arrived home fairly close to five in the evening, so he set the timer for four o'clock. From that time on, the cop would be shredded to dog meat when he reached the porch.

Carson opened one end of the container to expose a rocker switch and a red pilot light. He pressed the switch, and the light came to life, indicating that he now had a live bomb. He closed the container, got up and checked the street in both directions. All quiet. He gingerly took the container out of the bag, climbed the stepladder and placed it on the ledge.

His morning dose of Methedrine peaked as he drove away and back to the Pine Street apartment. He looked at his watch. 10:30 a.m.

He could hardly wait.

. . .

"Believe me, I don't want to rain on your parade," Detective Linehan said as he gazed at the sketch of the bomber. "But this guy looks like about a zillion street freaks you'd find between here and downtown."

Stone raised his elbows off his desk and leaned back in his chair. "I know. But when the time comes, it might be what seals the deal, so I see it as one step ahead."

"Yeah, could be," Linehan said. "Anyway, what's up with this Hells Angels dynamite business?"

"It's a long shot, for sure," Stone said. "I've got nothing linking it to the bomber, except a hunch."

"That's great, but a hunch isn't going to get you a warrant."

"I know," Stone said. "It looks like we're back to a waiting game."

"For now," Linehan said with a trace of optimism. "We're close. One more break is all we need. You'll get 'em. Hang in there."

"That's my plan," Stone said as Linehan got up and took off.

Before Stone could delve into the precise nature of this plan, the phone rang. Christine.

"Hi. I think it's time to get back together," she announced with no preamble. "I'm going to take the afternoon off and go down and check out. What do you think?"

"I think that'd be just fine." He felt elated, but not surprised after the passion of their recent encounter. "Can I expect you for dinner?"

"Yes, I believe you can." Even over the phone line, he could hear the twinkle in her voice.

"Anything you'd like in particular?" he inquired.

"Shrimp linguini sounds good. That okay with you?" she asked.

"That'll work just fine," he said.

"Okay, see you then."

When he hung up, he looked out the window just as a dark-eyed junco landed on the window ledge. It instantly became his favorite bird.

. . .

"All assets in place," the little speaker in the rear of the van told Special Agent Peter Trobe. He certainly hoped so. They'd been forced to throw this operation together on the fly, which presented ample opportunities for failure. It all started on the other side of the country in Chicago, where agents were keeping tabs on an attorney with known ties to the Weather Underground. He'd walked into a Western Union office, identified himself as Herman Schaefer, and sent a money order for $650 to one Duane Lee Compton in San Francisco. They knew for a fact that the attorney was not named Schaefer and suspected that the transfer was a ruse to send money to a radical sympathizer in the Bay Area.

The Chicago office contacted the San Francisco office, and the ball picked up speed as a plan was quickly sketched out. When "Herman Schaefer" showed up at the downtown Western Union office, they would put a tail on him that might eventually point to one of the hardcore Underground suspects holed up somewhere in the city.

Some of the field agents questioned the wisdom of putting together a sizable operation to latch on to someone who might or might not be an actual sympathizer. But Trobe overruled them. He had a hunch that this incident was the real deal and was willing to gamble on it. To hedge his bet, he outlined his plan to Aaron Andrews, the Special Agent in Charge of the San Francisco office, who was just on his way out the door for eighteen holes of golf at the Olympic Club. Andrews nodded impatiently as Trobe made his case, and said yeah, yeah, do whatever.

With this hierarchical insurance policy stuffed in his pocket, Trobe immediately swung into action. Several agents took up positions inside the Western Union office, with more out on the sidewalk, and others parked in nearby pursuit vehicles. They were locked and loaded. All they needed was a target, the so-called Duane Lee Compton, to show up and collect the cash from the $650 money order.

But that was hours ago, and Trobe felt a chill tide of anxiety eroding his optimism. He couldn't keep this many agents tied up indefinitely in the speculative pursuit of someone who might not have any useful connection to the Underground people. At some point, he'd have to pull the plug and suffer the consequences of what would be deemed a fool's errand.

"This is four. We have a hit. He's at the counter right now, picking up the money."

Trobe turned to Storlin, the other agent in the van with him, and gave a big thumbs up. Payday.

"This is three. I have him on camera." Agent Three was filming the encounter from a back room. A tall man with bushy blonde hair filled the lens. "Hey, this guy sure looks a lot like Jeff Jones."

Trobe soared. Jeff Jones was one of the big three at the center of the Weatherman organization, along with Ayers and Dohrn. They'd been fishing for a minnow and caught a whale. He grabbed the mic. "All units stand by. I need a positive ID on the target."

Agent five checked in from the street out front. "Five here. Just looked in. It's gotta be Jones."

"Six here. I concur."

Strobe was just about to order an arrest when Storlin tapped him on the shoulder. "Hey boss, I'm afraid we've got a problem here."

"What do you mean we've got a problem?" Trobe shot back. "We've got a major bust here. We gotta go right now."

"There's a protocol issue," Storlin said. "If we get someone in the top ten, we have to have the Special Agent in Charge to make an arrest."

Strobe sank. Storlin was right. Jones was on the FBI's current Ten Most Wanted list, which required the presence of his boss to make an arrest. But Special Agent in Charge Aaron Andrews was out somewhere on the verdant links of the Olympic Club. By the time they contacted the club and sent someone out to fetch him, their target could be halfway to Mars. Strobe pressed his forehead against clenched fists. There was no worse crime within the organization than usurping the authority of your superiors. No matter what he did, he was looking at a major catastrophe. He could blow the bust of the decade, or he could violate the most sacred of official directives.

"Six here. He's leaving the building. He's heading toward a Volvo sedan that just pulled up."

Trobe grabbed the mic. "All units: Let him go and initiate pursuit." That said, he leaped out of the van and looked up to the far end of the block, where Western Union was located. Sure enough, a tall blond male was opening the door to a blue Volvo and climbing in. "Shit!" He jumped back into the van, where Storlin was already in the driver's seat. "Stay behind unit two," he instructed, referring to a nondescript black sedan that had already pulled out up ahead. "We're way too obvious in this rig." He got back on the radio. "Units three and four, stand by until we get a lock on them."

The Volvo made a right onto Mason Street and headed north. "Okay, we're on Mason," he informed all the pursuit vehicles. Unit three, track parallel with us on Powell. Unit four, take Stockton." Up ahead, Trobe could see unit two's black sedan trailing a couple of cars behind the Volvo as they approached California Street. He still hoped for a positive outcome. Maybe Jones would lead them right into the lair of the radical beast and buy them some time to get his boss to the scene.

Then it happened. Just as the light went to yellow, the Volvo made a sudden left turn onto California. Unit two's black sedan found itself stuck at a red light with no way around. "Shit!" Trobe yelled. "Three and four, we just lost him on California going west toward Mason. Take up pursuit!"

They did just that and came up empty. No Volvo, no Jones. Even worse, one of the pursuit vehicles got a glimpse of the Volvo before they lost it for good in traffic. A woman was driving. Most likely it was Bernadette Dohrn, divine empress of the radical underground and a companion of Jones on the Top Ten list.

Trobe sighed. "We're screwed. Take us back to the office. It's going to be a long night."

He anticipated a massive epidemic of finger pointing from the top down and he was right. The processed photos from Western Union strongly indicated that it was indeed Jones, and fingerprints lifted off the counter confirmed it. They'd gone fishing for minnows, landed a whale, and wound up with absolutely nothing. Jones – and possibly Dohrn – had floated off into a vast sea of urban anonymity.

. . .

Christine got lucky and bagged a parking place right in front their house on 43rd Avenue. It was about an hour until quitting time so there were still a few vacant slots. She wheeled her Chevy Vega up to the curb and left enough space for Stone to pull into the driveway when he got home. She'd bought the car new a few months back and Stone teased her about how far she had fallen. When they'd met, she was driving a 1954 Buick Roadmaster convertible, a true classic the minute it rolled off the assembly line. But for traffic-choked San Francisco, the scaled-down Vega was an expedient choice.

She climbed out, opened the hatchback, and pulled out two suitcases. Her timing would give her a chance to shower and freshen up before James arrived. She regarded this as a special occasion, and she was sure he did too, even if he didn't let on right away. To properly christen their reunion, she'd bought a bottle of Domaine des Justices, a wine of impeccable provenance.

She'd just put one foot onto the sidewalk when she spied Kitty coming her way with his hyper inflated sense of entitlement. She had to smile when the cat cut her off without even acknowledging her. They were back to a familiar and comforting domestic rhythm.

Kitty proceeded to bound up the steps and onto the porch, and the world ended.

34.

SAN FRANCISCO

Stone first noticed the column of smoke while driving west on Lincoln Way along the southern edge of the park. He'd given in to a surge of romantic anticipation and wanted to beat the traffic home to see Christine. This particular route avoided all the usual traffic lights and gave him a straight shot down to 43rd.

He periodically glanced up at the smoke, which formed into a dirty, ragged spire as it rose into a sky of clear blue. It looked like it might be somewhere near his neighborhood, but it was difficult to judge at this distance. Its volume suggested that it wasn't a major conflagration but definitely cause for concern. Ever since the earthquake-driven fire of 1906, the city took fires of any size quite seriously. As if to emphasize this, he had to pull over to let two fire trucks speed past with sirens bellowing.

He came closer now, close enough to confirm that the smoke was originating from somewhere near his house. He hoped it wasn't close enough to distract from their homecoming and downshifted to turn left onto 43rd, which gave him an unobstructed view up the few blocks to where he lived. A calamitous scene played out up ahead, a cluster of flashing emergency lights, a tangle of fire hoses, a crowd of responders of every sort. Firemen, police, paramedics.

All centered on a single dwelling. His house.

Christine. His heart danced wildly. Where was she? Was she there? Was she okay? He drove crazily up 43rd, to where a traffic cop was directing cars around the scene. He screeched to a halt at a haphazard angle and leaped out. The cop gave him a dirty look, but let it go when he ripped out his badge and shouted "Police!"

He sprinted down the sidewalk, badge still out to deflect any interference. Christine's Vega came into view, with a smashed passenger window. And there she was, just beyond, lying on a gurney, her eyes shut, her head heavily bandaged, her mouth and nose covered by an oxygen mask. A paramedic held it in place while a second opened the door of a nearby ambulance.

"Oh my God, Christine!" he exclaimed when he reached her. He looked at the paramedic in desperation, a look the guy had seen many times before. "Her pulse is fine, her breathing is normal. Her blood pressure's a little low, but nothing serious. Probably just a concussion, but we'll have to wait for the doc on that. You family?" he asked.

"Yeah, I'm family," Stone said weakly.

"You want to ride with us?"

"Yeah, yeah," Stone said impatiently. "What happened here?"

"The neighbors say it was an explosion. We found her propped against the side of the car over there, underneath the busted window. She has some lacerations on the back of her head, so it's a good bet that she hit the window and blew it out – which is a lot better than hitting the door or the fender."

"Okay, let's go," the second paramedic said from over by the open doors.

Stone had a moment to survey the devastation while they loaded her in. The roof above the porch was completely gone and walls on either side were shattered. From there, the damage extended back into the interior, where the fire still smoked and hissed. The property damage was probably horrific, but right now he could care less. He'd give it all up in an instant to ensure that she was okay.

He took a quick look at the Vega as he climbed into the ambulance. A handful of random indentations pocked the doors and fenders facing the house. Shrapnel. He was sure of it. Thank God it hadn't hit her. As they pulled away, he noticed her suitcases on the sidewalk. One had burst open, and clothing items spilled over its sides. It felt like a gross invasion of privacy, a personal disembowelment of some kind.

. . .

She regained consciousness about halfway to the ER, the same one where she worked five days a week. Her mouth opened and her head rotated slightly. The paramedic removed the oxygen mask just as her eyes opened briefly then shut again. Stone sighed in relief and held her hand firmly but gently.

"Oh my God," she said softly. "What happened?"

"There was an explosion," he told her. "You were thrown against the side of your car and took a hit on the head. But you're going to be okay."

"Oh," she said weakly with eyes still closed. "Okay."

There was an explosion, he repeated to himself.

A bomb. And it was supposed to kill me, but instead it almost killed you.

All because I was too stupid to listen to you. I should have never gone back to being a cop.

An avalanche of guilt crashed over him, a dirty, muddy wave full of agonizing fault and recrimination. *I'm a fool. I don't deserve you. I'll make it up to you. I don't know how, but I'll make it up to you. Please let me try. Please.*

"What about Kitty?" she murmured.

"The cat?"

"It went up on the porch. That's all I remember. What happened?" she asked.

"I don't know," Stone said. But he had a pretty good idea. The cat had somehow triggered the blast. The bomber hadn't counted on the cat.

. . .

Stone remembered the ER doctor from some of the social gatherings of the ER team over barbequed hotdogs or holiday ham. He liked them. It was one group that came in regular contact with the police and empathized with their position out on the grim edge of human discourse. This particular doc was a mid-life guy who had managed to maintain a positive attitude in a workplace saturated with distress and death.

"I do have to say, it's really strange to have one of our own come in through those doors," the doc told Stone. "The good news is it looks like a happy ending. The X-rays don't show any fractures to her skull or anywhere else. She did have a few lacerations on the back of her scalp, and we stitched those up. Shouldn't be a cosmetic problem. Her hair will cover it all up. Anyway, we're going to keep her here under observation for a day or two, then she's yours. They just took her up to a room on the third floor."

"Thanks, doc," Stone said and headed for the elevator.

Christine smiled softly when he entered the room, and it flooded Stone with relief. It meant she didn't hate him, even though he was sure he faced some kind of reckoning in the near future.

"Hey babe." He bent over the bed and kissed her softly. "How do you feel?"

"Pretty good," she said as he sat and took her hand. "I'm ready to go home. But I guess that might be a little difficult right now, huh?"

"A little difficult," he echoed with a nod. He didn't elaborate because he didn't know himself. But the smoke billowing through the roof did not bode well for the interior. "Maybe it's back to the Charlton for a while. Only this time with a king instead of a queen."

"James?" she said.

"Yes?"

"I know what you're thinking."

"You do?"

"I do. And the answer is, I don't hate you."

It was all he could do to keep the tears at bay.

"I just have one thing to say," she went on. "And I'm only going to say it once."

"What's that?"

A mischievous smile came over her. "Told you so."

· · ·

Stone sat in his car in the hospital parking lot. The bombing and Christine's injuries had left him in a highly agitated state, and he needed some time by himself. Off to the west, the evening sky melded from gold to copper over the ocean, but its beauty failed to touch him.

Whether by error or intent, the bomber had nearly killed her, and she was all he had. He was certain the assailant knew what happened and cared less. Just a little collateral damage, nothing to it. It reminded him of documentary footage showing predacious animals eating their prey before the victims even expired. They went about it in a casual and methodical manner, utterly devoid of compassion. If there was any justice to be had, it originated from higher up the food chain, where the hunters themselves would be taken down and devoured with the same callous expediency. A closed loop of perpetual savagery.

For the moment, this bestial world held sway over his soul, or what remained of it. He would stalk the bomber, corner him and kill him. Forget about process, procedure and compliance with the law of the land. Forget about the captive finally cuffed and surrendered to a system riddled with caprice. Forget about all the maneuvering and machinations that might set him free. Close the loop. Take him down and out. Ignore his squirming and pleading. Visit all the violence upon him that he had visited upon others. Bring the balance beam back to where it belonged with six rounds ripping into his torso.

Stone watched the light slowly fade while he sat immersed in a Stygian world of righteous anger. Some ancient, unspoken code granted him license to seek the most immediate and devastating compensation possible. It felt good. It gave him purpose and direction. It dissolved all fear and anxiety. He became immortal, unstoppable, the sole instrument of God upon the face of the earth. The time had come to strike out with unshakable purpose and resolve.

But then again, maybe not. He paused to consider the consequences of following a path of vengeance as opposed to legal redress. How big a price was he willing to pay? Was he willing to forsake his lifelong conviction that the rule of law transcended all others? Was he willing to serve prison time? Was he willing to essentially leave Christine a de facto widow? What justice was there in that? The bomber might be dead, but he would leer at Stone from beyond the grave and revel in his misfortune. No, the best option was to track him down and keep the faith that justice would prevail, that he would suffer countless days on death row waiting for the inevitable.

The rage within him begin to gradually subside, along with waning light over the ocean. But like that light, it didn't really disappear. It simply receded over the horizon and waited for a new day.

35.

SAN FRANCISCO

"We're not putting any crime scene tape up," Sgt. Dillon, the bomb guy, explained to Stone. "The fire department's going to announce that it was a gas explosion. That'll keep you out of the papers."

"Appreciate it," Stone said. He'd insisted on spending the night with Christine at the hospital and dozed fitfully in a bedside chair. It left him anything but rested. They stood a few steps below the ruined porch, with the smell of burnt wood and roofing still fresh in the morning air.

"Your bad guy keeps getting better at what he does," Dillon said. "This time, the trigger was probably a combination of a clock and some kind of sensor device."

"Yeah, the cat," Stone remarked.

"The cat?"

"We had a stray cat that came up on the porch all the time for handouts," Stone explained. "Christine saw it go up there right before the bomb went off. It must have activated the sensor somehow."

"How's she doing?" Dillon asked. "We'd like to talk to her."

"She's good," Stone said. "Already wants to go back to work, but they're going to keep her down for another day or two."

"Whenever she's ready." Dillon pointed up to the clear sky where the porch roof had once been. "He positioned the device so the roof over the porch focused the blast mostly downward." He pointed to the pitted surface of the porch's cement floor where the shrapnel had struck. "If you'd been standing here, you would have been shredded into a pile of hamburger."

Stone nodded. Dillon didn't need to add that the same thing would've been true if it was Christine standing there. He had to struggle to compose himself.

"Thanks for the update," he told Dillon as they descended the steps. "Let me know what you find when you look at all the scraps."

"Will do. See you later."

Stone sat in the sun on the steps and watched Dillon drive off. The thought of Christine in jeopardy had once again triggered a subterranean urge to cast off all legal constraint in his hunt for the bomber. He sighed, tamped it down and headed back to the station.

. . .

Special Agent Trobe spread the city street map out on the trunk of the government-issue sedan. He sensed progress but had no way to confirm it. Earlier this morning, they finally got the break he'd been praying for. They found the blue Volvo abandoned in back of a building not far from where they'd lost the trail yesterday near California and Mason. He knew that during the pursuit, the suspects had no way to call for help from their radical subjects, so they had to ditch the car to seek shelter. He also doubted that they would risk traveling very far on foot, not with a veritable army of federal agents pursuing them. All of which led him to conclude that they were within relatively short walking distance of a hideout of some kind, maybe a sympathizer's place or better yet, a safe house full of faithful followers.

He ran this assumption by his boss, Andrews, who okayed a massive operation to canvas fifteen city blocks, house by house, apartment by apartment. Once again, the application of brute force looked like the best option. In a gesture of confidence, Andrews arranged to be available at a moment's notice to swoop down and make an arrest. Nobody wanted a repeat of yesterday's bureaucratic fiasco.

Trobe examined the map, where he had checked off one block after another as they failed to produce any useful information. At this point, there were only a couple of blocks left, but Trobe sensed they were approaching a payoff. A neighbor, a janitor, a store clerk, a plumber, a delivery boy. Someone would come through.

· · ·

Stone banged the door of the Hells Angels house on Ashbury Street, using the hand that held his pistol, a Colt .38 Special. When it started to open, he put the weapon behind his back and brought his other hand forward holding his ID and badge. A generic biker appeared sporting a ponytail, goatee and a small gold earring. Stone's aggressive knocking had obviously irritated him. "So what the fuck?" he demanded.

"Police," Stone announced as he held up his badge. "Get out of my way."

"Oh yeah? You got a warrant?" the biker asked with a wily grin. Like most Angels, he had a basic grasp of street-level legalities.

"A warrant? Right here." Stone swung the pistol around and into the biker's face. The Angel's mouth dropped, and his arms started up in capitulation. "Hey man…" he began.

Stone's right foot came up and kicked him in the gut, sending him down and sprawling backwards into the house with Stone right on his heels. Two other bikers looked on but were too shocked to react. Nobody did this to the Angels, not on their own turf. Stone caught a flicker of motion on the nearby stairs. Yet another Angel came into view, this one toting a sawed-off shotgun. Before he could bring it up to aim, Stone shot him in the upper right thigh in a thunderous report of noise and smoke. The shotgun flew loose, bounced on the staircase and went off with a blast that peppered the wall by the fireplace. The Angel sank down onto the steps and doubled up in pain.

"Alright, who's next?" Stone yelled at the remaining three.

None spoke and all brought their arms up in surrender.

"Which one of you is holding the dynamite?" Stone demanded.

In a dead giveaway, two of the bikers turned their head toward a third, whose eyes filled with dread. "Hey man, I thought it was okay to have it. Nobody told me…"

"How much have you got left?"

"I dunno. Maybe twenty sticks, something like that."

"Who you been selling it to?"

"Just one guy, man. That's all. Just one guy," the biker said by way of excuse.

Stone brought the police sketch of the bomber out of his jacket pocket and held it out. "Take it," he ordered.

The bomber grasped the paper and stared at the face in the sketch.

"That the guy?"

"Yeah, looks pretty much like him."

"What's his name?"

"Never said."

Stone aimed the pistol directly at the center of the biker's face. "You're gonna have to do better than that." He cocked the trigger.

"I dunno. I really don't."

"So what *do* you know?" Stone asked.

"I know where he lives, or at least real close."

"And how do you know that?"

"I gave him a ride home, man. He needed a ride."

"Where to?"

"It's over on Pine, between Jones and Taylor. An apartment beside an alley in the middle of the block. That's where I let him off, anyway."

"What's your name?"

"Lenny."

"Okay Lenny, here's what you and your buddies are going to do." He motioned toward their wounded companion on the stairs, whose face was contorted in pain. "You're going to take your pal to the ER and explain you had a little shooting accident over here. And that you've learned your lesson and it's never going to happen again. Got it?"

"Got it."

Stone lowered the pistol and headed toward the door. "Stay put. I'll be right back."

They didn't think he would, but they didn't want to find out the hard way. They stayed put.

. . .

His teeth woke him up. A couple in the back had fissures approaching the nerve, and they were letting him know about it.

Carson rose stiffly from the foam block in the bedroom and squinted out the window into the late morning on Pine Street. The apartment building across the street was still in shadow with its vertical columns of bay windows and fire escapes forming a stack of Zs in the center. The last time he looked out was maybe twelve hours ago, around midnight. He was still tired. With good reason. He'd once again run out of speed and was running a steep bodily deficit.

A single piece of paper caught his attention, a handwritten note on the pillow next to his. He immediately recognized Alice's careful schoolgirl script.

"Couldn't wake you up. Had to go. We got a call. The pigs are onto us. See you later."

Shit. Carson dimly remembered someone trying to rouse him, but the details escaped him. It no longer mattered. A wave of adrenaline filled in for the absent amphetamines. When did they get the call? Where did they go? Were the pigs onto this place? Was there going to be a bust? He had to assume there would be. He had to get out right now.

He grabbed a small knapsack and hustled down the hallway to the closet where he'd stashed his bomb-making gear in a large cardboard box. He'd needed to do a quick sort and take what he could easily carry and get the hell out of here. Everything else could wait. He dumped the box's contents out on the floor and started to pick and choose.

. . .

Stone spotted the apartment immediately when he rounded the sidewalk onto Pine Street from Jones. It sat on the opposite side of the street and was the only one with an alley next to it. It appeared well maintained, with a pair of large flowering bushes with pink petals flanking the steps up to the first floor. He felt for his pistol in its shoulder holster under his jacket and waited at the intersection for the light to change so he could get to the right side of the street.

"Well look who's here."

Stone whirled around. Special Agent Peter Trobe. Two of his associates trailed slightly behind him, with telltale aviator sunglasses and close-cropped hair.

"And just what are your intentions, detective?" he asked Stone.

"Want to guess?" Stone asked.

"I'd say you've probably tracked your bomber down to a location right up the street. Small world, isn't it?"

"You got a problem with that?" Stone challenged.

"As a matter of fact, I do. This time, your bomber's only the sideshow. There's a very high probability that we've just cornered the entire leadership of the Weather Underground in that very same apartment building. And that makes it our show, not yours."

Stone knew they had him. He'd gone rogue in his pursuit of the bomber, which meant the SFPD would no longer back him in a showdown. "So what are you going to do?" he asked Trobe.

"We're gonna go in there in force and take down everyone we find. Which means you might get lucky. If the bomber's in there he's going down."

"I'm the only one that can identify him," Stone countered.

"No problem. All you need to do is wait for the dust to settle. Then you can pick your guy out of the crowd. Be our guest."

Stone resented Trobe's condescending tone, but maybe it was all for the best. He'd fully intended to shoot the bomber point blank and sort out the legalities of it later. After what he and Christine had been through, no one would blame him, at least none of the cops. But the rest of the world might not be so forgiving. "Alright," he conceded. "When's this going down?"

Trobe checked his watch. "In about five minutes."

. . .

Carson shouldered the knapsack and looked at the tools and materials he'd left on the floor. No room, no time. He considered leaving out the front but deemed it too risky. He had no idea how long it had been since they got the warning call. For all he knew, the pigs were assembling a small army out there. He trotted on down the stairs, hustled through the kitchen, and out the back door. The space in the rear dwelled in perpetual shade from the surrounding buildings and stretched behind three other apartments. Two token fences marked the property boundaries, but Carson found them easy to negotiate.

He'd never been this far and stopped to contemplate the rear of the furthest building. The street-level unit had a door and a small landing with steps down to the ground, but beneath it was a second door that looked more promising. At the bottom of some recessed steps, it contained a glass window protected by some heavy-gauge chicken wire. He descended and peeked into a utility room with a washer and dryer. Good. He pulled a set of wire cutters out of his knapsack and methodically cut a hole in the corner nearest the knob. After stowing the wire cutters, he fished out a jeweler's hammer and some tape, which he applied to the exposed window. A single tap with the hammer broke the taped glass. He pulled the glass out intact, reached in, felt the deadbolt and unlocked the door.

A careful trip up the basement stairs brought him to a small alcove just inside the front entrance. He walked on through it and out onto the porch landing, where he squinted into the noontime brilliance. Two men sprinted past on the sidewalk, both wearing sidearms and T-shirts stenciled with "FBI" in big yellow caps. He froze in place as they continued on down the block toward the safe house. Several black sedans skidded to a halt in front of the place and agents seemed to converge from every direction.

It took him only a moment to realize he'd caught an extremely lucky break. The pigs' entire focus was on the raid itself. He could leave the scene with impunity. The raid rendered him invisible. He went down the steps and headed west on Pine Street where people looked right past him to all the commotion in the middle of the block.

. . .

Stone knew the operation was botched when he saw Trobe come out the front with his face in the middle of a nosedive.

"So?" Stone asked. He resisted the urge to throw a counterpunch. His career was already in flames, and it would just add more combustible material.

"Gone," Trobe said. "Someone got the word to them. Looks like they left in a hurry. Damn!"

"Mind if I take a look around?" Stone asked.

"Sure. Why not? You know the rules. It looks like your boy left some toys."

Once Stone was inside, he concluded that Trobe had it figured right. They obliviously dropped everything and ran. The living room remained cluttered with all manner of radical literature. Maoist tracts, the gospel according to Che, Debray's take on revolution, back issues of the *Berkeley Barb*, and so on. Uneaten food still occupied the kitchen table. The receiver on the wall phone dangled from its stretched coil.

Nothing pointed directly to the bomber until he reached the top of the stairs and looked down the hallway. A linen closet was open at the far end, with various tools and electronic components scattered on the floor. Long-nose pliers, wire cutters, soldering iron, several spools of single-stranded wire, and a blank wiring board. But more directly to the point were three blasting caps. He moved in for a closer examination. It didn't tell him much he didn't already know. His prey had bomb-making skills not possessed by the rank and file of the radical community.

He stepped into a bedroom to his left where wads of dirty bedding sat atop old mattresses, and a random scattering of foam pads covered the bare wood floor.

A strange tribe born of strange times. One that harbored a monster.

. . .

Carson slumped on a bench in the inner recesses of Lafayette Park, where the tree cover gave him at least some anonymity. The adrenaline rush had faded, and fatigue was setting back in. This temporary respite gave him time to think about the pig, Stone. It appeared that the bomb hadn't worked. During his flight, Carson had stopped and grabbed a copy of the *Chronicle* and scanned the headlines. The assassination of an SFPD cop on his own doorstep would have been front page news, but he found nothing of the sort.

Now he picked the paper back up and took the time to search the inner pages. Finally, on page 17, he came across a brief mention of a minor explosion and fire in the Sunset District, probably caused by a gas leak. That was it. No mention of death or injuries. He threw the paper in a trash container next to the bench and slumped down even further. At least he could take consolation in knowing that the trigger worked as intended. Once again, fate was the spoiler in the game.

So Stone was alive, and untouched, and probably enraged. A dangerous combination. As Carson considered the possibilities, paranoia settled in. What if Stone was teamed up with the FBI? What if the feds decided to let the dog off the leash? What if they put aside the Weather Underground and focused their massive resources exclusively on him? How long would he last out here homeless and broke on the streets of San Francisco?

He struggled to remain coherent and assess his present circumstance. His days with the Weather Underground were over. Their entire clan had proven naïve, incompetent, and incapable of all that they preached. Their reckless blundering had nearly led to his capture. He needed to seek shelter elsewhere. Immediately.

Nyanga.

At the time, he'd found the black man's proposition interesting, but set it aside as he bore down on Stone. The guy had a way with words, and Carson still remembered what he'd said: "I think maybe it's time you hooked up with some people who take this shit seriously. Dead seriously."

Carson also remembered the slip of paper Nyanga handed him with a phone number. He looked in the recesses of his wallet and it was still there. Maybe something could be worked out. Maybe Nyanga would meet him halfway. But halfway to where? They'd have to work that out. He came up off the bench and headed for a payphone at the park's far corner.

. . .

"Shouldn't you be resting?" Stone asked Christine. He'd found her up and staring out the window, still in her hospital gown.

"That's what they say," she said. "But what do they know? They're just a bunch of doctors."

Stone had to smile. Her wit was back in full force. "I was just at the house with the insurance guy, trying to figure out where we're at."

"Is anything left that will make our lives worth living?"

"It's not quite as bad as I thought, but it's going to take some time to sort through it. In the meantime, they're okay with us staying at the Charlton."

"Well good for them," she said as she plopped back down on the bed.

"I just came from the station, and I've got some bad news that I think you'll be quite happy with."

"Oh yeah?"

"For starters, I did a bad thing. I was more than a little upset about you nearly getting killed and I went off half-cocked. I had a lead on the Hells Angels holding a stash of dynamite that I thought might be connected to the bomber."

"So what did you do?"

"I went over to their house on Ashbury, charged in without a warrant and shot the place up. One of them went for a shotgun and I nailed him in the leg."

"Bad boy."

"Yup, bad boy. At least, that's what their lawyer is saying. He's going to file a lawsuit against the SFPD for a zillion dollars in damages for personal injury. I don't think it'll stick because of the shotgun, but there's still the matter of home invasion on my part."

"I'm failing to see happiness in any of this," she said.

"Well here it comes. I talked with the city's attorneys, and we all agreed that I need to resign. If I don't, they'll have to fire me to demonstrate that the department doesn't support rogue cops."

Christine closed her eyes. "Thank God."

Stone came around the bed and gave her a big embrace. "I kind of figured you'd see it that way."

"When are you going to do it?"

"Immediately. It'll take effect in ten days, which gives me enough time to hand the case over to someone else."

"And how do you feel about that?"

"It's fucked up both our lives for long enough. If I'd found him, I would've killed him. And then what? Are we any better off? Don't think so. It's just not worth it. I'd rather lose him and hold onto you."

"Not a bad idea," she told him, with the slightest trace of a grin.

Stone lit up. She was all the way back.

The Sleeper dutifully put the American flag in the metal holder on his porch every Fourth of July, where it hung lifeless in the heat of summer. He thought it an appropriate symbol of the nation's decline into civil chaos. Bombings, riots, demonstrations, racial strife, an unwinnable war. All the symptoms of an empire in decline.

At this point, he was ready to bail, to return to Havana and his reward for a long period of faithful service. An administrative sinecure of some kind. An apartment overlooking the ocean. A monthly stipend for life. Free public transportation.

Castro himself had promised The Sleeper these things during their encounter at the Palace of the Revolution. The IDG, the Cuban intelligence agency, had arranged the meeting because of the extraordinary nature of the assignment, a strange combination of boredom and danger. The bearded president had commended him on his dedication and loyalty throughout the revolution and spoke of the critical importance of his mission on U.S. soil. Only through the work of himself and others like him would the people's revolution spread like a wildfire through the Western world. Of course, there would be a certain amount of violence and suffering involved, but The Sleeper was already steeped in such things and would take them in stride.

The IDG people explained that his mission would differ somewhat from that of other operatives, who were embedded in departments and agencies throughout the U.S. government. Their role was to pass on substantive information through channels such as drop boxes and encoded radio or phone transmissions. His actions would be reserved for special cases, where the security and integrity of the overall operation was placed in serious jeopardy. Often, it would involve eliminating the source of the problem through execution. His extensive combat experience combined with his multi-lingual ability made him the ideal choice for this role.

It turned out to be sporadic yet critical work. An entire year might pass with no call to action. Each assignment represented a challenge all its own. In one case, he traveled to Washington DC, where one of his peers had become involved with a local woman who had discovered that he was a foreign agent embedded in the Department of Defense. Later, when they broke up, she threatened to expose him out of revenge. The Sleeper let himself into her apartment and surprised her in the kitchen when she came home with groceries. He slashed her throat with his gravity knife before she could scream for help. He preferred direct action of this kind rather than involved plots, which always increased the odds of failure.

He had no moral qualms about his work. It was simply a matter of balancing the books. At the direction of the U.S. president, the CIA had made numerous attempts on the life of Castro, all botched. So why should the U.S. citizenry be immune to similar attempts?

Not all his assignments involved terminations. He served as a contact of last resort in any case of extreme emergency. Over the years, he'd spirited people out the country, arranged for them to disappear, supplied funding for those on the run, and so on.

Bill. That's all they needed to know. Phone Bill and he'll take care of things.

Anything.

36.

HUNTERS POINT

The headquarters of the Universal Liberation Army occupied a rental property located on Hudson Street in the Hunters Point industrial area. Its rear deck faced toward a massive assortment of storage yards, warehouses, railheads and water channels bordering the Bay. In all, a marginal home in an extremely marginal neighborhood. Except for its occupants.

"Time to get you off the crank and on the coke," Nyanga told Carson as he chopped up parallel lines of the white powder on a hand mirror framed in tortoise shell. Carson snorted the product through a cut-off soda straw and felt the core of him come back online. "Thanks, man," he said to Nyanga.

"No problem," Nyanga said. "You help me, I help you. That's what the ULA is all about. Us against the pigs." He paused to snort the two remaining lines. "We are the conscience of the world. The people shall be avenged."

"Amen," Carson responded. He didn't feel put off by the man's blackness. In the jungle, a kind of de facto integration had emerged. If you didn't find a way to work together, the enemy would quickly find a way to kill you. After a while, a mutual acceptance set in, and it became a matter of the leadership versus the grunts rather than black versus white. Some had shed this attitude when they returned home, but not Carson.

A number of residents drifted by the dilapidated dining room table while they talked. None spoke to them, and Nyanga offered no introductions. They included the two stoic black men Carson had seen at the Pine Street apartment, plus a trio of young white women who looked like they'd been born angry. They dressed in loose-fitting sweats and had oily hair hanging in strings to their shoulders. Their pale bare feet padded across an aging shag carpet of sickly green. In the kitchen, a mound of dirty dishes overflowed the sink and invaded the counter space. Apparently, there was a standoff over the role of feminist revolutionaries in domestic labor.

"I know about your bomb stuff," Nyanga continued. "Now what about rifles and pistols? You good with things like that?"

"Depends," Carson replied.

"Okay, let me show you." Nyanga led them down the hallway to the rear bedroom, its door secured with a deadbolt lock. He took out a key and pushed it into the cylinder. "Bad neighborhood," he explained. "Gotta keep shit locked up."

The irony of this declaration was lost on Carson, who followed Nyanga in and beheld an entire array of weapons neatly arranged on the bed. M16 and AK47 combat rifles, various sawed-off shotguns, automatic pistols, and even a grenade launcher.

"So what do you think?" Nyanga asked him. "You know how to take this stuff apart if it needs to be fixed?"

"Some of it," Carson told him. "The rest I can figure out if I have to." He noticed boxes of ammunition stacked atop a scarred dresser, along with an assortment of spare clips. A portable safe protruded from the closet space, undoubtedly loaded with cash and drugs, the twin keys to material survival in the belly of the underground beast.

"Looks like you're pretty serious about all this shit," Carson commented.

"Like I told you before, we're dead serious," Nyanga said. "The time is upon us, brother."

"Yes, it is," Carson said.

"I've got a plan," Nyanga announced, "and you're part of it."

"What kind of plan?"

Nyanga smiled. "Let's go out on the deck. I'll show you."

Once on the deck, they sat in bargain-basement lawn chairs made of aluminum tubing and woven strips of white and green plastic. Nyanga made sketches on a yellow legal tablet and shared them with Carson who carefully took them in. From a military standpoint, the plan was quite clever and had an excellent chance of succeeding.

"Tell me what you need," Nyanga said when they were done.

Carson took the tablet and made a brief list, which Nyanga scanned. "Not a problem," he told Carson. "You're on."

Carson turned to the setting sun, and a bubble of memory surfaced as if released from the bottom of a stagnant pond far below. Sunset in El Paso. A burnt orange sky. He walks with his stepfather out into the wrecking yard, where the spent carcasses of automobiles form chaotic hills of dead metal. His stepfather carries a shotgun and reeks of one too many beers. Nearby, two mastiffs strain at their leashes, impatient to assume their nightly patrols. The air stays still and mild. Feral cats. You can't see them, but they're out there in profusion. They prowl the wreckage in search of birds and mice. His stepfather chambers a round, stops and listens. He swings the barrel toward an eviscerated 1949 Ford and pulls the trigger. The still of the evening magnifies the blast to colossal proportion.

"Let's take us a look," he says. They do so and find nothing but metal and upholstery pierced with pellet holes.

"You got something against cats?" Carson asks as they continue on.

"Not a damn thing," his stepfather says.

"So why are we doing this?" Carson asks.

"Because they were born to be target practice, that's why," his stepfather says.

Carson shifted in his chair and gazed out over the industrial sprawl. He was not born to be target practice. Quite the opposite. He turned to Nyanga.

"Let's have another snort," he suggested.

· · ·

"You're gonna owe me really big. You know that, don't you?" said Lisa Vaught's boyfriend of the moment, an attractive but mediocre guy named Tony.

"Yes, once again, I know that," Lisa told him. "And once again, I wouldn't ask if wasn't really important."

"I'm going to look like a fucking pervert," Tony complained. "Somebody might try to kick my ass."

"Well then, kick 'em right back," Lisa said. She knew Tony had a macho streak that wouldn't let him back down. The pair sat at a wooden picnic table outside the Bear's Lair facing Sproul Plaza. Less than an hour ago, a call came into the *Berkeley Barb* office, purportedly from the Universal Liberation Army, a new radical group that had pushed their way to the front of the status line through a series of bizarre declarations done in a prose style that bordered on insane. The caller identified himself as one Field Marshal Nyanga, who demanded to be put through to the managing editor. When informed that the managing editor was out on assignment, the caller reluctantly agreed to talk to one of the resident journalists, hence Lisa.

The caller's instructions turned out to be as odd as the organization he represented. Lisa was to proceed to the Bear's Lair, where she would find the group's latest communique inside the men's restroom. An unoccupied stall with a closed and locked door would identify the location. All the retriever had to do was crawl under the door, take down the message, unlock the door and walk out.

Easy enough if you were a guy; formidably difficult if you were female. At this time of day, the odds of the restroom being empty, even for a minute or two, were almost nil. Lisa imagined a scenario where some drunken guy took the action as a come-on and crawled in to join her in a raw sexual encounter. Not worth the risk.

"So when are you gonna get a real job with a real paper?" Tony asked her. "This whole thing is bullshit."

"Maybe for you, but not for me," Lisa retorted. "You're not going to chicken out on me, are you?"

She watched Tony struggle in the throes of a testosterone attack. "You gonna give me a blowjob for doing this?" he asked.

"We can talk about that once you've got the goods," she said. A clever ploy. It raised the possibility but stopped short of a promise.

Tony stared into the beer he'd been drinking. "Okay." He got up and headed back into the bar without further comment.

He returned ten minutes later, a single sheet of paper in hand.

"Now, let's talk about the blowjob," he said as he handed it to Lisa.

"Not right this second," she said and picked up her purse. "I've got to get this back to the office."

"Then when?"

"Later. Love you. Thanks."

"Yeah, right," he said glumly as she walked off at a brisk pace across the plaza.

. . .

Lisa couldn't wait to read the retrieved memo. Rather than wait until she reached the *Barb*, she sat down on a bench at a bus stop on University Avenue and pored through the text, which looked like the product of a well-worn typewriter:

```
UNIVERSAL LIBERATION ARMY

HEADQUARTERS UNIT SUPREME COMMAND

Communique No. 5.

Warrant Order: Death of Selected Police

Subject: Murder of Multiple Innocents by San
Francisco Police Department

Warrant Issued By: Field Marshal Nyanga

Charges: Indiscriminate execution of individuals
based on political, sexual and racial bias.

The SFPD has acted in collusion with the ruling
Pig Class to bypass their very own justice sys-
tem, which is thoroughly corrupt and fascist in
nature, and eliminates all manner of oppressed
peoples using the most brutal of methods in the
process.

We are all well aware that a fascist pig-run gov-
```

ernment will always allow some of us to get high
while the rest of us go to concentration camps of
the most horrific design, and that none will ever
know the taste of freedom henceforth.

We are also aware that the department is a con-
tributor to the Internal Warfare Tapes held in
the government's files, which identifies all citizens who have had the courage to speak out in
opposition to the government's biased operations
to eliminate all forms of protest. The SFPD has
repeatedly utilized these tapes to target individuals for execution.

Numerous pig-run governments throughout the
world are using similar bio-dossiers to murder all identified people who oppose their rule
or who do not serve and support the interests
of the wealthy. The SFPD has used their methods
as a template for their own local extermination
campaign, which is run in collusion with the FBI
and CIA.

For too long the porcine enemy has prostituted
our mothers, imprisoned our fathers, shot our
brothers and sterilized our sisters. So it is
that by the rights of our children and people
and by Force of Arms and with every drop of our
blood, declare Revolutionary War against the Fascist Capitalist Class and all the agents of murder, oppression and exploitation.

This Warrant identifies the SFPD and all its per-
sonnel as legitimate targets in these the opening
rounds of the Revolutionary War, which will end
in the freedom of all peoples. The War Council of
the Universal Liberation Army authorizes Field
Marshal Nyanga to command and execute immediately, by use of bullets and bombs, an operation to
demonstrate our intent to bring our growing force
to bear on the SFPD and all within it.

DEATH TO THE FASCIST PIGS AND ALL WHO FOLLOW
THEM. PREPARE YOURSELVES. THE TIME OF YOUR DEMISE
IS NOW AT HAND!

. . .

Lisa put the document in her purse and sat back on the bench to contemplate its significance. Part of it was the routine, semi-coherent political ranting she'd come to expect from pieces such as this. But the outright declaration of war with "bullets and bombs" deviated somewhat from the usual revolutionary banter of "taking to the streets" and the like. What made this one truly different was naming a particular police department as the intended target. Usually, there were vague references to "oppressive governments" or "all white pigs," and so on. This time, the announcement was very unambiguous and specific. And also either dumb or crazy. To inform your enemy in advance of attacking simply elevates their vigilance and defenses.

Lisa chose the crazy option. Field Marshal Nyanga, whoever he or she might be, was sailing out far beyond the bounds of rational thought. She needed to get this in front of her editor as soon as possible so they could decide on how to cover it. Sometimes they would print pieces like this in their entirety, other times just excerpts, and occasionally not at all.

Whatever option the paper chose, this latest document presented Lisa with the perfect opportunity to complete her atonement with Detective Stone at the SFPD. She needed to contact him directly and get him a copy of what she was looking at. While she felt no obligation to the department as a whole, she felt a very strong one to Stone. She'd been utterly blindsided by the FBI's COINTELPRO and put his life in jeopardy through her slipshod reporting. When she begged forgiveness, he gave it without hesitation, a gesture she would never forget.

This time around, Detective Stone needed to know immediately what was going on, before another swarm of roofing nails tore him apart.

37.

HUNTERS POINT

"A morning snort's a righteous thing," Moonstone informed Carson as she chopped the parallel lines on the tortoise shell mirror. "It gets you ready to go out and kick ass on the pigs."

She picked up a cutoff straw and vacuumed a pair of lines one by one into her flared nostrils. That done, she flipped a strand of stringy hair out of her face, leaned back and snorted loudly.

"All yours." She handed the straw to Carson and watched with empty eyes as he did the remaining lines. Her nipples popped through the thin cotton of a T-shirt silkscreened with a high-contrast image of a raging partisan thrusting her rifle toward some unknown sky.

Carson felt his nostrils tingle as the drug assembled the disparate parts of his psyche into a coherent whole. He still craved amphetamines, but this would do for the time being. Nyanga's supply of coke seemed to be bottomless, and all the residents indulged themselves at will. It served as a kind of social cement that bound them all together under his leadership.

"My thanks to the boss," Carson said as he put the straw down.

"There's no boss here," Moonstone corrected him. "We're all one. When Nyanga speaks, he speaks for the whole."

Carson shrugged. "Okay, so be it." He had no real interest in their internal politics and viewed Nyanga more as a bomb delivery system than anything else.

"You know what I was before I joined the revolution?" Moonstone asked him. "I was a fucking janitor. I cleaned up pig shit for a living. Can you believe that?"

"No I can't," Carson said, when really, he could.

"Know what else? I'm a fucking dyke. So forget about these tits. They're already spoken for."

"Got it."

Her hand, slender and pale, shot out and grabbed an open pack of filtered cigarettes. She plucked one out, scooped up a nearby lighter, and lit it. The orange tip glowed incandescent as she sucked a generous supply of oxygen through it. A cloud of transparent blue followed when she exhaled.

"You caught a lucky break when you got hooked up with Nyanga," she told him. "You scored big time. When it's all over, the truth will be known."

"The truth?"

"Yeah, the truth. The pigs aren't just the pigs. It goes way beyond that. They carry special genes that are different than the rest of us. And that's what makes them such assholes."

"Where do these other genes come from?"

"They come from other worlds."

"Other worlds?"

"Nyanga can explain it better than me, but anyway, that's the real problem. The bottom line is, they're not going to change. No amount of talking or writing is going to do it. In the end, we've got to wipe them out before they wipe us out. Simple as that."

Before Carson could respond, the front door opened, and Nyanga appeared carrying two shopping bags. He ignored Moonstone and spoke directly to Carson.

"Got what you wanted," he said. "Now let's get it going." He gestured toward the open door.

The pair walked around to a gated driveway that descended to an open area in the rear covered by leaf-strewn cement. An old house-trailer sat parked directly beneath the deck. Dirt and rust stains streaked its quilted skin of faded white. Its aluminum

window frames had weathered to a dull gray, and a solitary propane tank clung to the front above the hitch.

"Meet your new home," Nyanga said as he opened the door.
"Check it out."

They walked through the cramped interior, and Nyanga set the
bags down on a Formica table in a small dinette. Carson slid into
one of the seats and started removing items from the bags.

"We ran power out from the house, and you can sleep in the
back," Nyanga said. "It's all yours."

Carson completed a quick inventory of what Nyanga had
rounded up. Long-nose pliers, screwdriver, wire cutters, power
drill, small-gauge wire, 9-volt batteries, duct tape, soldering equipment, electrical tape, two blasting caps, two sticks of dynamite,
and a length of two-inch pipe with end caps.

"Got everything?" Nyanga asked.

"Pretty much. Except for a razor blade, a mirror, a straw and
big pile of blow to get it all done."

"Done deal," Nyanga said. Carson noticed that in their private dealings, Nyanga dropped all the political pretense and radical rhetoric. Business was business, and the business of extreme
violence was no exception.

"What time do we have to take off?" Carson asked.

"Around 8:30. Can you get it done by then?"

Carson nodded. It was a simple job that required a simple
bomb.

· · ·

A new bird made its debut on the window ledge at Park Station
and peered in at Stone at his desk. An attractive bird with bands of
bright red in its tail feathers. The new kid in birdland. He'd heard
that birds were highly territorial, but somehow they had deemed
this particular ledge a neutral strutting ground.

"Got a minute?" Stone looked up to see Sgt. Linehan taking a
seat opposite him.

"Absolutely."

Linehan sighed and scratched his receding hairline. "I've got to tell you, I feel pretty bad about all this. I was the one who hustled you into this job. And now, Jesus! What a mess!"

"Forget about it," Stone said. "You didn't make the mess, the mess made itself."

"How many days you got left?" Linehan asked.

"Six. Have you guys decided who's going to take this thing over?"

"That'll be me. Penance for what I have wrought, I guess."

"Spoken like a true Irish Catholic. Your mother would be proud. I just wish I had more to hand over. So far, all we've got are the facial sketches and the bomb pieces. I gave copies of the sketches to the FBI, and they peed all over them. Said they were too amateurish to be useful."

"Well fuck the FBI," Linehan said. He sighed again, looked out at the bird on the ledge, then back at Stone. "There's something we all want you to know. None of us blames you for stepping out of line about the dynamite over at the Angels. You had someone try to kill your family. When that happens, all bets are off."

"Thanks," Stone said. "That helps."

His phone rang just as Linehan was leaving. "Stone here."

"Hi. It's Lisa Vaught from the *Barb*. It's payback time."

Stone had to smile. "I hope you mean that in a positive way."

"I do."

"You wanted to know if anything new turned up about bombs or killing cops. "There's a courier about to bring you a copy of the declaration we got yesterday from this group called the Universal Liberation Army. We've gotten them before, and they've been pretty whacky, but this one's a little different. It mentions both bombs and bullets and then goes on to say that the target is the SFPD. It's the first time they've directly threatened a police department."

"Does it mention individuals or just the department as a whole?" Stone asked.

"Just the whole force. No individuals."

"You're a lot closer to this kind of thing than I am. What do you make of it?"

"I don't know. It's really hard to say. This is the sixth communique we've gotten from these guys, and none of them have ever been linked to any real violence. Like I said, they're so nutty and spacey they're hard to take seriously. But this time, I'm not so sure."

"Doesn't matter," Stone said. "Thanks for passing this on. You hear anything more, let me know, okay?"

"Will do. Bye."

Stone got up, went to the front office and retrieved the envelope. He brought it back to his desk with another cup of coffee and started reading. By the time he finished, he understood the Vaught woman's ambivalence. The text erratically veered between the absurd and the ominous. Was it worth putting the whole force on high alert? Maybe, maybe not.

It made him glad that he was almost out of here. Somebody else could pick up this ball and run with it. He took the document upstairs to the station captain. Let the Big Guys hash it out. That's what the Big Guys were for, right?

38.

INGLESTON DISTRICT

Ingleston counted itself as one the more sophisticated communities in the city and so chose to locate its shopping mall a respectful distance from the core business area. And at the far edge of this mall, Bank of America's rear entrance emptied into a large parking lot, where Carson and Moonstone now sat in her aging Datsun pickup. To shield the bank's overnight drop box from public view, a partition had been constructed along the sidewalk between the wall and the curb. It consisted of crisscrossed metal beams that divided it into glassed-in frames, each about two feet in length. Just large enough to rest a bomb along the top beam, ten feet above the walkway.

The stores inside closed at 9 p.m., and traffic quickly thinned to a trickle around the periphery as darkness fell. By 9:30 the lot was nearly deserted and the sidewalk along the back completely empty. Carson carefully set the timer for 15 minutes hence and put the bomb in a small knapsack. It was a simple device, with the stopwatch, battery and wiring taped to the outside of a two-foot pipe.

"Let's go," he commanded.

"Fuckin' A," Moonstone said, without further comment.

They drove through the empty lot and pulled up in front of the partition. Moonstone checked the rearview mirror. "We're cool."

Without hesitation, Carson hopped out with knapsack and bomb slung over one shoulder. He wore a hoodie and sunglasses to hamper surveillance. This was the riskiest part of the entire operation. The beams on the partition were just wide enough to afford toe and finger holds, and he quickly scaled his way up, then paused to make sure they were still unobserved. Lifting the device out of his knapsack, he gingerly placed it on the narrow ledge formed by the top beam. With the bomb secured, he pushed off, jumped down to the sidewalk, and hustled into the truck.

"Hit it," he commanded. Moonstone drove them out of the mall's parking lot to a second lot serving some professional offices across the street. From here, they had a clear view between two large trees of the rear of the bank and its partition.

They had done well. Nyanga had insisted that the bomb be placed so as to prevent or minimize collateral damage to non-pig civilians. He considered such people to be potential ULA recruits as the revolution marched toward critical mass. The bomb contained no shrapnel other than the pipe itself and was in an area scarcely traveled at this hour.

Carson checked his watch. "Ten minutes."

. . .

The woman they called Dancer stared at her reconstituted self in the cloudy bathroom mirror. Carefully sculpted hair, strawberry red lipstick, lavender eye liner.

"This is shit," she declared. "I look like a pig's wife."

"That's the whole idea," said Nyanga, who looked on. "Hot white pussy. Nothing like it." He chuckled.

"It's not fuckin' funny," Dancer said.

"I know," Nyanga said. "Truth is, you might save all our asses. Then you can go back to being whatever you want."

The plan called for Dancer to drive them up to a point where the Ingleston police station backed onto the 280 freeway. Here she would park in the emergency lane and dispatch Nyanga and two others, who would cut a hole in the chain-link fence behind the station and crawl on through to complete their mission. If the state patrol checked on her while she was waiting, she'd go all girly on them and explain that her boyfriend had gone to get help for their broken-down car.

Nyanga walked back into the dining area, where the two taciturn black men went about loading shells into a high-powered rifle and a 12-gauge shotgun. The taller of the two went by Quimbasa and his companion by Ashonti, although they were seldom referred to this way and opted for a noble sort of anonymity. Nyanga lifted an AK47 assault rifle off the table and popped the magazine out to ensure it was loaded.

"Let us pause for a moment and honor the revolutionary cause which we all serve," he said. Quimbasa and Ashonti stopped their work and stood with eyes cast down in deep reflection. Nyanga did the same before he went on to produce the revolutionary sacraments of straw, mirror and dealer-grade coke, 94 percent pure.

. . .

The brilliant flash seared Carson's eyeballs and lit up the pleasure centers in his agitated brain. He'd never witnessed his handiwork explode at night, and with such a clear view. An instant later, the shock wave arrived with a guttural boom that bounced off the windshield.

"Fuck yeah!" Moonstone exclaimed.

An interval of near-silence followed as the entire night recoiled from the force of the blow. Nothing moved under the cones of cool light cast by the parking lot's overhead lamps. And then the rain. Particles of roof, cement and glass fell from the blackness above and settled onto the oil-stained pavement. Finally, the alarms. Motion sensors far and wide reacted to the dense fist of air and bellowed in protest.

The blast had sheared off a portion of the overhanging roof and released the partition matrix from its anchors so that it leaned out over the street. Little tongues of flame begin to appear, along with approaching sirens in the background. Already, several onlookers had shown up to feast on the calamity.

"Maybe we should haul ass," Moonstone suggested.

"Maybe not," Carson said. It was a truly magnificent spectacle, one of his very own making. He wanted to embrace every nuance and detail as it unfolded.

. . .

It took about a half second for the peak of the blast wave to reach the Ingleston police station. It had traveled 1.6 miles and dissipated its energy over a broad and expanding wavefront, so it only registered as a distant thud by the time it arrived. Just one of the four officers in the squad room took notice and wrote it off to thunder or some such thing. None of the eight officers out on patrol reported hearing anything unusual from within the confines of their vehicles. The same was true for the station's front office, where Officers Joe Crenna and Frank Malovic were pulling desk duty, along with Grace Delano, a clerical assistant who was listening to a Dictaphone machine over earphones as she typed up its output.

"Dispatch to all Ingleston units," the radio suddenly barked. "10-80. Proceed immediately to the Bank of America branch on Filbert Ave. We have reports of a major explosion. Repeat 10-80."

Officer Crenna looked over to Officer Malovic. "You don't hear that one every day," he remarked.

"No, you don't," Malovic replied with a troubled look. A bank paired with an explosion didn't bode well for the remainder of the night.

The door to the squad room in back opened and one of the officers poked his head out. "You guys hear that?" he asked.

"We sure did," Crenna replied.

"We're outta here," the officer said and disappeared into the back. A minute later, all four officers hustled out the secured entrance on the side of the building. They formed into two pairs, piled into two patrol cars in the parking lot and roared off into the night.

Their departure left the Ingleston police station manned by just two officers and a clerk. Their reduced ranks didn't cause much concern. The front office was secured by a counter topped with bulletproof plate glass that separated it from the lobby. The only entry point was a door of armored steel off to one side.

· · ·

"Well it's about time, motherfuckers." Nyanga watched the last patrol car swing out onto San Jose Avenue and crank up its lights and sirens. He stood with Quimbasa and Ashonti in the shadows on the edge of the parking lot. A half hour earlier, they had cut an opening into the chain link fence between the station and the freeway and crawled on through. Now their wait was over. Just a few moments ago, they'd heard the blunt report of the bomb going off at the bank, triggering the exodus from the station.

"How many you think are left in there?" Ashonti asked while clutching his high-powered rifle.

"Two, maybe three," Nyanga said. "This is a balls-out deal, so they're going to send everyone they can." He chambered a round into his semi-automatic shotgun. "And every pig that's left is going down. Power to the revolution."

"Power to the revolution," Quimbasa echoed as he cocked his AK47.

"Let's go," Nyanga commanded, and they started across the parking lot to the front entrance. "Remember: Weapons down until we're ready, then follow my lead."

. . .

Officer Crenna studied the document on his desktop intently. It listed all the guests for his wife's thirty-second birthday party, and he needed to ensure that they hadn't left anyone out, like her cranky aunt Jill. He was also dithering about what kind of gift to give her. Something practical? Something elegant? Hard to know.

He looked up to the sound of someone entering the lobby, and saw three black men file in. From his seated standpoint, the counter blocked the lower half of their bodies. The nearest of them approached the speaking hole in the bulletproof glass and Crenna got up to go meet him. "Can I help you?"

"Yeah, I think you can," the man replied. In one continuous motion, he brought a shotgun up, poked it through the speaking hole and let loose a blast that caught Crenna square in the chest. He flew backwards from the impact and crashed onto the floor, the first stop on his journey to the hereafter.

Grace Delano whirled at the sound of the shotgun's discharge; and this circular motion saved her life. It moved her to one side of the pellet cluster from a second shot intended to rip open her back.

A few bits of shot stung their way into her left arm as she fell to the floor and crawled behind a metal filing cabinet.

Officer Malovic, seated in the rear of the office, heard the first two shots and saw Crenna and Delano go down. He dived onto the floor and worked his way to one side and then toward the front as the gunman continued to pump more rounds into the office. By hugging the floor, he was able to avoid the shooter's line of sight and reach Crenna, whose cratered chest leaked a river of red and burbled in a futile attempt to suck in air. "Help me," Crenna whispered in that final precious moment before he expired.

A second weapon opened fire and raked the entire length of bulletproof glass. It produced a flurry of crystalline spider webs, but none made it all the way through. A third weapon sounded like it was firing at the lock on the armored door but failed to open it.

The firing ceased. The front door opened and slammed shut. The assault on the Ingleston police station had ended.

. . .

"Watch your speed," Nyanga instructed the woman called Dancer. "Three black guys and a white chick won't look good if we get pulled over."

The four of them traveled north on 280 in silence. As they approached the Evans Avenue exit, Nyanga spoke up in the mythical voice of a wrathful god. "I am not pleased with our action tonight. It only delivered a single dead pig. The revolution will hold us accountable. We must atone."

"But how?" Ashonti asked.

"It will come to me," Nyanga replied. "I will have a vision that points the way to our redemption. Trust me."

And they did.

39.

SAN FRANCISCO

"So you heard?" Linehan asked Stone.

"How could I not?" Stone answered. The morning papers and news stations couldn't get enough of it. Three intruders killed a cop inside an SFPD police station and wounded a civilian clerk, then made a clean getaway. A second officer survived the attack and identified them only as black males in their twenties. A nearby bank bombing had drained off all the other officers, and it was suspected that the explosion was meant to do precisely that.

"What about the bombing part? Could it be our guy?" Linehan asked.

"If it is, he's joined a whole new club," Stone said, and pushed a copy of the ULA declaration across his desk to Linehan. "You see this?"

"Yeah, I did. It's pretty weird."

"I think they just delivered on their promise," Stone said. "Bullets and bombs for the SFPD. Now we know they're for real. But that's about all we know. Are they pals with the Weather Underground? Don't think so. Their communiques have an entirely different style."

"Why would our bomber switch horses and go with these guys?" Linehan asked.

"Because he doesn't give a damn about the politics. He's on his own wavelength and fighting his own war. If that's true, he sees these different groups as allies, but doesn't consider himself one of their chosen. He's a kind of free agent."

"Interesting theory," Linehan. "But where does that leave us?"

Stone grinned. "I don't know where it leaves you, but it leaves me with just a few days until I'm out of here."

"Gonna miss you, buddy," Linehan said.

. . .

"It has become clear to me what must be done," Nyanga told Carson. They sat at the cramped little dinette in the trailer behind the house in Hunters Point. The interior had the musty smell of imprisoned air left to molder. The late morning sun shone in through a dirty window and cast its compromised light upon them. A halved straw and razor blade rested on the tortoise shell mirror on the table between them. Its surface bore traces of ghostly white lines.

Carson looked into Nyanga's eyes of deep almond just a single shade lighter than his dilated pupils. Dark on black. They glowed with a singularity of purpose that bordered on mesmerizing. Field Marshal Nyanga. The first among equals, or so it was said.

"To compensate for our failure, we have to off a great number of pigs in a single stroke," he continued. "Only then will the revolution come to life and unite the masses behind us. People of all colors, all sexes, all beliefs of the spirit. They await us. We can't let them down."

"And how do we do that?" Carson asked.

"Fate is about to present us with the perfect opportunity," Nyanga responded. "Let me show you."

As Nyanga laid out his plan, Carson had to wonder if genius and madness were indeed synonymous but decided that ultimately it didn't matter. It was the outcome that counted; and in this case it promised to be as devastating as it was brilliant.

"I'm going to need something stronger than dynamite," he said when Nyanga had finished.

"Name it," Nyanga said.

"There's a plastic explosive called C4. That's what we need. Only problem is you can't get it without a blasting license."

"I don't see that as being a problem," Nyanga said. "All we need to know is where to get it. The rest should be fairly simple."

Fairly simple, Carson thought. Of course. He should've known that.

. . .

The CBS news announcer related to Stone and Christine how the Milwaukie Bucks beat the Baltimore Bullets in four games straight to win the NBA championship. A four-game sweep had only happened once before. A very big deal in some circles, but not Stone's.

KRON TV's national coverage ended, and the local news fired back up. It detailed how police were still baffled by the assault on the Ingleston police station and the murder of Officer Joe Crenna. An inside source claimed the SFPD had been warned of a pending attack by a fringe terrorist group but had taken no precautions. The mayor promised an investigation, whatever that meant.

Stone tipped his gin and tonic to the television screen and all its frantic little pixels. "Adios amigos," he said, and then took a generous sip.

"Are you going to the funeral?" Christine asked.

"Yeah, I suppose so," Stone said. "It's my last day on the job and it seems like a good way to go out."

"Yes, it does," Christine agreed.

The news droned on about an escaped monkey in the Castro district. It once worked in a traveling carnival in Texas.

40.

HUNTERS POINT

Ten pounds of the world's deadliest putty. An initial blast velocity of 26,400 feet per second. A compression wave of astounding density. A monstrous destructive capacity. The choice of political and criminal outliers worldwide.

Carson admired the simplicity of the C4's packaging. It came wrapped in plain brown paper, as if for mailing at the local post office. Except that this package bore the label "C4 EXPLOSIVE" in enormous, unambiguous letters that occupied the entire top side.

He tore it open to expose four bricks, each with its own wrapping of transparent plastic. He picked one up and pulled off a corner of the pale gray putty with no apprehension. The substance remained inert unless exposed to the power of a blasting cap. During the war, they often lit small pieces of it on fire to heat their rations. For this particular project, he would roll it into a pair of elongated cylinders, as if it was a grade school silly putty project.

Nyanga had given him a quick rundown on how they procured it. As he'd predicted, it was fairly simple. A couple of brief phone calls had identified a supplier, and they entered the warehouse dressed in mechanics' coveralls and concealed themselves until the place shut down for the night. The only technology involved was a flashlight and a bolt cutter, the universal master key to much of the industrial world. The C4 turned out to be lightly secured in a framed enclosure lined with chicken wire. A single snap of the bolt cutter popped the lock, and the C4's bold packaging quickly identified it. They did set off a security alarm on their way out but were long gone before anyone could respond.

· · ·

The trailer's metal siding snapped and popped as the noonday sun beat down upon it. Carson snorted a couple of lines of high-grade cocaine and tore more putty off the brick he'd opened. He placed it between his palms and rolled it into a sphere the size of a base-ball. A compulsion overcame him to bring the bland, gray surface to life, and he used a pencil to punch in two deeply recessed eyes. He pulled out the space between them to form a sharply pointed nose and teased two satanic ears out on the sides. A severe crease under the nose completed the figure and gave it a macabre grin.

Welcome, Mr. Bomb Man.

He set his creation atop an old radio near the table's edge, where it would bare mute witness to the rest of his efforts.

· · ·

The woman called Dancer had once again been called upon to play the part of a pig's wife. She stood in the glass and metal con-fines of a phone booth at the intersection of 3rd and Hudson and stared at the mutilated remains of a phone book slowly rotating on its chain. She got an answer on the fourth ring to a number she'd just dialed.

"Good afternoon, St. Brannon's Parish," a woman answered.

"Hello, I'm sorry to bother you, but I have a question about a funeral you've scheduled for an Officer Joe Crenna. My sister wants to attend because she's friends with Joe's wife, but she's really worried about the casket."

"The casket?"

"Yeah, she's a very nervous kind of person and is afraid that the body might be visible, which would totally freak her out. She wants to be absolutely sure it will be closed during the service."

"I'm sorry to hear that, but she really doesn't need to worry. It's always a closed-casket service, right from the time the deceased leaves the mortuary."

"Would you mind if I called them, just so I can say I double-checked? It would be very helpful."

"I don't see why not. Let me check here. Yes, for the Crenna service it's the Seven Hills Mortuary."

"Seven Hills. Thank you so much. I really appreciate it. Bye now."

The Dancer woman shoved open the booth's folding door and stepped out into the whoosh of traffic and warm exhaust. She walked two cars down the sidewalk and got in next to Nyanga.

"You're on. The casket's closed all the way and the mortuary's called Seven Hills."

"Well done," Nyanga said. He handed her a bullet-shaped coke inhaler. "The revolution applauds you."

41.

SAN FRANCISCO

Stone looked into the rearview mirror on the back of the bedroom door and saw himself transformed by the SFPD dress uniform he thought he would never wear. He'd always considered himself an approachable person, a valuable asset for an investigator, but the stark military cut of the uniform made him appear stiff and inaccessible. Its navy-blue wool, brass buttons and shoulder epaulets were topped by a peaked cap replete with shiny black visor. In all, he looked more like a monument than a real person.

Nevertheless, the funeral announcement had made it clear that dress blues were the uniform of the day, and he had to admit they fit the formalized gravity of the occasion. They were to assemble at 9:30 in front of St. Brannons Church prior to filing in and filling the pews behind the grieving family at 9:45.

He took the uniform off and put on some jeans and a sport shirt and sandals. Much better. Today had been his last official day at the office, and his only real job was to receive all those who drifted by and wished him well. He cleaned out his desk, gave his official files to Linehan and was on his way home five minutes after quitting time. It turned into a melancholy trip as he thought about all those good souls he would inevitability lose touch with. It reminded him of the transient nature of all things.

He checked his watch. Christine would be home soon, and he'd decided on grilled halibut, risotto and cooked carrots for dinner, with perhaps a little wine sauce on the fish. Maybe something with

a dry Riesling, shallots and garlic. The kitchen was still under res-
toration following the blast, but he'd make do.

So much for being a cop.

. . .

Nyanga knelt in the nave of St. Brannon's Church halfway between
the altar and the vestibule. He rested his elbows on the pew in front
of him and clasped his hands in a display of prayer in case someone was looking. A black man in a white church was an anomaly
in this neighborhood. Statues of Joseph and Mary flanked the altar
and gazed down benignly upon him, as if to forgive him for that
which he was about to do.

He remembered asking his mother why Christ and all the saints
were white, and she said that their color didn't matter; it was the
goodness in their hearts that we should hold dear. If that was so,
why hadn't that goodness reached out and intervened as his life
lurched ever further into darkness and chaos? Why had he endured
the horror of a chronically violent father, sadistic policemen and
corrupt prison guards? Why had all his attempts at prospering in
business collapsed into ruin? Why had his family ultimately for-
saken him?

At one time, he'd decided that it was simply because he was a
black man in a white man's world. But then he came to realize that
the flagrant abuse of power was more than a matter of color and
was visited upon people of all races, persuasions and genders. Its
cruelty knew no bounds. But to what end? It took considerable
time, study and thought to construct the answer. The legion of
pigs at the top and their cronies at the bottom were not actually
human. They were a species unto themselves, so inhumanity came
naturally to them. Eventually, it would be proven scientifically
through genetics, but he couldn't wait for that day. The only way
to defeat them was to grow an underground collective and then,
without warning, rise in revolt and wipe them from the face of the
earth. Much literature pointed to the possibility of realizing this
goal, such as the works of Debray, Guevara and others.

And thus, Field Marshal Nyanga.

History had appointed him to be the ultimate catalyst that would set the revolution in motion. It wasn't a matter of personal choice; it was a matter of public destiny. Through his leadership the revolution would take on a life of its own and become a global force without precedent in human history. He was simply bowing to its will and giving it shape and direction.

And this place, this church, would become the ignition point. He looked out to the center aisle and visualized the casket positioned there, near the altar. The ideal blend of explosives and shrapnel to destroy over a hundred pigs in a single blast. The news of it would quickly radiate over the media, and the masses would spontaneously interpret it as a signal to take to the streets. It was the cue they had awaited since the moment they were born into this troubled age.

Long live the revolution.

On the way out, he lit a votive candle in its honor.

. . .

The front of the Seven Hills Mortuary faced Geary Boulevard with a church-like architecture in keeping with the solemn spirituality within. The business side of things faced a less-traveled feeder street off to the right. Here a recessed entry sat next to a closed garage used by hearses for transporting deceased clients to various services and burials, depending on religious preference.

Sometime around 8 a.m. one such hearse would back into this garage to load the remains of Officer Joe Crenna for his mournful journey to St. Brannon's Church. But now, around 12 a.m., it became the target of a break-in by the Universal Liberation Army. The intrusion proved to be relatively easy. As a precaution, they had already located the junction box for the phone line and severed the connection to prevent a possible alarm. That done, there was little chance they'd be discovered. Funeral homes ranked quite low in terms of burglary attempts. They retained little cash and stored no narcotics since their patients had all passed beyond the realm of earthly pain.

Carson watched from across the street as Ashonti jimmied the lock on the front door and gave the high sign as it swung open.

Carson hopped out of their car and popped the trunk as Ashonti joined him, and they each grabbed a canvas bag. Carson's contained the bomb components. Ashonti's held twenty-five pounds of roofing nails.

Once inside, Carson pulled out a flashlight and let the beam play over the interior. A short corridor on the right led to a suite of offices and a longer corridor straight ahead had three doors spaced at even intervals. They moved to the first door, opened it, and found themselves in a chapel of the kind used for viewing and memorial services. It had a non-denominational feel to it, with rows of generic pews and an altar-like staging area in front for the casket, but there was no casket.

They backed out, walked to the next door and came upon a similar chapel, also with no casket. Carson began to feel slightly anxious. If the casket wasn't in one of the chapels, they'd have to search room to room until they found it.

They went on to the last chapel and there it was, in the center of the staging area, devoid of flowers and ready to transport. Ashonti hung back, but Carson approached without hesitation. Two years of war had immunized him to the presence of death in all its flavors. He quickly located the latch and opened the lid of polished cherrywood. The lifeless form of Officer Crenna reposed on a white velvet lining, dressed in a civilian suit. Carson had brought a picture he'd clipped from the paper for identification purposes but didn't need it. They had the right person.

"Hold the light for me," he instructed Ashonti, who took it and shone it down into the open casket. Carson reached in, grasped the body by the shoulder and the hip and rolled it toward him. He opened his bag and pulled out an elongated five-pound cylinder of C4 putty and placed it in the vacated space on the far side of the body. Next, he produced a blasting cap with a trailing wire and inserted it into the C4. With the explosive in place, he rolled the body to the opposite side, and repeated the process. Finally, he brought out the detonation device, which he'd installed in an empty cigar box. An alarm clock, two 9-volt batteries and a simple switching circuit with two terminals for the blasting cap connections. He carefully set the alarm for 10:30 a.m. and secured the two wires to their respective terminals. To complete the operation, he flipped an arming switch, which caused a small red pilot light to come on. He closed the box and rested it on the dead man's chest.

"Now the shrapnel," he said to Ashonti. He opened the second bag and began pouring the roofing nails into the coffin. In the silent chapel, they made a clinking sound like the rush of coins from a slot machine jackpot. As he listened, he reflected on the brilliance of his bomb design. In essence, it was a pipe bomb writ large. At the moment of detonation, the casket would contain the explosion for an instant, allowing the burning gas to accumulate enormous pressure before bursting. He tried to imagine the devastation it would cause in the packed church, but failed. When catastrophes reach a certain scale, the human dimension becomes an abstraction.

He closed the lid and secured the latch on his masterwork.

42.

"Too bad you have to spend your last day doing something like this," Burke told Stone.

"I don't know," Stone replied. "Somehow, it seems appropriate." It was strange seeing the old detective in his dress blues. He was used to watching him amble through the office in an ill-fitting suit that reflected all the weight he'd lost after his heart attack. Now he looked like he might be going to a costume party.

"So what's your plan?" Burke asked. "What are you gonna do now?"

"Good question," Stone said. "Right now, my plan is no plan."

Burke nodded thoughtfully. "I like that. Stick with it."

They were standing on the sidewalk in front of St. Brannon's, along with over a hundred of their fellow officers, waiting for the funeral mass to commence. A marine overcast obscured the sun and set an appropriate mood for the occasion. In a few minutes, they would form up and file in to fill up the pews as the organist played Adagio in G minor.

. . .

Carson found a good location to the right of the church which offered both concealment and protection from the imminent blast. It contained a well-kept lawn and garden with a tool shed at the far end flanked by a cluster of large rhododendrons. He could peer out onto the sidewalk where the large cluster of blue-suited pigs had started to file into the church. He checked his watch. 8:45. It seemed rather early for them to be seated, but they must have scheduled some kind of preamble to the main service. Probably a lengthy series of testimonials to the character of the fallen pig and the resolve of the department to bring his slayer to justice. In any case, the funeral announcement clearly stated that the mass itself would commence at 10 a.m. and he'd set the bomb for 10:30 to guarantee a full house.

. . .

The casket occupied a spot in the center aisle near the communion rail. A funeral pall covered its polished wooden top with a brocaded material centered on a golden cross. On the inside, the bomb's alarm-driven timer ticked on resolutely toward the appointed moment. Its main spring slowly uncoiled and set in motion a series of gears and wheels that regulated its advance, which was scheduled to terminate at precisely half past ten on this most auspicious of mornings.

But half past ten according to whom?

While constructing his bomb, Carson had to swim upstream against a continuous cascade of drug interludes, confusion and distractions. But in the end, every detail, every issue was accounted for and managed.

All save one.

At 2:00 a.m. this morning, Daylight Savings Time had kicked in. What the bomb knew to be 10:30 a.m. was now 11:30 a.m. in the world outside the casket. The funeral service would be right on the cusp of conclusion when it went off.

. . .

Stone filed in and sat between Linehan and Burke. Linehan, an Irishman, was Catholic and had explained that what they were attending was a Requiem Mass, also known as the Mass of the Dead. It would be largely conducted in Latin and follow a strict protocol in terms of events.

To Stone, the flow of it all quickly became incomprehensible. Three priests and an entire flock of altar boys moved according to some ancient choreography accompanied by sad yet beautiful strains of a Gregorian chant. His mind soon sought shelter in a string of memories that used the music as if it were a film score…

…New Year's Eve, 1954. He sways drunkenly on the lawn of his newly minted suburban ranch-style home, which he just lost in a divorce. As the fireworks reach their crescendo, he chips in by firing his police revolver into the smoky sky…

…He stands with aching feet at the gate of the Paramount lot, where he's been reduced to working as a security guard, and tips his pseudo-cop hat to William Holden as he drives off in his Ferrari…

…He stares at the body of a dead girl in the Kern River, whose dress billows out to take the form of a pale blue jellyfish…

…He chats with an 18-year-old Merle Haggard, who explains his theory about Genius Listeners while they stand in the parking lot of a Bakersfield dive bar…

…From the 12th floor at Capitol Records, he watches angry billows of black smoke rise from the Watts district as it descends into civil chaos…

…He drifts westward on foot across San Francisco, screaming high on LSD that has reached in and grabbed his soul and won't let go, but somehow, it's all right…

· · ·

Matt Carson's watch lied to him. It was still set to Standard Time, and registered 10:28, just like the timer in the casket. He retreated behind the tool shed and covered his ears in anticipation of the blast. It never came. After three minutes, he uncovered them and looked at his watch once more. He could scarcely believe it. It was such a beautifully simple design. What could have possibly gone wrong?

· · ·

The homily yanked Stone out of his reminiscences. The priest stood at the pulpit and praised the life of Officer Joe Crenna as an exemplar of Christian living at its very best, a life of public service devoted to others. He drew upon the recollections of many fellow officers, some sad, some touching, others laced with humor. The prayers of the faithful followed, then communion, which took some time because of the many Irish within the ranks of the department.

The final song and prayer commenced at 11:20 a.m. At its conclusion, the assembled officers began to file out row by row, followed by friends and family.

Up at the altar, the priest removed the pall from the coffin while the widow and one of her daughters looked on. The funeral director stood back discretely and watched as the priest handed it to the one remaining altar boy, who retired back into the vestibule. That done, the director started down the central aisle to summon the attendants who would roll the casket into the waiting hearse.

11:29 a.m. had come and gone when he took his first step.

. . .

Matt Carson stood in the open next to the tool shed. A steady stream of blue pigs flowed out of the church. What went wrong? Maybe someone had opened the casket and discovered the device. He hadn't seen the coffin come out the front, so it was still inside. Maybe it had been opened and the bomb discovered and disarmed. He had to know. He started across the lawn toward the windows on the side.

. . .

The explosion erupted with staggering force. It literally raised the church roof several feet before it settled back. A giant crack appeared in the steeple, and its top half tore loose and tumbled onto the front lawn, where the spire burrowed into the turf.

Stone felt the blast wave pummel him. *It's happening all over again.* It knocked him to his knees and slammed his ears shut. All around him, officers were down or staggering. The main force of the blast followed the path of least resistance, the rows of windows on each side of the nave. A spray of glass shot out, along with a torrent of roofing nails. The front of the building fared much better because it had no windows, so its stucco walls absorbed the onslaught and largely spared those out in front. Stone waited for the sting of shrapnel to set in, but it never came.

Not so for those inside. The explosion generated a horrific blizzard of roofing nails moving at hypersonic speeds. A priest, the funeral director, the widow and her daughter were all shredded into red pulp and powdered bone.

. . .

Out on the street in front, one of the station captains spontaneously took charge. "If you're hurt, come over to me!" he yelled. Not everyone heard him. Some were temporarily deaf or close to it. The herd of cops began to cluster into groups composed of fellow station members.

"You guys okay?" Stone asked Burke and Linehan. Behind him, smoke and dust poured out of the shattered windows.

"Yeah, we're okay," Burke answered and Linehan nodded.

Christine. I've got to let Christine know. After all that had happened to them she would be frantic, and with good reason. A quick scan of nearby homes told him that virtually every resident had come out to witness the unfolding catastrophe. He sprinted across the street to the nearest house, where a middle-aged couple stood on their porch.

"Emergency!" he yelled. "I need your phone."

The man led him inside and pointed to a phone in the kitchen. "All yours," he said and went back out to watch the fire trucks arrive with their banshee sirens and jittering red lights.

Stone had the hospital put him through to the ER, where they paged Christine. While he waited, he stared at the Kitty Kat Clock on the wall above the sink. Its bulging eyes rotated endlessly from side to side, and it grinned as if all was right in the world, which it wasn't.

"James?"

"Yeah, it's me. A bomb just went off at the funeral, a really big one."

"Oh my God! Are you okay?"

"I'm fine. We were pretty much out of the place when it went off. Whoever did it screwed up the timing, thank God. It was a huge explosion. It brought down the steeple and blew out all the windows and sprayed glass all over the place. I don't think this is going to generate much traffic for you. Nobody left inside stood a chance."

"You've got to get over here. I need to take a look at you. I need to make sure you're alright."

"I'll do it, but it may take a while. It's absolute chaos here."

"Promise me you'll do it as quick as you can, okay?"

"Okay. Gotta go now. Bye."

. . .

The bellowing of the emergency sirens awakened Carson where he sat propped against the plywood wall of the tool shed. He'd been tossed a good ten feet backward from his position when the bomb went off. The back of his skull throbbed where it had slammed against the wall, and he felt a trickle of blood down the base of his neck. He started to bring himself upright, and abruptly sat back down. The effort had triggered a sharp pain just below his bellybutton. He looked down and saw the cause. A shard of glass protruded from his abdomen. An inch or so wide, it cleared the surface of his T-shirt by maybe two inches and glistened in the late morning sun. It produced only minimal blood, which formed a shiny red disc around the wound.

Carson had seen such wounds before. In fact, he had seen all manner of wounds during his time in combat. He'd spent numerous hours discussing their nature and consequences with the medics. This type tended to be self-sealing, so the bleeding out the front would remain fairly minimal. The real problem was the bleeding inside his gut, and that was hard to assess. There was no way to gauge the length of the shard and how far it had penetrated; but the deeper in it went, the greater the odds that it hit a vein or artery. Even a nick would trigger a steady flow of bleeding that would eventually kill him. If it hit a bowel, it would produce a flood of fecal matter into his abdominal cavity, with equally horrifying consequences. Either case mandated immediate surgery.

He looked to the street where several ambulances had arrived, but it was alive with pigs, who were swarming like angry blue hornets. Given his disheveled appearance, he'd immediately become a suspect, and he had a good idea what they'd do to him after what he'd tried to do to them.

He considered his options. One was to stay put until the area cleared and risk bleeding to death while he waited. Another was to hope the ULA would somehow mount a rescue, which seemed nearly impossible. In the end, they were criminals, not soldiers.

Finally, there was The Sleeper.

He had the contact number. All he needed to do was get to a phone and make the call. Difficult, but not impossible. He was only a block or two from a business district that undoubtedly had a payphone. If he made contact, The Sleeper could pick him up and drive him to an emergency room and they could fabricate a story about what had happened to him.

He rose slowly and carefully to his feet. The pain was insistent, but tolerable. He buttoned his shirt over the wound. Any attempt to pull the shard out might cause even more internal damage. He started down the block, away from the disaster.

. . .

Stone shook his head in dismay. A massive hook-and-ladder fire truck occupied a spot that completely blocked his car off from the street. And it wasn't going anywhere soon. Multiple fire hoses sprouted from a panel on its flank and snaked down the street toward the church, which still smoldered fitfully.

He shrugged in resignation and headed back up the street where the ranks of cops had thinned considerably as they headed home in shock and disbelief. They came to bury one of their own, and now this. Their outrage had yet to fully surface.

Two ambulances remained out front, and their paramedics were starting up the walkway to the vestibule entrance, which had taken on the form of a burnt-out cave. Stone joined them to see if he could get a look inside, but they were all stopped by a fire captain. He dictated that they could peer in from the entrance, but no one could enter because the blast had destabilized the entire structure. Stone looked in through the haze of smoke and steam. Nothing remained intact. The pews were splintered into firewood and the altar was riddled with shrapnel. The casket had apparently been vaporized. Not a trace of human remains was visible.

"Jesus!" one of the paramedics exclaimed.

"Sorry," the fire captain said. "Don't think we're going to need you here."

"I guess not," another paramedic said, and the group walked off, leaving Stone alone with the captain.

"What about the family?" Stone asked.

"Don't know yet," the captain replied. "The wife and one of the daughters aren't accounted for. That's all we got right now." They both knew what that meant.

"I've got a favor to ask," Stone said. "One of your trucks has me blocked in down the street and I need to get to the emergency room at the UCSF Medical Center. Any chance you could let me out?"

"Yeah, maybe," the captain said. He had an air of profound exhaustion about him, the kind that might never completely recede.

. . .

By the time Carson reached the payphone, he knew that things weren't going well inside him. His pulse was shallow yet rapid, and the pain was relentless. He'd found The Sleeper's number in a remote corner of his wallet on a scrap of dirty paper and now dialed it. He had no idea what to expect.

"Hi, Bill here," the male voice said cheerfully. Perfectly fluent. Not even a trace of an accent. It was like he was talking to a clerk in a hardware store in the middle of Omaha.

"My name's Matt. We met at Alegría de Pío. You remember?"

"As a matter of fact, I do," the voice said in a more neutral tone. "How are you these days?"

"Not so well," Carson said. "I'm going to need a ride to the hospital."

"I see," the voice said. "Where are you right now?"

"I'm at a payphone on Shannon at 53rd."

"Well you're in luck because that's close by. Just give me a few minutes and I'm on my way."

"The sooner the better," Carson said.

"Understand. See you soon."

Carson hung up and propped his elbows on the little shelf below the phone to support himself. He felt his legs began to quiver.

. . .

The first paramedic took one last look at the shattered remnants of St. Brannon's Church as he climbed into his ambulance. Wisps of smoke still drifted out of the vacant windows, and the fallen steeple sprawled across the front lawn like a giant felled tree. Its plunge had decapitated a statue of St. Brannon, whose head now rested on the sidewalk.

"Fucking incredible," he remarked to the second paramedic, who simply nodded his assent.

He started the ambulance, turned north and threaded his way through the fire trucks and their tangle of hoses.

"Back to base?" the second paramedic asked.

"Not yet," the first one said. "I think we owe ourselves a little coffee and maybe even a scone."

He turned right at the end of the block, traveled one more block and turned onto Shannon Street.

"Hey, what's that?" the second paramedic said. He pointed up ahead to where 53rd intersected with Shannon. Several people stood around a phone booth, where a pair of legs stretched out onto the sidewalk.

"Uh oh," the first one said. "There goes our coffee."

They pulled up to the curb, got out and approached the phone booth, where a white male slumped half in and half out, eyes closed and jaw slack. "Give us a little room please," the first paramedic said to the bystanders.

"Anyone see what happened?" the second one asked.

"He just kind of slid down," a bystander volunteered.

The first paramedic knelt and put his index finger on the subject's jugular vein. The pulse was rapid and weak. He scanned the body and noticed a slight bump in the man's shirt. After a few opened buttons, the cause of his distress became obvious.

"Oh yeah," the paramedic remarked to himself. A big sliver of glass protruded from the subject's abdomen. "Get the gurney," he instructed his partner.

. . .

"Doctor Harmon to the ER. Dr. Harmon," the wall-mounted speaker barked.

It roused Christine out of acute somnolence from where she sat on a leather couch of hideous green in the physicians' lounge. Stone had phoned again to tell her he had just gotten loose and was on his way, which brought her considerable relief along with a palpable wave of fatigue.

She shook it off and headed down the hall. Stone had said that they shouldn't expect much traffic from the explosion at the church, and that was turning out to be the case. He said he'd explain why later, meaning it must be something awful. She went on through the ER's double doors and one of the nurses looked up at her and said, "Bay three."

She knew him the instant she saw him. They were just lifting him off the gurney and onto the exam table, so his face wasn't obscured by an oxygen mask.

Altamont. It was the Vietnam vet, or at least that's what his drug-fueled ravings had suggested. She'd had no way to treat him and let Stone take him up to the psychiatric interns in the other tent. She still remembered the raw panic in his eyes as the psychedelics and God knew what else plunged him back into combat.

She put it all aside and let her training kick in as she mounted her stethoscope. The nurses applied an oxygen mask and prepped the IV lines for blood and antibiotics. An aide cut the patient's clothes off with a large scissors, starting with the shirt and undershirt. And there it was. A shard of glass embedded in the abdomen a couple of inches below the bellybutton.

"I need blood pressure and a hematocrit count," she ordered and put the stethoscope to his chest. The heart maintained a normal rhythm but presented a pulse both rapid and feeble. There was a good chance he was bleeding internally. A minute later, a blood pressure reading of sixty over thirty reinforced her diagnosis.

She stepped back and let the nurses and aides work while she waited for the hematocrit test to come back, noting that the tip of the glass missile had penetrated to some unknown depth. The guy was lucky that an ambulance happened by when it did. A few more minutes and he would have been in mortal trouble.

The hematocrit count came back low and confirmed the diagnosis of internal bleeding. She prepared to hand him over to the surgeon, who would open him up and carefully explore his innards, looking for severed or nicked blood vessels.

She wasn't a forensic expert, but the shard must have entered nearly perpendicular to the body and at an extreme velocity. Stone had mentioned that the explosion blew out all the windows in the church at the funeral. That would produce precisely the kind of wound she was now looking at. Should she be suspicious? She'd wait and ask Stone, who was a seasoned expert when it came to suspicion.

43.

SAN FRANCISCO

The Sleeper listened to AM radio as he drove down Shannon Street. Several stations had already picked up on the deadly bombing at the murdered cop's funeral, a story as sensational as it was provocative. They couldn't get enough of it. Field reporters telephoned in constant updates and the TV people prowled the scene with their Bolex 16-mm cameras. Film at eleven, they promised. The decapitated head of the sculpted saint was the most favored shot for B-roll.

His caller's connection to the bombing was blatantly obvious. The phone booth he'd designated was only a couple of blocks from the church. Somehow the fool had been injured in the explosion and needed safe passage to medical treatment.

Before he'd left home, The Sleeper had communicated with Havana via an encrypted shortwave radio link and relayed his assessment of the situation. The reply was swift and decisive. The subject was to be terminated without delay. There was no need to transmit the reasoning behind the order. The bomber had succeeded all too well in his role as a political agitator. His latest work would spark international outrage and condemnation. If he was apprehended, he would eventually give up his connection to Cuba. The nation's carefully cultured image as a benign and model socialist state would suffer grievous damage.

It would be a relatively simple operation. He'd drive the contact to a secluded location and hold him there until he died of his present injuries. An investigation would not uncover any evidence of homicide.

Of course, there was always the possibility that the contact would offer some resistance. He was, after all, a combat veteran. But in the end, it wouldn't matter. The Sleeper checked the gravity knife in his pocket just to make sure.

He looked ahead to the appointed intersection and saw a complication, potentially a big one. The phone booth in question was empty. Why? He pulled up to the curb beside it, got out and gave it a brief inspection. Sure enough, he spotted several small drops of fresh blood on the metal floor.

"You lookin' for that guy?"

The voice belonged to an old man in a wheelchair tucked in the shade of an awning in front of a book shop.

"As a matter of fact, I am," The Sleeper replied.

"Ambulance came and got him. Looked like he was damn near dead. Had a big piece of glass in his gut."

"Did they say where they were taking him?"

"Didn't hear. Hope they got him there in a hurry."

"Me too," The Sleeper said. "Thanks."

"Nothing to it," the old man replied, obviously pleased with his active role in the drama.

The Sleeper already knew what had to be done. He got in his car and headed down the street, looking for the next available payphone, which was several blocks away. A quick check of its yellow pages showed about a dozen hospitals within the city, a manageable number. He'd need to phone each one until he tracked down his target.

. . .

Stone and Christine fervently embraced the moment they encountered each other in the ER waiting room. Ellie, the receptionist, looked on with an approving smile. Stone was a familiar figure, although she'd never seen him formalized in a dress uniform.

"You look pretty good, everything considered," Christine told him. "Come on back."

They headed through the double doors and down the hall toward the lounge.

"You're not going to believe this," she said.

"Today, I'd believe just about anything," he said.

"Right after you phoned, we admitted a guy with a big piece of glass sticking out of his gut. I just checked with the ambulance people. They picked him up only a couple of blocks from where you were."

"Where is he now?"

"He's just come out of surgery for internal bleeding. But that's only the half of it."

"And the other half?"

"Remember when we were at Altamont, and you had to help me with the guy who was over the top on psychedelics? The guy who thought he was back in the war?"

"I do."

"It's the same guy."

A circuit formed within Stone. Switches closed, gears meshed, relays shut. Matt. He'd seen the guy not once, but twice. First at Altamont, then again during his undercover stint at the Caffe Mediterraneum. That time, he was with a woman who went on endlessly about the coming revolution.

The circuit hummed. Information flowed. A drug-addled, radicalized Vietnam vet who caught a piece of flying glass during a massive act of terrorism that landed him in the ER. The connection was complete.

"I've got to see him," he told her. "Right now."

They found him in the intensive care unit, still unconscious. An oscilloscope displayed his heartbeat, and several IV lines fed him various liquids. An oxygen mask obscured his face.

"Does he really need all that stuff?" Stone asked.

"Probably not, but it's standard procedure under the circumstances," Christine said.

"Can you take the mask off for a second?"

"Sure." Christine lifted the mask up and Stone moved in for a closer look at the stringy long hair, patchy beard and hollow cheeks. It was the same person, the one he'd seen both at Altamont and Berkeley.

"You're looking at our bomber," he announced.

"You're sure?" she asked.

"Let's say ninety percent." He gazed down at the pitiful, wasted figure with the pasty skin, hollow cheeks and rotting teeth. A man ironically undone by his own twisted behavior. Stone felt no urge to visit retribution upon this sad piece of human wreckage who had become a graphic object lesson in the futility of revenge.

"The way I figure it, he worked with the Weather Underground to get his chops up, but then he met these Universal Liberation Army people, who are as crazy as he is. They gave him a shot at the biggest prize of all, a hundred cops all at once, and he nearly pulled it off. Anyway, I'll have to have a long talk with him when he wakes up."

"That might not be for a while," Christine said. "And just remember, you're only a cop until midnight."

"I know. How soon can we move him to a private room?"

Christine peered at the instrumentation. "It looks like he's pretty well stabilized. I'd say tomorrow."

"How about right now?"

"Right now? I don't know. There might be some risk…"

"I don't want to cloud your ethical sensibilities, but most likely, this is the guy who tried to kill me twice and nearly killed you in the process. So, unless you think the move is actually going to kill him, let's do it."

Christine sighed. "Okay. But only if you tell me exactly why it's necessary."

"Simple. I want to see if he has any visitors and what their intentions might be. If he's who we think he is, he's going to attract some interesting attention."

· · ·

Stone stared at the galactic swirl of cream as it blended with his coffee in the blue mug on the cafeteria table. Christine had been called back into the ER to deal with yet another crisis. Some drunk downtown had driven into a streetcar. Fortunately, she was moving at a crawl when it happened, but the crash had spawned multiple minor injuries that spread out to ERs all over town. It struck Stone as trivial in the extreme compared to what he'd witnessed today. The magnitude of the tragedy at St. Brannon's made it impossible to absorb in a single dose. Officer Crenna's widow, one of his daughters, a priest and a funeral director, all gone, almost without a trace. You had to consume it in manageable chunks that didn't overwhelm you.

The hospital had assigned Stone a pager to connect him with the front desk and the telephone operator. They'd been instructed to alert him about any callers inquiring about an ER admission. The patient had been moved to Room 350, located at the far end of the corridor from the nurses' station in a wing that was mostly empty. Room 351 across the hall was vacant and gave Stone a surveillance location to see who, if anyone, showed up. Once they entered the room, he could come in behind them and see what they were up to.

He felt conflicted about failing to notify anyone at the station about what was going on. Since the suspect was completely incapacitated and in no danger of fleeing, he felt partially justified. Also, he couldn't be interrogated until he regained consciousness. By then Stone would probably be off the job. In the meantime, his last shot at being a cop was to see if he could identify potential co-conspirators. Not a bad way to go out.

The pager beeped and displayed the front desk number. He took a last sip of coffee and went to a nearby wall phone and dialed the number.

"Hi, James Stone here. You just paged."

"Yes, Mr. Stone. We received a call a few minutes back from a man inquiring about an ER admission. He said he was just a block away and would be right over."

"Did he say anything else?"

"He said his brother had been carrying a big pane of glass and tripped. The glass broke and he got stabbed by one of the pieces."

"Did you give him the room number?"

"Yes, we did."

"Thanks."

Stone took off immediately. He'd screwed up. He didn't expect anyone would show up on such short notice. There was no telling how soon the man might arrive. Or what he might do when he did.

. . .

The Sleeper instantly made a favorable impression on the two women at the third-floor nurses' station. His middle-aged features still carried a youthful presence and magnified his disarming smile.

"Hi, I'm inquiring about the patient in 350," he told them. "How's he doing?"

"They just brought him up from the ICU," one nurse told him. "I'm afraid he's not conscious yet."

"How did the surgery go?"

"Good. They located internal bleeding in a couple of spots and patched it up. You'll have to ask the doctor, but he should be in pretty good shape."

"Wow, that's great. If you don't mind, I'd like to go take a peek at him. I'm with the family and they're all going to want to hear."

"Alright, but don't disturb him and keep it brief, okay?"

"Absolutely. And thanks."

The Sleeper walked at a casual pace down the hall and glanced briefly back toward the nurses' station before he entered room 350. Both women had turned their attention elsewhere.

Once inside, he quietly closed the door behind him and took in his target. The man lay face up and wore an oxygen mask of transparent plastic and had several tubes stuck in his forearms. He exhibited no motion save for some shallow breathing, and his pasty skin had the color and texture of a freshly picked mushroom. The Sleeper moved closer and gently lifted off the oxygen mask, which caused the jaw to go slack and reveal a mouthful of rotting teeth. They put off a foul odor that The Sleeper found deeply repellent. Fortunately, he'd have to endure it for only a few moments.

He looked over to the bedside stand holding the monitoring equipment and saw a box full of latex medical gloves. After slipping a pair on, he pulled them taut and returned to the task at hand. He pinched the target's nostrils shut with his left hand and covered the mouth with his right palm. The target showed no reaction. In his heavily compromised state, the man would be dead in maybe a minute or two. All The Sleeper had to do was watch the scope that monitored the heartbeat. Soon the instrument's waveform would dance its last.

. . .

Stone departed the elevator on the third floor and hustled down to the nurses' station, where they looked up at his approach. His dress blue uniform made it clear who he was.

"You had anyone visit 350?"

Both nurses had a look of alarm, like maybe they'd been duped. "Yeah, somebody just showed up and..."

"Call security," Stone commanded on the fly.

He stopped just short of the door to 350, which was shut. He had no idea what the intruder's intentions were. Was he here out of respect, or to snuff out an already flickering candle? What if he was armed and showed deadly intent?

Stone made a snap decision that it was better to rush in than walk in, which would give the intruder more reaction time. He pushed down on the handle and rammed the door open with his shoulder. A man stood bent over the patient with his back to Stone. He started at the sound of the door flying open and whirled around as he took in Stone's cop uniform.

"Move away from the bed!" Stone ordered.

The intruder raised his arms in surrender. "Whoa, man, you scared me," he said with an apologetic smile.

"Move!" Stone yelled. The man's presentation was utterly unconvincing. He seen it hundreds of times in his career.

The intruder moved away slightly and to the right. "It's my cousin. He was carrying this glass and ..."

He lowered his arms and his right hand reached down to his pants pocket, where Stone saw a rectangular outline. A knife or a small caliber pistol. Stone knew he had to make the first move. If he didn't, the intruder would have a nearly insurmountable advantage. He launched himself straight ahead and hit the intruder with a flying tackle.

As they sprawled onto the floor, Stone deliberately rolled to his left, released his right arm from the intruder's waist and brought it up around his neck in a chokehold. He completed the move by shoving his left hand against the back of the man's head.

Normally this would have given him complete control. But not against someone armed with a knife. The intruder reached down with his free hand, extracted the gravity knife from his pocket and clicked the blade into place with a flick of his wrist. He extended his arm backward and struck.

Stone felt a sharp pain in his oblique right above his hip and immediately knew its source. Stab wound. He didn't dare yield. If he released his grip on the intruder's neck, they might separate, and the knife would prevail when they rejoined.

A second jab. More pain. One more, and he'd slip into shock and be doomed.

He had one last option. For a brief instant, he relaxed the pressure of his forearm on the intruder's trachea. He moved it forward so the man's throat was caught in the crook between his bicep and forearm. He squeezed with all his strength, which shut off the blood flow through both carotid arteries.

A third stab. But not as painful, not as deep. His opponent was losing consciousness. Stone held tight to his grip. His life literally depended on it.

A fourth stab. This one so weak it failed to penetrate his uniform. Seconds later, his assailant went limp, and the knife clattered to the floor. Outside, Stone could hear the security people rushing down the corridor. He resisted the urge to continue his pressure on the intruder's arteries and kill him. The whole point of this exercise was to uncover how the bomber was connected to a wider world of political terror. He rolled off the limp body just as two security officers rushed in.

"Cuff him. He's dangerous," he told them.

"Are you okay?" one of them asked.

"More or less," he said.

They handcuffed The Sleeper and dragged him into the corridor, where he rapidly regained consciousness. "I want a lawyer!" he screamed. "Get me a lawyer!" They brought him to his feet, grabbed each arm and forced him on down the hall.

Stone unbuttoned his uniform jacket and felt his blood-soaked shirt where the stab wounds had landed. No gushing, no pulsing. He'd escaped the worst. He knew that when the adrenaline died down the pain would increase, but for now it was tolerable. He looked over to the bed. The patient was indeed the bomber. No one would've risked an attempt like this for anyone less.

So, in the end, he'd just saved the life of the person who had tried repeatedly to kill him. Stone was not a serious student of irony but knew that this case most certainly qualified. He'd let Christine fill in the blanks.

He removed his jacket and walked into the hall. Three nurses and a doctor were heading his way and staring at the glistening red blotch on his white shirt.

"You're injured," the doctor said and turned to one of the nurses. "Get him on a gurney."

"A ride would be nice," Stone commented. "Thanks."

. . .

Stone reclined on the bed in Bay 4 of the Emergency Room, where Christine looked down on him in wry amusement.

"You're pretty incredible, you know that?" she said.

"How so?" The morphine had left him a little woozy, but still functional.

"You had just a few hours left of being a cop, and you go do something like this."

He had to smile. "I just couldn't help myself."

"I know," she said and squeezed his hand.

"Am I okay?" he asked.

"Basically, yes. As long as you're a good boy and take your medications."

"I promise. Now what about the bomber? Did he survive through all this?"

"Yep. He's still with us. Security contacted your fellow offi-cers, and they were here in a heartbeat. I didn't want to spoil your show, but I did tell them how you figured that our patient and your bomber were one and the same. They wanted to talk to you, but I told them not right now. Doctor's orders."

"And what about the guy who jabbed me?"

"He was still yelling for a lawyer when they cuffed him and carted him off. They've posted two armed guards on your bomb-er's room, just to make sure there's no second act."

"Good. Anyway, I've got a big favor to ask."

"What's that?"

"Would you fix dinner tonight?"

He saw just a trace of moisture in her eyes. "Maybe."

. . .

It should have felt odd being back at the Park Station as a civil-ian, but it didn't. Mainly because neither Stone nor his peers had adjusted to his outside status. Linehan and Burke considered it routine police business as the three of them sipped some morning coffee in the squad room.

"You got it right," Linehan told Stone. "We just received a report on the fingerprints. Your bomber is an army vet named Matthew William Carson. Came from El Paso. Did a tour in Nam. Made corporal before he was discharged, for what it's worth. Looks like he never got over the war."

"I guess not," Stone said. "Anything else?"

"Almost zip," Burke said. "The only other connection would be through the girl you saw him with at Altamont and Berkeley. But good luck with that one. Anyway, we're going to have a nice long chat with him when he wakes up."

"It's a no brainer that he has some kind of link with the Universal Liberation Army," Stone said. "You can start with that. And what about my pal with the gravity knife? What's the con-nection there? The guy was screaming for a lawyer last time I saw him. Has he clammed up on you?"

Linehan and Burke exchanged troubled looks. "You're not going to like this," Burke finally said.

"Try me," Stone said.

"It seems that somebody high up in the department contacted the FBI and told them what went down with you and the bomber and the guy with the knife. Why? Doesn't really matter. Some kind of political back scratching maybe. Who knows? There's a couple of thousand people in the department and all it took was one to make the call."

Stone knew instantly where this was going. "Don't tell me: The feds came and grabbed the guy."

"Yup," Linehan said. "Just like that."

"And just what do they plan to charge him with?" Stone asked.

"Didn't say."

"So where are they holding him?"

"Didn't say."

"Have you checked with his lawyer on all this?"

"Doesn't have one. They took off with him before the guy showed up."

"Let me get his straight. He's being held at some undisclosed location with no scheduled arraignment or legal counsel?"

"That's it," Linehan said.

"Wow," Stone said. He had every reason to wish his attacker the very worst. But not at the expense of the entire U.S. legal system.

. . .

Stone borrowed Burke's desk and phone to make a couple of calls. The first was to the U.S. Attorney's office at the federal courthouse. They had no record of anyone being held in federal custody on an assault charge or anything like it in the last forty-eight hours.

The second call went to the FBI field office in San Francisco, where they put him through to Special Agent Peter Trobe.

"Agent Trobe here."

"Yes, Agent Trobe, Detective Stone here. I assume you'll be wanting to interview me about the assault on my person at UCSF Medical. Can we set something up?"

"Not right now, detective," Trobe said as if they'd never met.

"Then when? It's my understanding that you have the suspect in custody, which means you have to arraign him in something less than forty-eight hours. I don't see how you can do that without making me part of the criminal complaint. So when?"

"I can't say." An extended interval of silence followed. "Look, I suppose I owe you one, so I'm going to go slightly off the record, but just slightly, understand?"

"Understand."

"At the church, you were witness to one of the worse acts of terrorism in the history of this country. A fallen officer was being buried and look what happened. His body was totally desecrated, and his widow and a daughter were blown to bits along with two other people. If the bomber hadn't somehow screwed up, you and dozens of other cops would've been included. Right?"

"Right."

"Now I don't know much media you follow, but the public outrage is unprecedented. The same goes for the mood in Washington, both in Congress and at the White House. A new consensus is forming about where we go from here."

"What kind of consensus?"

Again, a moment of silence. "I can't give you the specifics because I don't know all the specifics. Let's just say that this time, the gloves come off."

"I see."

"Good day, detective."

Stone hung up. The gloves come off. Five minutes ago, he lived in one country. Now he lived in a very different one.

44.

SAN FRANCISCO
APRIL 26, 1971

Stone pulled off 43rd Avenue and parked in his cramped driveway just as the workmen were winding up their day and packing their tools. They'd made enough progress that the place was once again quite livable. Exterior painting would be last, and until then a big smoke stain cast a dark shadow across the creamy beige stucco out front.

As promised, Christine was chopping up vegetables for dinner when he entered. She failed to look up and acknowledge his presence. Not like her. Something was wrong.

"The hospital just phoned," she reported. "The bomber's dead."

"What?"

She looked up and put the knife down. "Pulmonary embolism."

Someone finally got to him. "Do they know the cause?"

"I know what you're thinking," Christie replied. "And that's not it. We see this sometimes, following major surgery, especially abdominal surgery. It's just the way things go."

"Just the way things go," Stone repeated. "Yeah." He pulled up a stool and sat down at the counter. "Makes me want to have a glass of wine."

"As well it should," Christine said. "How are you feeling?"

Stone touched the bandaged wounds on his side. "Still sore, but better."

"Good. That's what we in the business like to hear," Christine said, and blew him a kiss.

Stone got up and opened a vintage bottle of French Bordeaux. It seemed fitting given that today was his permanent retirement from law enforcement. He poured each of them a glass and sat back down.

"Cheers," he said and raised his glass in a toast.

"Cheers," she responded and went back to the vegetables.

In truth, things were substantially less than cheery. Maybe he should have raised his glass to all the souls killed, maimed or injured over the past year, himself and Christine included.

The death of the bomber and the apprehension of his assailant did little to resolve the matter, although it did remove a significant threat to public safety. In the end, it simply pushed the whole business ever deeper into the turbulent interface between justice and politics, where fate alone seemed to be the arbiter between winners and losers.

Stone took a sip of his wine. They were living through bad times, about as bad as he ever remembered. So how were good people supposed to find their way? How were they to keep their souls afloat when everything around them was sinking into the abyss?

Christine paused to take a sip of her wine, and a deep quiet filled the room as the evening settled in solid.

"Did you hear that?" Stone asked her.

"Hear what?" Christine said.

"I'm not sure." He'd detected a faint sound coming from near the front door, so he got up and walked over. The sound increased in volume, but just slightly. It came in a series of muffled pulses. He opened the door and looked out onto the porch.

A small cat stared up at him, slightly larger than a kitten. It stood its ground and let loose an arrogant meow. Stone had to smile. His time with Kitty had taught him the language of feline entitlement. He turned to Christine. "Check this out."

"Oh my!" she exclaimed when she reached the door.

"Okay, okay," Stone said to the cat. "Hang on, little buddy."

He went inside, opened a can of tuna, brought it out and set it down on the porch tiles. "This gonna do it for you?"

The cat stared at him without the slightest trace of gratitude before starting in on the fish.

"Do you suppose they're related?" Christine asked, obviously referring to Kitty.

They might be, but it didn't really matter. In the end, they were both products of life's relentless continuity as it rolled forward with a terrible beauty and majesty. Ultimately, it would wash over bombers, cops, radicals, journalists, politicians, criminals, students, and every other creature without pausing to discriminate on its journey into an unknowable future.

For some inexplicable reason, Stone took comfort in this.